Look Around

Darrin May

Martin Pearl Publishing
www.MartinPearl.com

Published by
Martin Pearl Publishing
P.O. Box 1441 Dixon, CA 95620

First Edition: 2013

ISBN: 978-1-936528-09-7
Library of Congress Control Number: 2012919336

Digital ISBN: 978-1-936528-10-3

PRINTED IN THE UNITED STATES OF AMERICA

10 9 8 7 6 5 4 3 2 1

DEDICATION

To my parents, John and Rose May. You have always been my role models. Thanks for being amazing parents, but more than that, thanks for being the two best people I've ever met and known.

ACKNOWLEDGEMENTS

This project couldn't have come to fruition without the help of my publisher, Angelina McKinsey and editor, Kelly Norris. Thanks to both of you. It's been a pleasure working with you. I also want to thank Mark Deamer for the cover design and Maria Christie for the photos.

Special thanks goes out to Amanda Carstenson, whom I've leaned on for advice and feedback while writing this book and for putting up with me.

Accomplishments in life are rarely made alone. I wouldn't be here without the help of the following people: Julie Fie, thanks for hiring me as intern in the Kings' PR department while I was in college. Arthur Triche, thanks for taking a chance and hiring me in the Hawks' PR department fresh out of college. That was a great 10 years working for the Hawks and living in Atlanta. (Kenny Smith, thanks for putting in a good word for me with Arthur). Troy Hanson, thanks for hiring me this time around with the Kings and bringing me back to California. It's been an enjoyable 13 years.

I've had an unbelievable support cast of friends throughout the years. Thanks Dave Montano, Tony Piver, Laurence Humphries, Chad Lee, Joel Hardy, Brian Maxwell, Manny Arreguin, Maurice Egan, Terry Hall, Pat Kennedy, Robert Pinto, Janet Anderson-Bennett, Kim Parlett, Margaret Katz, Malcolm Means, Paulette Abegglen, Susanna Bravo, Kristen Zellmer, Sean Harris, Molly Carter and J.R. Parquette.

Thanks to Ebony Chambers, Dana Simondi, Sue Costa, Kathleen Skelton, Emily Begley, Karin Kotite, Kimberly Hellwig and Luc Luzzo for the feedback and to Darryl Arata for the early edits.

Thanks to my Kings Basketball Operations family (Geoff Petrie, Wayne Cooper, Jerry Reynolds, Scotty Stirling, Mike Petrie, Shareef Abur-Raheem, Shelli Gotlieb, Devin Blankenship, Chris Clark, Lafayette "Fat" Lever, Pete Youngman, Daniel Shapiro, Manny Romero, Dwayne Wilson, Joe Nolan, Hakeem Sylver, Steve Schmidt, Tiffany Valdez, Melanie Stocking, Keith Smart, Bobby Jackson, Jim Eyen, Alex English, Clifford Ray, Miguel Lopez, Joe Cook, Christina Vasquez and Travess Armenta.

And last but not least, thanks to my sister, Melanie May-Johnson for always having my back, brother in-law JaHarvey Johnson, nephew Kyri Johnson, niece Kamari Johnson and brother Dwayne May (may he rest in peace).

1

HUNTER

"**T**AKE your shit and leave! I don't ever want to see you again!" Hunter yelled at the top of her lungs. "What did you think we were doing all of this time?"

As I stammered and stuttered, the words escaped me. And really, they should have. What could I say? She was right. For the past two years I was simply passing time. I liked her. We had fun together. We were attracted to each other, but did I really view her as a possible partner for life? I didn't think so. Though, the sex was incredible. Hell, who was I kidding? It was off the charts!

"Uh, well…." I started, before she cut me off.

"Uh, well, my ass! Just get out. Take your shit, and your tired, trifling ass and leave!"

"Baby, let's talk about this," I pleaded.

"Talk about this?" she said. "What is there to talk about, Matisse? Oh, I know, let's talk about how we dated for two years, and how you're still not ready to go there. Let's just keep things the way they are, huh?"

"Well, yeah," I said, without my usual confidence.

"I'm not getting any younger, Matisse. Like I said before, take your sorry, trifling ass and get the hell up out of here. You obviously haven't heard…I'm not the one!"

This seemed like the story of my life, or at least when it

came to my dealings with women. For some reason, I've always had trouble going the distance. Don't get me wrong, I love women and, for the most part, I've always enjoyed being in a relationship. I've just had a problem with commitment. I never really admitted to having such a problem, but my friends, and of course my mom, were always ever-so-quick to point it out.

"You're not getting any younger," my mom would say. "I want some grandkids. She's a nice girl. What's wrong with her? You're just afraid of commitment. Marriage is wonderful, Matisse. Look at how happy your father and I are."

"I'm all right," I would tell her. "I'm just not there yet."

"Well, I just don't want you to end up a lonely old man. I worry about you, Matty." To my mom I was still a kid, even though I was thirty years from being her little boy. I wasn't worried about being lonely, though. I always had women around me. Keeping them around was a different story.

Getting women has never been much of a problem for me. Why, I couldn't tell you. What they saw in me, I have no idea. Maybe it was my bald head like my man, Jordan. I guess you could say I wanted to be like Mike. I started shaving my head a few years ago. His Airness made it popular and in-style for black men to walk around with bald heads back in the day. And now, what can I say? That's just how most brothers play it these days, especially when their hairline starts to recede. Anyway, after I started shaving my head, I figured, damn, I might as well grow a goatee to compensate for my bald head. And if that wasn't enough, I figured, shit, why not sport an earring? I like wearing an earring so much that I now sometimes wear one in each ear—never while I'm working, though.

It's funny, but when I think about that whole thing—you know, brothers walking around with bald heads—it's cool, but it cracks me up. I mean, think about that. No one is tripping; hell, it's even fashionable. However, when a white cat does it, more often than not he looks like a skinhead or a serial killer, like Woody Harrelson in *Natural Born Killers*. And don't have a white cat who is a professional athlete prancing around with a bald head, because people automatically assume he's trying to be like a brother. Take

Campbell Kennedy of the Minnesota Timberwolves for instance: he's a white boy who shaves his head bald, wears a goatee, and wears an earring in each ear. Of course, he only wears the jewelry when he's not on the court. Never mind the fact that he's one of my clients, people swear up and down that that fool is a brother. Go figure! I like to call him the Jon B/Robin Thicke of the NBA. Talk about some cool white boys—who can sing, too.

2

ERICA

HERE I was with Erica in our usual position—at least for the past month or so. For some reason, she only liked having sex one way: standing, with me behind her. While I hit it from the backside, several thoughts ran through my mind. The main one was, *What the hell am I doing here?*

It had been six months since Hunter saw the light and told me to step, and I had gone through about nine different women in that time. With Erica, I was now on my tenth. Talk about sad. I didn't feel anything for any of the nine women, and I was quickly finding out that my feelings for Erica were no different. This brought me back to the question I had asked myself moments before, *What was I doing here?* It's strange, I knew I was tripping, and yet it didn't stop me from fondling Erica's breasts, still from behind, and continuing to maneuver my johnson in and out of her.

"Shit, baby!" Erica moaned. She turned and looked back at me. "Your balls feel good slapping up against my ass." I smiled back while thinking, *Ditto! This shit is doing the trick for me, too!*

Men! Sometimes I think we have it all wrong. The louder she screamed, the more masculine I became. Little popular, *player* phrases popped in and out of my head like, *I'm doing work!* and *I'm the man!* And let's not forget, *I'm tearing this shit up!*

Yeah, I wasn't proud of it, but my head wasn't in the right

place. Somehow, my value system was out of whack. I was doing women simply because I could. After 38 years, I was officially burned out. I hadn't connected mentally with any of the many women I had dated. I guess I just liked the way they looked, and hoped their good looks would lead to good sex. In most cases, it did. I know…it's pitiful.

"You were on top of your game tonight, Matisse," Erica said. She turned and faced me. Her caramel skin looked soft and inviting. Erica's long, curly hair was naturally black, but the light highlights reddened it a bit.

I studied her for a moment before responding. She was absolutely beautiful. Her lips were full and perfectly shaped, which went well with her bubbly personality. With Erica, I had the best of both worlds. Not only was she lovely and intelligent with girl-next-door qualities, she was also a freak in the bedroom. For some reason, though, none of that seemed to matter. My ideology was a little off.

"Is that right?" I said unemotionally. The guilt was beginning to set in. Then I thought about something my old man said to me a long time ago. "Son," he said, "there's no need to run down the hill. Take your time. Walk down that hill; you'll pick off more cows that way."

I think that was the problem. I had always taken my time. I was never the one to rush into things, especially relationships. Once I entered into a relationship, I was never too eager to take it to the next level. Along the way, and in between the many insignificant relationships, I definitely picked off more than a few cows, as my old man put it, coming down the hill. Though I like to refer to them as foxes. Yeah, I've crawled down the hill like a fat snail on his way to his own funeral. As much as I hate to admit it, sadly enough, I still don't think I've reached the bottom yet.

"Baby, let's do it again," Erica said. She looked at me with a huge smile like a kid who was about to open presents on Christmas morning.

"Again?" I said slowly, without any excitement. I was hoping she would get the hint. I know this sounds terrible, but I was ready for her to leave. It's funny how you can spend all day thinking about how you can't wait to be with someone and, one minute after you go there, you're ready to be rid of this person—at least for the night. It's wild and I can't explain it. I hated the fact that I was at that point in my life. I was living foul!

"Baby, I can't get enough of you. Why do you think we're so good together?" she asked. We lay in bed and cuddled. Her hands ran up and down my chest in such a soothing way that I was beginning to tire.

"I don't know," I responded softly, with one eye open. "It must be you." Don't ask me why I said that. Hell, I didn't even know. I mean, I did, but the hole I had dug was getting deeper and deeper, and I was sure I was about to fall in. I think I was so conditioned to tell women what they wanted to hear that when it came time to put up or shut up, I was usually the one whose mouth looked like a closed Ziploc bag.

"Matisse, do you love me?"

Somehow, I knew this was coming. I liked to think of it as a sixth sense, but I knew it was just a result of my being in the game way too long. I tried to stall my response. As I looked at her, I thought, *Am I stupid? Tell her you love her. She's damn-near a perfect ten all the way around. She's going yard every time she steps up to the plate. She's a winner, Chief!* But the words failed me.

"Yeah, I love hanging out with you, Erica," I responded, trying to soften the blow. She immediately removed her hand from my chest.

"Hanging out?" She sounded somewhat puzzled, but her face said it all. Her expression was like one of those sunny days suddenly darkened by clouds. She still looked lost in pleasure, but now was hurt at the same time. I felt hollow.

"Erica," I said. It was obvious I was stalling for time. I didn't know what to say beyond her name. I had been in this particular situation many times before and somehow always found a way to bullshit my way out of it. Clearly, I was at the end of my rope. There wasn't any more bullshit left in me, nor did I want there to be. I wasn't the type of guy who got off on hurting people. In fact, I hated it; what always overshadowed it was my love for women.

"Matisse, I asked you if you loved me." Her eyes began to well up. "Is that all you can say—my name? And how you love hanging out with me?"

"It's more than that, Erica," I said, picturing myself on a bike and back-pedaling as fast as I could.

"We obviously have a communication problem, Matisse." Tears rolled down her face as her voice cracked. "Do you know I spend the majority of my time thinking about you? While I'm at work, all I can think about is how I can't wait to see you. I relate everything about me as it relates to us—you and I! And you can't even say whether or not you love me? I can't do this, Matisse. I need more, and I deserve better."

I couldn't dispute what she had said, and I certainly couldn't convince her that I had simply used a poor choice of words. Crying uncontrollably, Erica dressed quickly, gathered her belongings and left. I sat in my bedroom feeling empty and in a daze.

I didn't understand it. I understood her actions, but I didn't quite understand mine. How could I not feel anything for a woman like Erica? She was the complete package: looks, personality, values, goals. I mean, you name it, she had it. And my dumbass just let her walk out like that.

3

RODGER'S
BARBER SHOP

I had to stop off at the barbershop to get a cut before picking up my boy, Miles, who was flying in for his wedding. As happy as I was for Miles, it made me think about how foully I was living. It seemed like my life was just one woman after another, and here was Miles, ready to do the damn thing. He had found the person with whom he wanted to spend the rest of his life. Isn't that what we all strive for? I remember a time when Miles and I were cut out of the exact same cloth, where women were mere numbers to us. But he overcame it and got there. Why couldn't I settle down with one woman? It was definitely something to which I aspired. Was I chemically imbalanced? After all, I'd certainly been involved with some good women throughout my years in the game. Or was it just not in the cards for me, kind of like the woman who has always wanted kids, but is physically unable to bear one? It made me wonder if I was destined to be a career bachelor.

***

"Matisse Spencer, you truly are a creature of habit."

"Why do say that, Rodger?"

"Man, look, every Friday at four o'clock I can count on you walking through my door."

"What do you expect, Rodge. You're the best barber around. And besides, maintaining a bald head is hard work. And let's not forget about my goatee. You know I need your magic touch. You keep me groomed, Rodge."

A pair of clippers in Rodger's hand was as natural as Angela Davis's afro back in the day. The two just went hand in hand. He was even more talented with a blade. Rodger was just one of those cats who could flat-out *cut*. It didn't matter either, whatever you wanted, my man Rodge was about it. I started going to him about four years ago. Granted, I was still wearing a boxed fade back then, if you can believe that. Talk about not being able to let go, I was holding onto something that was in style (and for only a minute, mind you) a *decade* prior to four years ago. Thankfully, Rodger updated my look as he always tightened me up perfectly. Black folks and hair—we crack me up. Every weekend, you can count on hair salons and barbershops doing much business in black communities all across the nation, and especially in the ATL. Rodge's place, like most barbershops, was in *The Hood.* Why is that? Why can't we have some shit in Buckhead, or Beverly Hills, or in the heart of Manhattan? That's all right, though; I like going back…and being around *the folk*. A trip to the barbershop—there was nothing like it. Talk about getting educated. It was always like sitting in someone's classroom. I've learned some good stuff there throughout the years.

Even though I was beyond late in being down with the Jordan look, I was finally down. And, don't sleep; brothers and bald domes are still very much in style.

Rodger's cutting skills around a head were undeniable as he always put me in there with a nice phatass shave. You know what I'm talking about: real close, so your head just shines. And, his art form didn't rest there, either. He got his Picasso and Michelangelo on when it came time to tightening up some facial hair. He always had my goatee looking straight. I mean, he consistently had it trimmed, lined and brushed perfectly, and that's not an easy thing to do—and brothers know this. Needless to say, I was in good hands with Rodger. It was one of those things that when it was all said and done, you just felt better. Well, that's always been the case with me, anyway.

"You're up, Matisse," Rodger said. I sat in the chair and dapped Rodger with a pound.

"You all right?" I asked.

"Aw, you know me, Matisse. I'm doing fine. Business is good. Hell, it's better than good. It's great."

"Is that right?"

"Shit yeah, Matisse. I can't enjoy it, though."

"Huh! What do you mean, you can't enjoy it?" The chair was beginning to feel comfortable.

"Man, do you know…well let me stop myself before I say anything. I don't want to be a bad influence on you." Rodger tied the strings to the sky blue apron around my neck. He also donned an apron, but his was much longer, spanning the length from his chest to his knees, and more stylish because it was made of leather. The barbershop was long and narrow, and Rodger's chair was the farthest from the door.

"What! Oh, that's foul. You can't stop. You have to tell me, Rodge. You already put it out there. I hate when people do that."

"Look it here, Matisse. All I'll say is don't ever get married." Rodger stopped everything he was doing, stood in front of me, and looked into my eyes. His eyes were wide open—I think for effect. It was working. I could tell he was serious.

"You're barking up the wrong tree, Rodge. I can't keep a woman around. They always seem to find me out. These women are for real. They're playing for keeps. They aren't just trying to hang out and have a good time. They want to know for sure that you're in it for the long haul. Damn anything else!" I explained. Rodger still hadn't begun to work. "Anyway, getting back to you, Rodge, what nonsense are you talking about today? Why are you telling me not to get married? I thought you were single."

"Brother, I am," Rodger quickly noted. His voice grew louder. "It's my three ex-wives. Do you know, Matisse, I feel like I'm working for them. Every last dime I make goes to them. It's crazy! They aren't trying to get re-married, either."

"Damn! That's some bullshit!"

Rodger shook his head. "I mean, they aren't cutting a brother any slack!"

"Damn, Rodger, you were running through them like that? Three?" I said with a slight chuckle.

"Like what?"

"Man, you went down three times. I'm having trouble getting to the altar just once."

"I know, Matisse. Women are my weakness, especially if they have a nice smile. Once they get me with the smile, they always seem to know just how to close the deal." He applied the shaving cream atop my head.

"How are they booking you, Rodge?"

"Man, Matisse, I must have a sign on me or something because it seems like all of these women know that all they have to do is put it on me in the bedroom, and I'm toast. It's over. They got me."

"Wow. Yeah, I kind of know what you mean. It can put you under—that shit can be some powerful stuff sometimes," I agreed.

"You know what I'm saying? I guess most men have a weakness for women," he said. His strokes were steady and precise. Thank God for that! Call me a scaredy-cat, or whatever you want, but I trust only a few people with those long shaving blades. Luckily, Rodger is one of those people, but every now and then I have second thoughts even with him.

Rodger's barbershop wasn't one of those big, popular places where people went just to be seen. It was an incognito place for the most part. The reason why his business did so well was the fact that he rarely lost a customer. He had a total of four chairs that resided on top of a black and white checkered floor. More often than not, the piles of hair that fell to the floor were quickly swept up by one or two kids who lived in the neighborhood. It seemed like a good way for them to make some extra money as Rodger and the other barbers would each pitch in and give them cash at the end of the day. His walls were adorned with a lot of signed pictures of professional athletes, most of whom were my clients. Rodge tightened up most of the athletes that I represented—at least the ones who lived in Atlanta.

Like Rodge said, Fridays were my day—at least most of the time. Every now and then, I'd show up on a Saturday, but only if I was out of town or if work prevented me from making it on Friday. Rodger had an oversized refrigerator in his shop. During the week it was filled with soft drinks and bottled waters. On Fridays and Saturdays, though, that thing was filled with brew. It wasn't the best brew, but it quenched a brother's thirst. It was the perfect way to end a long workweek. In this fairly small barbershop, Rodger had five 62-inch flat-screens mounted and a surround-sound system that wouldn't quit. In case you haven't guessed by now, Rodge was a sports *junkie*. When you were at his place, you had about two programming choices: some type of game (football, basketball, baseball, or hell, even hockey) or ESPN's *SportsCenter*. Take your pick. That, by the way, was probably another reason why so many of my clients liked going there.

"How they treating you, Matisse?"

"Like I said, Rodge, I can't hold one down. I don't know what it is."

"What do mean, you can't hold one down?" Rodger stopped what he was doing. He elevated my chair, and turned it so that I was facing him. This was one of the only things that irritated me about Rodger. Why couldn't he do two things at once? Why was it that every time he found something interesting through our conversations, he had to stop everything he was doing? As much as I enjoyed going there, I had places to go, and things to do, too. Damn! He always acted like I was on his clock! Shit! "That doesn't sound like you, Matisse."

"Well, actually, I can hold them down," I said. I thought about it more intently. "I think that's the problem."

"You're losing me, Matisse. What's the problem?"

"Man, I have trouble going the distance. Most of the women I've dated, especially lately, want more. You know what I'm saying?"

"Yep!" Rodger nodded.

"I mean, they really want to go there. They're trying to be Mrs. Spencer. Don't get me wrong, Rodge, I'm flattered that someone would actually like to spend the rest of their life with me. I'm puzzled because when I think about getting married, having a wife and starting a family, I get goosebumps. You know what I'm saying? It's appealing to me. And why shouldn't it be? Hell, my business is going all right. I have a little loot, and I'm pushing 40. You know what I'm saying? I've been there and done that, right?"

"Right," Rodger agreed. He still hadn't done a damn thing to my goatee or my head.

"For some reason, Rodge, when it's staring me straight in the eye, I freeze and bitch up."

"It sounds to me like you may be set in your ways. You've been a bachelor all of your life. Sure you've had many girlfriends for long periods of time. But I bet in each of those relationships you felt like you were married. Either she was at your place, or you were at hers all the time."

"You got that right," I said.

"I know I do, Matisse. I ain't no spring chicken. Shit, you know that. I've been around the block more than a few times. I specialize in women, boy! I'll admit, you good with them, too." Roger still had the blade in his hand. Every time he said something, he dangled it at me like he was scolding me with his index finger.

"You think so?"

"Matisse, listen to me. Listen to the age." When he said that, I looked down at my watch. Rodger was about to climb on top of his soapbox. *Damn!* I thought. *How long is this going to take?* "Now, look, age equals knowledge. Like I said, I've been around – especially a lot longer than you."

He had that right. If I had to guess, Rodger was somewhere between his late fifties and early sixties. Though he was completely gray, you could tell he grayed prematurely. Rodger was one of those guys who was older than he looked—even with the gray hair. His face was wrinkle-free. His dark chocolate skin was smooth and youthful. Rodger's mustache and beard matched the color of his hair. I always cringed, though, whenever he smiled. Yuckmouth was in full effect. He needed some serious dental attention. Roger always wore jeans and some played-out pimp daddy shoes that had a theme to them. If he was wearing a blue shirt, he wore blue loafers. If he had a green thing going, he sported the green loafers. This always gave away his age. I don't know, I guess that's how they played it back then. He rotated several gold watches, with Gucci and Rolex being his top two choices. Not that I'm an authority on watches, but I could tell Rodger's were fake as hell. He didn't smoke, but for some reason he always gnawed on an unlit cigar.

"It's easy to play house, but there comes a time, Son, when you have to shit or get off the pot." Rodger paused and looked at me like he had just said some profound shit. *That was it? Shit or get off the pot? This was his sage advice gained through experience and wisdom?* I felt like saying, *No shit, Sherlock. Tell me something I don't know.* However, I managed to hold it in. *Ain't this a bitch!* I thought. *Finish tightening me up so I can get the hell up out of here.*

"These women don't have time to play house, Matisse. You know that, right? Hell, it's like you said, these women are trying to get married."

"Rodge, you don't feel me. All this shit you're talking about, I know. Let's not forget, I've been around the block too!" I forgot I was talking to a man with a sharp razorblade in his hand. I probably should have toned it down a bit. "What I'm talking about is, why am I having such a problem committing? Like I said, I wouldn't mind being married and having kids. Granted, you made a valid point about being somewhat set in my ways, but for some reason, I just can't commit. And it's not like I'm running three and four women at the same time, like I used to when I was in my twenties. I'm talking about monogamous relationships."

"You not gay are you?" Rodger asked. Based on the lack of facial expression he possessed at the time, I knew he was serious, which pissed me off. I felt like bitch-slapping him. There was nothing gay about me. Believe that!

"Come on, man! You know the answer to that," I said.

"Oh, no I don't!" he replied in a matter of fact way. "Got a lot of brothers on the under these days, especially in the ATL!"

"Whatever, Rodger."

"Matisse, don't get mad at me for asking a question. You

may not be in touch with yourself. I see stories like this all the time on *Springer*, and what's that bald-headed black cat's name?"

"Montel?"

"That's right, *Montel*. They got guys coming out of the closet all of the time. Most of those cats are married too. So, you never know."

"Well, let me assure you, Rodger, there's not a gay bone in my body. I like women. Ain't a thing wrong with it, but I'm not gay. Okay?"

"Okay, fine, Matisse."

"By the way, *Montel*'s been off the air for years now. What you need to be watching is *Dr. Phil*!"

Me, gay! Shit! Please, I'm not the one.

After ten minutes of silence, Rodger knew he'd touched a nerve. I had acted young, and I knew it was up to me to break the ice. Before I could say anything, Charlie, one of the other barbers in the shop, leaned over to Rodger and said, "Kind of quiet over here."

"Oh, he mad, Charlie," Rodger responded, without looking up at him. At least he was back on the job. He was almost finished with my head.

"Look," I said, "let's just drop it."

"It's dropped," Rodger replied. "Want some fruitcake?"

Oh, uh-uh. I couldn't believe he went there. "I said, let's drop it! Damn!"

"Matisse, it's dropped."

"Well, what the hell was that all about?"

"It's about fruitcake! Here, you want some?" Rodger pulled out a loaf of what appeared to be homemade fruitcake. I forgot it was the holiday season.

"Naw, I'm good. Thanks."

"This is good stuff, Matisse. Suit yourself." Rodger stopped what he was doing to my head. He cut a piece of the cake with a butter knife, broke it in half with his hands, and wolfed it down in one bite.

"I have a buddy coming in from out of town tonight," I confided. My chair was fully tilted back.

"Is that right?" Rodger said. His mouth was full, so it was hard understanding him. "He flying in?"

"What?"

"He flying in?"

"Yeah, I have to pick him up in about an hour." I hoped he'd get the hint and hurry his ass up. Man, sometimes people kill me. What are they thinking? He must think I just have time on my hands. I had no one to blame but myself. I was a regular and I went through this almost every visit.

"What's the occasion?" Rodger asked.

"Huh?"

"Why is he coming to town?"

"Oh, he's getting married," I said. Finally, he was finished with my head. I didn't even have to look in the mirror; I knew he hooked me up. But he still had to attend to my goat.

"Married! Shoot, bring him by here. I'll change that. I'll make him see the light."

"I bet you will."

"He getting married here?" Rodger asked. He was trimming my goatee with scissors. My chair was upright.

"Yep."

"You in the wedding?"

"Yeah, I'm the best man."

"Best man! You in charge of the bachelor party, huh?" Rodger had a smile on his face.

"Yep," I said, while I thought, *Why'd I even mention this to him? This is doing nothing to help me get out of here.*

"You need some girls for the party? I can call my girls over at The City, or if you really want some party girls, I can hit my Decatur spots, the Pink Pony and the Blue Flame. Yeah, Matisse, I got girls for you. Let me know; I'll take care of you."

"Oh, I think I'm good there. But thanks, Rodge," I said quickly, hoping he would leave it alone. Not to talk about anyone, and especially not Rodger, but I kind of questioned his eye. I didn't think he was all that particular when it came to women. While he was telling me about his girls at his clubs, I kept picturing fat, ungroomed women with teeth missing.

"How she look?"

"Who?"

"Your boy's fiancée."

"She's straight," I said. In truth, she was better than straight. She was fine. She was about an eight, maybe a nine. My caveman system of grading women with numbers is probably one of the reasons why I can't seem to keep one around for too long.

"You like her?"

"Yeah, she's cool. What's with all of these questions, Rodge?"

"Huh, oh, I don't know. Shit, Matisse, you brought it up!" Based on his response, I knew I had struck a nerve. Rodge got riled easily.

"Well, can we relax on the questions?" I said, hoping he would concentrate less on my boy's upcoming wedding and more on finishing me up so I could bounce.

"Aw, Matisse, you still mad about that gay shit, huh."

"I'm over it, Rodge. Life's too short."

"Ain't that the truth!" Rodger replied. He handed me a mirror. "How's that look? You straight?"

"As always, looks good. Took your old ass long enough," I jokingly said.

"Old! Who you calling old? You not too far behind. Shoot, you better hope you look this good when you reach my age."

"Yeah, okay, Rodge. Whatever you say," I said with a chuckle. I gave him a twenty. He gave me back eight, and I slipped him the standard five-dollar tip. Rodger's price hadn't changed in over seven years—probably another reason why he did so well.

4

MILES

I was happy for Miles. I knew he'd find his way to the altar sooner or later. Who could blame him? His fiancée, Shelby, was a knockout. Superficially, like I said, she was fine—a little shapely, petite, redbone. I have to admit: I like mine a little taller. I've always liked long, muscular, shapely legs. Shelby was straight, though. Miles definitely had a looker on his hands. Lookers—sometimes they're more trouble than what they're worth. You know, high maintenance. Talk about an automatic turnoff.

As well as Shelby was physically put together, the Lord didn't half-step on her inner parts either. She was nice, smart, giving…I mean, he really broke the mold with this one. He did good work.

Miles and I had been best friends since the third grade. We did everything together—went to the same elementary, junior-high and high schools. We even went away to college together. It's a wonder we didn't still live in the same city. But, that was about to change due to the fact that Miles and Shelby had recently purchased a new home in Atlanta. I guess what I'm trying to say here is that we're tight. He's my N-word!

I owe a lot to Miles. He's the very reason why I'm a sports agent. The thought of representing professional athletes never once crossed my mind while I was in law school. We did our undergrad work at Hampton University. When I think about it, it's funny—I've always looked at Miles as a tall, lanky, uncoordinated cat. Though I'm a bona fide six-footer, he stood around six-six. Miles came into his own in high school. He was the center on our hoop team, but at Hampton, Miles was a swingman. He could put the ball through the hoop. Yeah, Miles used to kill them in college. He could really fill it up. Our last year of school, Miles was one of the top scorers in the nation. His 'J' was out of this world. When it came time to get drafted, Miles's name wasn't called until late in the first round. Not bad for a guy who played at Hampton, though I expected him to go a little higher. You know how they do: even though my man was one of the top scorers in the nation, they kind of played him because he didn't come from one of the top Division-I schools, and, on top of that, he played at an HBCU.

Anyway, when it was time to renegotiate his contract after a few mediocre seasons in the league, Miles, unhappy with the representation he was getting from his agent, came to me. I was working for a small firm that had nothing to do with any type of sports. The tie-in, however, was the fact that I was the firm's main contract guy. And Miles, being my best friend, naturally knew this.

I guess the rest is history. I negotiated his second deal, but he only lasted another couple of years in the league. That's just something a lot of people don't realize—as the levels get higher, so does the competition. Just because you were a great high school player doesn't mean you'll be a great college player. The same goes for making the jump from college to the pros.

I like what I do. I guess you could say I built the company from the ground up. I say I did it, but that's not really the case. I don't care who you are, if you've achieved any type of success, it wasn't without the help of someone. I'm a firm believer in that. Some people crack me up with that stuff. It's weird, but a lot of us are so concerned about getting all of the credit all of the time. Relax! Whatever happened to being humble? Because chances are, somebody helped us get there.

Miles was my first client, and now I have about fifteen guys. Even though I'm still enjoying it, it's getting tougher and tougher simply because of the athletes. By and large, they're a bunch of knuckleheads. It's like a double-edged sword. On one hand, we're friends. Friends and colleagues. I work for them. They hired me to do a job, and I do my job well. But they also turn to me for advice on a lot of things, which I give. On the other hand, some professional athletes (including a few of my guys) are just so out of touch with the common person, and what the average person's concerns are on a daily basis, that they come off as pompous, arrogant, overpaid, spoiled brats—and unfortunately, a lot of these cats are.

Anyway, enough of that. I'm just excited to see my man, Miles. He's coming to town a little early. The wedding won't take place for another few weeks. It's one of those New Year's Eve weddings. I like that idea. I mean, hell, someone's always getting married in the summer months. Why not start the New Year off right? I just hope Miles is ready for it. Marriage is serious business— and not that Miles isn't a serious brother, because he is. I just hope he knows what he's in for. Hopefully, a lifetime of happiness, right? Who am I kidding? I sound like I'm trying to convince myself. I'm one of those old-fashioned, idealistic guys who believe that marriage is a one-time thing. Once you tie the knot, it's all good forever. But who really knows? And of course, realistically, it's not all good forever. I guess all relationships have their conflicts here and there, but in the end, if your life was enhanced by being in the relationship, that's probably what it's all about. I guess. By now you know my track record in the relationship game is somewhere between shit and shit! So I really wouldn't know.

Being the best man, I had to make sure I sent Miles off properly. Bachelor parties are kind of tricky. On one hand, you want everyone to have a blast. So you just want to really set it out—girls, girls, girls, and plenty to eat and drink. That kind of stuff makes or breaks bachelor parties. As much as I hate to admit it, as men, that's how we roll. A bachelor party isn't on point unless there are plenty of naked women prancing around, good food and something to sip on, preferably adult beverages. On the other hand, if you set it out too ridiculously, you know, tits and ass all over the place, with the women doing a little more than dancing, you ended up feeling kind of guilty, especially seeing all of the married men and cats with girlfriends taking part in all of the festivities. The worst part was facing their wives and significant others in the following days leading up to the wedding, and knowing you were the one responsible for putting the bachelor party together. In the back of my mind I kept thinking, *It's all innocent fun*. Besides, I was no one's keeper. After all, I'm talking about grown-ass men. We're all responsible for our actions, and actions have consequences. So there it was, it was settled. I was going to set this shit out. Talk about parties—this was going to be the bomb-ass party of all. It had to be—Miles was my boy! It was that simple.

5

AIRPORTS,
OLD FRIENDS
AND EX-LOVERS

THE drive to the airport took about twenty minutes and by the time I arrived I was in a great mood. The fact that I was meeting my boy should have been good enough, but what really got me there was the Isley Brothers' *Greatest Hits* CD I listened to on the way. If you know anything about the Isleys, it's hard to beat "Take Me to the Next Phase." Believe it or not, my old man turned me on to the Isley Brothers back in the day. Not that I wasn't around while they were still making hits, but he was the one who put me down. Speaking of my old man, I needed to make it over to my parents' house to check in on them sometime next week.

My parents moved to Atlanta about two years ago. The winters in Chicago were always cold, and with them being retired and all of the kids grown and gone, they figured, *What the hell?* and moved down here. It's nice having them around, but at times it can get kind of tight, especially on those evenings when my mom shows up at my front door unannounced, if you know what I mean.

Here I am talking about Chicago and, at the moment, it was pretty damn cold here in the ATL. I parked in the hour lot and made my way to the baggage claim. It was a good thing I wore my three-quarter leather jacket because Jack Frost wasn't bullshittin'. He was on a brother's ass and trying to take a nasty bite. On cold days like this, I also always wore some type of hat, usually a skullcap. It kept my bald head warm and, at the risk of sounding self-centered, I have to admit it went well with my jacket. My look was kind of relaxed. I didn't have on a suit, only a pair of slacks, a turtleneck sweater, and earrings in both ears. Hey, I wasn't working, so I could do that. My goat was trimmed and groomed, so I felt good. It's amazing how valuable your facial hair becomes when you're lacking hair atop your head.

I was a little early, so instead of waiting at the baggage claim, I made myself comfortable at the bar where I sipped on a Stoli on the rocks. I positioned myself in a way that I was sure to see Miles walk by.

"Matisse, is that you?"

I felt a hand on my shoulder. I turned and looked. Pure beauty stood before me. "Hunter? Hey," I said awkwardly. As always, I was immediately drawn to her eyes. Her hazel-colored eyes were captivating, and almost piercing to the point that once your eyes locked in on hers, it was all over. She had you and there was no escaping. Hunter's skin was chocolate brown and her thick, jet-black hair fell just below her shoulders. She obviously had kept up with her daily workouts. Her body appeared svelte and lean, just as I remembered it. I've seen a lot of beautiful women naked, but Hunter was definitely tops in my book. As much as I enjoyed making love to her, I remember all of the times I lay in bed with her and marveled at how beautiful she was in her most natural, naked state while she was sleeping. It's funny how things turn out, though. I guess there's a lot to be said about getting to know a person. When the smoke cleared, it was obvious that our personalities clashed and the entire relationship fell apart right before our eyes.

Obviously, I was somewhat shocked and surprised to see her, but I was uneasy because I was uncertain as to what was coming next. Was I about to be pummeled by a group of hit men she'd hired, or was she going to take me out on her own? A quick slash of the throat, or maybe these days she was packing and a simple pull of a trigger could have me eighty-sixed. In any event, I was bracing myself for something—at the least, a good old pimp-slap across the face. Considering the way things ended between us, with her telling me to take my shit and leave, I didn't know what to expect. What I did know was that she looked good. There was a glow to her. Why is it that every time you bump into an ex they always look like a million bucks? Hunter looked outstanding—sexy as hell.

"I thought that was you," she said. Just as I expected, she wasn't giving up any smiles. "How have you been?"

"Not bad," I responded. I didn't want to give her the impression that everything was great now that she was out of my life. "And you?"

"Things are great, never better," she said bluntly without hesitation. "I'm just here to pick up my boyfriend."

Oh, here we go, I thought. I knew what that was all about—clearly a case of a woman scorned. Hunter wanted to make sure I knew she was over me and had moved on. Obviously, she had. I mean, damn! She didn't waste any time. We stopped seeing each other only about six months ago. I guess that's beyond the pot calling the kettle black. Who am I to talk? I had my fair share of women in the aftermath of Hunter.

"His plane should arrive any minute now. What's your story, Matisse? You waiting on a client or something? Wait, let me guess. You're probably waiting for some sweet, innocent girl who has no idea what she's gotten herself into—especially if she's dating you!"

I knew it. I knew she couldn't let me off by just being cordial. If she wasn't going to take me out physically, I knew she had to get a couple jabs in verbally. "That was kind of below the belt, Hunter. It's nice to see you, too." I hoped my sarcasm was felt.

"Oh, save it, Matisse. I shouldn't even be talking to your trifling ass!"

"So, why are you?" I asked. I took a sip of my drink, and played with the ice inside my mouth for a moment. If you haven't guessed by now, *trifling* is her favorite word when it comes to me.

"Because I'm over it. Besides, I have a new boyfriend, and we're in love." She climbed on top of a barstool next to me, and motioned to a bartender. "So, you see, Matisse, I should buy you a drink because leaving you was the best thing that could have ever happened to me."

"Well, I'm glad I could be of help." Hunter was beginning to irritate me. I don't care how good she looked. I remember thinking that often when we were still together. It was one of those classic relationships where I loved looking at her. She made for great eye-candy and, granted, she was nice, but in the end she just irritated the hell out of me.

"So, Matisse, I'm waiting. What's your story? Why are you drinking alone at a bar in the airport?"

She didn't see it, but I looked at her out of the corner of my eye like she was crazy as I managed to keep my poise. "I haven't been doing much, outside of work. And no, I'm not waiting on a client. Remember Miles?"

"Yeah, how's he doing?"

"He's doing well. In fact, I'm waiting on his plane to get in. He's getting married in about three weeks. The wedding is here, so he's coming a little early to make sure everything turns out okay." Though I was a bit peeved with Hunter, I still couldn't stop myself from sneaking peeks at her smooth, long, chocolate legs.

"Miles is getting married?"

"Yep, he's tying the knot."

"Miles?"

"Yeah! Why? Is Miles not allowed to get married?"

"What?" Hunter administered a soft blow to my shoulder with her fist. "Shut up, Matisse."

"Well, what's up with that dumbass, sophomoric, Miles?" I mimicked her whiny, annoying voice.

"I'm just a little surprised. You and Miles are like clones. If I ever hear of you getting married, I'll react the same way."

"Oh, here we go," I said, rolling my eyes.

"Wow! Good for him! When are you going to grow up and follow his lead? You're getting up there in age, Matisse. Isn't it about time you started thinking along those lines?"

"You sound like my mom. No! I don't have a biological

clock. Hell, I could be fifty and marry a twenty-one year old bombshell." I turned and looked her straight in the eye. I could see the steam rising from her head. I could tell it got to her because there was complete silence—at least for a moment.

The thought of being fifty and marrying a woman half my age repulsed me. If it got to that point, so be it. I'm one of those guys who believe everything happens for a reason. There was obviously a reason why I had so much trouble holding onto a woman. I have a couple of theories, but who really knows? My commitment issues were obvious and my attention span mirrored that of a two-year-old's. It seems my mind is conditioned to think that there's always something better around the corner.

Hunter's drink arrived. She still hadn't said a word to me. Knowing Hunter the way I did, considering we had dated for two years, I knew having kids and being married were among her top priorities in life. I shouldn't have gone there, but I was weak. I let her bitterness get to me, causing me to stoop to her level. Don't get me wrong, Hunter's a nice woman. What can I say? I hurt her. She was obviously still mad and hadn't gotten over it. All that love and boyfriend shit she was talking was just that: talk. It was a farce. I guess what I'm trying to say here is that I understood. She baited me, and I took it. I didn't feel good about it, even as much as she pissed me off.

"Here you go," Hunter said. She handed me another Stoli on the rocks.

"I didn't order this"

"I know you didn't. I did. Remember, I told you I owed you a drink," she replied irritably.

Stay cool, I thought. *She's acting young. Don't stoop to her level. She's a woman scorned. But damn, I wish she would leave me alone.* I took the drink out of her hand and placed it on top of the bar.

"Thanks," I said.

With much sarcasm, Hunter blurted, "Anytime." Her eyes rolled.

"Looks like Miles's plane is late," I noted, trying my best to switch topics, which was why I chose to just accept the drink without commenting any further.

"It seems Jeff's plane is late also," Hunter said.

"Where's he coming from?" I asked. My fingers were crossed. I had hoped this would change the direction of the conversation.

"New York," she responded.

"New York?" I looked up at the Big Man upstairs. "What's his flight number?" My stomach was beginning to feel upset. She pulled out a piece of paper from her purse.

"It says, 510."

"Delta?" I said with much anxiety. My voice even cracked.

"Yeah. 510 Delta," she replied. I wanted to ask her again, but I knew it wouldn't do any good. We were waiting on the same flight. Somehow, considering this chance meeting with Hunter, I knew the inevitable without even looking at the flight information I was holding. *I could be wrong,* I thought for a moment, knowing I wasn't. I looked at Miles's flight number, shook my head in disgust, and said, "Well, it looks like we'll wait together."

"Huh?" Hunter had a puzzled look on her face.

"Miles and…what'd you say his name was? Jeff?"

"Yeah, right! You know what his name is. It's swimming around your head as we speak. Yes, my boo's name is Jeff."

"Oh, anyway…." I paused and took a deep breath before giving her the disturbing news. "Miles and Jeff are on the same flight."

"Great. Maybe I'll introduce you to his fine, sexy self. I just love showing him off. Unlike you, Matisse, he loves public affection."

I didn't respond, but I knocked back that Stoli on the rocks. It was right on time. It was hard, but I was committed to taking the high road. Some people can take it, some people can't. I prided myself on knowing I was one who could take it. I could give it as well. Hunter, on the other hand, could dish it out, but couldn't take it. I'd have that poor girl boo-hooing if I went there. It was a struggle to stay cool, but she was pushing it with her young-ass comments.

"I guess this is to be expected this time of year. I hate

traveling around Christmastime. As nice as this airport is, it's one of the busiest. We could be waiting for a while," I said, and cringed at the thought.

"So I'm just curious, Matisse," Hunter started. Her tone changed to a serious one. She looked me in the eye. I felt like I had just committed a crime and was now about to be interrogated in a dark, smoke-filled room with only a single light shining above me. "Had I not have put you out when I did, would we be here today, continuing to go through the motions as a couple?"

What kind of shit is this, I thought. *Look, just pick up your new man and bounce!* "Hunter, come on."

"No! Really."

"Look, Hunter, let's just call it a failed relationship."

"Failed!" Her voice grew louder. "I didn't fail. You failed! You failed me!"

Man, this damn plane better hurry up and get here. I'm tired of this, I thought. "You're right," I conceded. "I failed you, and I'm sorry. Maybe I'm just a career bachelor who can't get it right when it comes to women and relationships. How pitiful is that?"

"Very," Hunter snapped. She turned and ordered another drink. Once again, she was mad. And once again, it was my fault. At this point, I didn't care. It was nice having silence between us. I used the time to people-watch. Airports are great places to watch people, especially during a busy time like the holidays. It seemed like everybody was in a hurry. People were either running or walking extremely fast, and many of the people had Christmas bags of some sort. Another thing I noticed about airports was the amount of attractive women it had running in and out of them. I attempted to distract myself from Hunter by looking at all of the beautiful women. I saw some dime pieces.

"It looks like their plane has arrived," I said. Hunter was facing the bar. She stirred her drink with one of those little straws. I had my back against the bar. "Well, it was nice seeing you, Hunter. I think I'm going to go make my way to the baggage claim area." Before I could say, *Take care,* as it was on the tip of my tongue, I saw Miles making his way through the airport. "Miles!" I yelled. Hunter turned quickly.

"Jeff!" she screamed. She smiled. Then her mouth dropped to the floor like it was filled with a bag of concrete.

Upon what I saw, I was startled too. The guy who was walking next to Miles responded to Hunter's yell. They were talking like they'd been boys for years. That sight alone should have caused my hair to stand straight. But, as unsettled as I was by it, I was totally freaked out by something else. Speechless and white-knuckles to boot, I saw a ghost from my past in that airport and no one can say shit-else to refute it. I know what I saw.

6

SURPRISE! SURPRISE!

I'VE always been pretty good about putting on a poker face when needed. This was one of those times. I had to quickly gain my composure and put what I know I saw in the back of my mind. As much as I was tripping, I had to focus, Academy Award-style, and put that shit on the back burner. My man, Miles, was in town and the night had to be about him. So, on the way back from the airport, I got my Denzel on and acted like everything was copasetic. I didn't ask Miles how he knew Hunter's boyfriend, or bring up what else I saw, which was bothering me even more. It was jacked up. I had two major issues swirling around in my head, but had to play them off. Miles and I had a lot of catching up to do.

It was a short drive from the airport to midtown. Miles wasn't too hip on listening to the Isley Brothers and, I'll admit, who could blame him? I could understand him wanting some music that was a little more upbeat. So, once again I dug into my bag of vintage tricks and hit him with Atlanta's own, Outkast. Yeah, I put *The Love Below* on him. He didn't know what to do, it sounded so good. Actually, Miles was already up on Outkast, but I always kidded around with him about who was down with the group first.

We made a quick stop at my place to drop off his bags. I live in a high-rise condo in midtown. I like it. I'm on the 26th floor, facing Piedmont Park. It's only a three bedroom. I converted one of the bedrooms into an office. Though I work out of my regular office in Buckhead most of the time, there are days when I work out of my home. I think one of the biggest reasons I like my condo so much is because of its location. I have a skyline view of Buckhead, as well as Atlanta's downtown. Most of my friends and, of course, my parents, are always on me about my place. They think because I do pretty well financially that I should be living in one of those big houses somewhere in the suburbs like most of my clients. Talk about a drag. Who wants to make that commute on a daily basis? I know I don't. And besides, I'm not married and I don't have any kids. So why would I want to live in a big house in the suburbs? Hell, if I ever get married and have kids, I still don't think the suburbs is an option for me. There are plenty of nice in-town neighborhoods. Another reason I like my place, in addition to the location, is the fact that it's modest. It's all I need.

That's the thing about some of my clients. As soon as they get a little change, instead of paying their bills or investing in a home or in stocks, they go out and buy the most expensive Benz on the lot. And if that's not enough, what's the second thing they do? They buy some loud, ugly-ass rims to put on the car. Why is that? What are they thinking? Then they buy more cars and more rims, and, oh, let's not forget about the ice that's required in the ears and around the necks and wrists. In the ATL you see all kinds of brothers and sisters driving nice, expensive luxury cars, and living in apartments. What kind of shit is that? If they want to collect expensive things, they should collect houses and real estate. Don't get me wrong, I'm not talking about all of my clients, just some of them, which leads me to this: on the flip side, and there most definitely is one, I have just as many clients who are business-savvy and invest their money well. It's kind of funny how we very seldom hear about those people via the media. When it comes to athletes and entertainers, more often than not, all the media wants to report on are the negative aspects of their lives. That's my rant for the moment. Paradigms are a bitch because everyone has one and they tend to differ. To each his own.

We walked over to Al's from my place. Al's was one of my favorite watering holes. It was right around the corner from my condo. The neighborhood pub was usually densely-populated and dark. Al had only a couple of televisions in there, but he had all of the sports packages. You see where I'm going with this? I could catch all of the games. It was my little place to quietly relax.

"I knew this would be the first place we hit," said Miles. He chuckled. Entering the pub before me, Miles stopped just inside the doorway.

"Over here," I motioned, pointing to the bar.

Miles laughed, "Man, you are funny. Of course you want to sit at the bar, Matisse. That's your shit; sitting at the bar so you're close to the televisions."

"What can I say, I'm a creature of habit, and you know this!" I responded. We each took a stool. The place, as usual, was dimly lit. Unfortunately, smoke filled the air. Sometimes you have to take the good with the bad. Al's bar was long, spanning the length of the place. It was made of redwood and had a shiny lacquer finish. It was beautiful. The barstools were extremely comfortable due to the thick padding on the seats and backs. There weren't many people in there, which made for a quiet setting. Al was old-school. All of the pictures on the walls, and he had many, were black and white. He didn't limit them to just sports, either. Don't get me wrong, most of the pictures were of various sports figures like Jackie Robinson and Jim Brown. However, Al also had pictures of men like James Baldwin standing alongside Martin Luther King, Jr. He had signed pictures of Lena Horne and Dorothy Dandridge. There was a picture of W.E.B. Dubois and one of Benjamin E. Mays. The list went on and on. Al did a great job of mixing the entertainers and scholars in with the athletes.

"Back in the ATL!" Miles blurted. "What's up, man?"

"What's up?" I said. "What's up is your wedding, player. You ready?"

"Am I? Matisse, have you ever known me not to be? I'm ready to do this, man!"

"Are you?" Miles could tell I was serious by the way I asked.

He looked at me, paused and then chuckled before

responding, "Man, come on. Am I ready?" Miles's voice grew louder. "Hell yeah, Matisse! I love her. She's the one."

"All right, Chief! Damn! You don't have to get all loud on me."

"Well, shoot! We haven't even ordered a drink yet, and you're already questioning me. Can't a brother be in love? Can't a brother want to spend the rest of his life with someone?"

As I listened to Miles, I thought to myself, *Wow, it must be nice to be where he is, knowing that this is the person you want to spend the rest of your life with, and not wavering one bit.* "Hey, man, I'm happy for you," I said. "You know, as your friend, and as your best man, part of my job is making sure you're straight. I'm just looking out, pimp! You've always been a good decision maker, and if I came off wrong, I apologize. It's just that marriage is a big step in anyone's life. That's all."

"True. You're right, Mat, it's serious business. I'm so ready for it, though. It's weird, but she's all I really think about. She's on my mind twenty-four/seven. You know?"

"Yeah," I responded. But did I? If I had, I'd probably be trying to get married as well. Unfortunately, I didn't know what he was talking about. In theory I did, but in truth, no. I never had one woman on my mind all day and all night. The times I had been close were always clouded by the thoughts of forever, and with the same woman. How weak is that?

"What's up, Al? It's been a long time," said Miles. He stood and gave Al a cross between a pound and a hug. Like many former professional athletes, Miles's once perfectly-toned body had softened a bit. His face was no longer chiseled. It was now round. A tire took the space where the six-pack once was. By no means was Miles now a fat boy. The extra weight he carried complemented his tall frame. During his playing days he was often referred to as skinny, and it bothered him. His looks were still youthful. Miles had a full head of hair and there wasn't a gray strand in sight. His copper skin was free of wrinkles.

"Yeah, it has," said Al. "Congratulations on your upcoming wedding. Matisse told me he was going to bring you by tonight."

"Well, you know—coming to Atlanta and not spending any time at Al's is like going to a baseball game and not eating a dog. The two just go hand-in-hand."

"Oh, here you go!" said Al. He let out a loud laugh. Al was a large man. He stood somewhere around six-eight, and was a good two-eighty to three-hundred pounds. His deep voice matched his massive physical appearance. When he spoke, it was like the entire bar vibrated. James Earl Jones didn't have anything on Al.

"What are you drinking, Miles?" asked Al. "I know what this one's having." He motioned in my direction.

"I'm just going to start off with a brew," said Miles. "What do you have on tap?"

"You name it, we basically have it."

"I'll go with the Bass ale."

"You got it. You're looking good, Miles."

"Thanks, Al. You know how it is, black don't crack."

Al let out another laugh. "I know that's right!"

Miles's Bass ale arrived in a frozen 16-ounce mug. Al placed a Stoli on the rocks in front of me.

"Some things just don't change, huh, Al," Miles said, referring to my drink.

"It's the damnedest thing, Miles. He won't drink anything else. It's always Stoli on the rocks."

"What can I say? I like what I like. Y'all need to back up off me," I kidded before taking my first sip. Al knew just how to make my drinks. Not that it's tough. I mean, come on, Stoli on the rocks is just vodka over ice. His trick was adding a little water to it. It took the edge off a little, making it easier to drink.

It was Friday night, and early December, which was my favorite time of year. I loved the holiday season, and I especially reveled in the fact that there were plenty of sports to watch. You had all kinds of hoops going on, and you also had football at the height of its season, both college and professional. Needless to say, I was a happy camper sitting in Al's with my Stoli, catching up with my boy Miles, and watching the Bulls do mad work against the Knicks on one television, while enjoying a UCLA/Cal basketball game on the other. I was straight! Oh, and let's not forget, even though Al's was a quiet little neighborhood pub, that didn't mean it was void of quality women stopping in for a couple cocktails from time to time.

"So how you doing, man?" said Miles. "You still liking Atlanta? It's obviously been good to you."

"Aw, you know, I'm just trying to do my thing," I responded while messing around with my goatee.

"Well, it looks like you're doing it. I guess business is going well."

"I'm doing all right, Miles," I said. "I'm just trying to make it. You know, keep my head above water."

"Huh!" Miles laughed. "Whatever, Matisse. You're doing a lot better than just trying to make it. I can see that quite clearly."

"Oh, please!"

"Oh, please, my ass! Look at you, pushing the fully loaded Mercedes. You got the phatass in-town condo, across the street from the park, I might add. And to top it off, you're looking like a million bucks. Nigga, what!"

"You can't judge a book by its cover, player. Like I said, I'm just trying to do my thing. I'll tell you what, dealing with those knuckleheads sometimes is a pain in the ass. Some of those cats haven't a clue. But then again, some totally get it."

"They can play ball, though," Miles said, "and they're making you some good money, too!"

"This is true," I agreed. "Enough about me. You're the one who has the world by its tail."

"Huh?" Miles said. He looked puzzled. His beer was half-empty, or half full, depending on your point of view.

"Don't 'huh' me. Look at you. Job's going well. You're making money. You just bought a new house. And if that's not enough, you're about to get married to the woman of your dreams. It doesn't get any better than that." *Lucky bastard,* I thought to myself.

"I have to tell you, Matisse, I am pretty happy," Miles admitted. "It's strange, I thought I'd be nervous, but I'm not. I can't wait to marry her. In fact, I wish she was with us right now, you know? I mean that's how it is for me. I can't get enough of her."

"That's deep. Some powerful shit there," I replied. I turned away from the bar for a moment to focus my attention on a pair of legs that were so inviting I could feel my mouth watering. They were dark brown and had a fresh, shiny glow to them. She wore open-toe heels. Her feet were so pretty they gave a brother goosebumps. The chills ran all up and down my body. Miles was still talking, but I didn't hear him. I had tunnel vision. Now was the crucial part: how did her face and ass look? If the face was through, what's the point? And if she didn't have any ass, again, what was the point?

She walked towards us. Her face was the bomb, and she had much ass—which was usually a deal-closer with me. I didn't like those skinny, scrawny girls. I liked a little thickness. She was in there, Chief, to the point that it was ridiculous. When she walked by, I could hear Miles, *Mr. Happily-in-love, I-can't-wait-to-get-married*, stumble over his words until he just said forget it and stopped talking to admire the beauty with me.

"Woo," Miles said. He shook his head.

"Yeah," I agreed. "I bet she can't put two sentences together, though."

Miles laughed and said, "You're probably right."

"It's tough finding that total package," I said. "How'd you do it, Miles?"

"I don't know, man. Sometimes it's staring you right in the face, and you don't even know it. We're always chasing, thinking there's something better around the corner, and taking what's right in front of us for granted."

"That's the story of my life," I said shamefully. Erica came to mind.

"Aw, come on. Though you have let some winners get by." He took the last swallow of his beer. "Hey, you hungry?"

Ignoring Miles's question, I said, "You just had to remind me."

"I can't talk. Remember when Denise and I broke up when we were in school?"

"Do I!"

"That's what I'm saying. 'Member that? Man, I couldn't

sleep. Couldn't eat. Couldn't do anything. All I wanted to do was lay in bed all day. I thought she was the one. She had me open. You know it's bad when you can't even function. I look at that, and then look at where I am now, about to get married and all. It's a trip because I didn't think I'd ever get over Denise. I thought I had let one slip by. But I didn't. It just wasn't meant to be. And I now know that I had to go through that and a whole lot more in order to get where I am now. Life is funny, man. You hungry?"

"So, it sounds like you're saying there's still hope for me."

"Oh, hell yeah! Hope for you? Man, come on! Matisse, ever since I've known you, you've had women—fine women, and many of them. I don't know why you insist on playing this game."

"Game? What game?"

"This game about wanting to settle down and get married. Man, you and I both know if that was the case, you'd be on your way to the altar, too."

"That is the case! I'm not saying I'm trying to get married right now," I explained, "but I'm definitely tired of going through all of these women. I've just been in the *game* way too long."

"My advice to you is maybe you should try being alone for awhile." Miles motioned to Al for another beer.

"That's no fun," I replied. "But I hear you."

"Look, Matisse, you aren't the cat who has trouble with women. I know you swear up and down you do, but we both know it isn't so. Like I said before, you've always had women. And lots of them."

"Miles, I know I do all right with women from that standpoint. The hard part for me is finding *The One*, and being able to identify her as such when she crosses my path. I seriously think I'm one of those guys who think the grass is always greener on the other side."

"If that's the case, you haven't found *The One* yet. Believe me, you'll know when she's staring you in the face."

"I hope so. I hope I haven't already let her get away."

"Naw, it doesn't work like that. If she has gotten away, she'll come back. You know the old saying: 'If you love someone, set them free. If it's meant to be, they'll come back.' It's all about timing, my brother. It's all about timing."

"Well, since it seems topical at the moment, and mind you, I told myself I wasn't going to say anything, but I'm tripping right now, Miles."

"Tripping? About what?"

"I saw her tonight."

"Who?"

"Think about it." I shifted in my chair. "You know who?"

Silence filled the air. Miles' eyes widened. His lips smacked. "Please! Anyway, Matisse, you are tripping!"

"You know damn good and well I'm not tripping!"

"Where?"

"At the airport. She wasn't too far behind you."

"So, you saw her and didn't say anything?" Miles smirked like I was crazy.

"She acted like she didn't want to be seen."

Miles let out a loud laugh, "Oh, this story just gets better and better. She didn't want to be seen? How do you know that?"

"By the big-ass sunglasses she was wearing and by the way she quickly dipped out of sight." Now, I was irritated, but was also beginning to second-guess myself.

"Matisse, let that shit go. Has Al over served you already?"

"Okay," I shook my head, "you know what? I am going to let it go. You're such a dick!"

Al set a Bass ale in front of Miles. "You need another, Matisse?" he asked.

"No, I'm good right now," I responded while glaring at Miles.

"Hey Al, can we see a couple of menus?" Miles asked. "Damn! I'm starving."

Al handed each of us a menu.

When it came to food, I wasn't the daring one. I knew Al's menu from top to bottom, yet I still always perused it, only to order the same exact items I had the last time I was in there. This time, however, I took a timeout from looking over the menu. As Miles studied it, I thought about what he had said moments before. It made a lot of sense. It made me feel better, too. But, looking at Miles and how happy he was, and knowing the reason why he was so happy was because of the woman he was about to marry, made me feel kind of incomplete. I felt like I was missing something. It was sort of like how Jordan used to glide through the air on his way to one of his spectacular slam-dunks without his tongue hanging out. *Am I going to be a career bachelor for the rest of my life?* I wondered. But Miles's words really put things in perspective for me. Upon hearing them, I added my own slant on the topic. What will be, will be. Everything happens for a reason. And I was comfortable with that. Though I had botched many relationships, and let some good ones go, it all happened for a reason. I guess.

"You guys ready?" Al asked. He had a notepad in one hand and a pen in the other. Al also always had an extra pen resting between his ear and head.

"I'll take a bacon cheeseburger," Miles said. "Fries come with that, right?"

"Yep," Al responded.

"Then, that'll do it for me."

Al turned to me. He looked and just shook his head from side to side. "Wait, let me guess," he said sarcastically. "Buffalo fingers, fries and a Caesar side salad."

"You know it," I said, without any shame. Some things never change.

On his way to placing the order, I saw Al point the remote towards the television closest to us. The Bulls game was over, so he changed the channel to one of the local stations. There she was right before my very eyes. She was in Atlanta. Everything changed.

When the commercial break finally came, I looked over at Miles. He hadn't said anything the whole time either.

"Am I still tripping?" I asked loudly with much bass. Miles said nothing. He knew exactly who she was. Life as I knew it was about to change drastically.

7

A BLAST FROM
THE PAST

I spent the night tossing and turning. A morning person I wasn't, but this was one time I was up before dawn. I used the time to go for a run, which was extremely uncommon for me. Don't get me wrong, I usually saw to it that I got my runs in, but it normally took place after work or at some point during the course of the day.

What was she doing here, I kept thinking to myself. I couldn't get her off of my mind. Why the ATL of all places?

Though the drive to my office was a short one, I drove to work completely dazed. My mind was cluttered with images of her. It pissed me off. I barely had time to notice how nice the weather was. It was awesome! The air was cold and crisp. The sun shone brightly, and the sky was as blue as the ocean. It was my type of day. There wasn't a cloud in the sky, but to me it seemed cloudy. Yeah, this girl was getting the best of me.

I had a busy morning scheduled. One of my clients, Jerrell Jackson, one of the best centers in the NBA, was holding out for more money. Granted, he was good as hell, but even I know when to say when. I mean, every time we go to the table and have an agreeable contract, this fool goes and vetoes it. As his agent, I can advise him on this and on that, but what can I really do? I work for him. If he's unhappy with the deal, I guess I'm unhappy, too. I keep telling him he's pushing it. Greedy bastard! He won't listen. All he knows is that he needs—or, bump it, I'll call a spade a spade—he *wants* more money. Unbelievable! So, anyway, it was one of those mornings. I had a ten o'clock conference call with Jerrell and the Knicks' General Manager. That's part of the problem—because he plays in the number one media market, Jerrell thinks he should be the highest paid player in the league. He doesn't deserve it, but I'm doing my best at getting him the money he wants. After all, I do get a nice percentage of that money.

Upon entering my office, I was floored by pure beauty. The earth's most physically appealing creature was sitting in the waiting area, and chatting it up with my receptionist like they were best friends who hadn't seen each other in twenty years.

"Hey!" Sullivan said. She was adorned with a huge smile. The shock I was experiencing was beyond words. I mean, simply put, I was paralyzed. I tried to take another step forward, but I couldn't. I stood in the doorway looking ghostly white—and that's damn-near impossible, considering I'm a brother with much color. Some people say brown-skinned, while others say dark-skinned. Take your pick because I don't mind either one just as long as my ass stays black. Though the rest of my body wouldn't function, I somehow managed to speak.

"Sullivan?" I said hesitantly. I felt as though I needed to be pinched. *Was it really her? If so, what was she doing in my office?*

"Uh-oh, by the look on your face it's obvious I shouldn't have come."

"Huh? Oh, don't pay any attention to me," I said, trying to play it off. It was too late, though. My cool points were not in effect. My body language had said it all. All of the bones in my body were still on vacation. They wouldn't budge. I just stood there stiff as a board. "Well, I have to admit, I am a little surprised to see you. After all, I didn't think I'd ever see you again."

"That makes two of us," Sullivan agreed. Finally, I was beginning to loosen. I looked over at my receptionist, who was sitting there with the widest of eyes, like she was witnessing the

Second Coming, Idris Elba in the flesh or a tsunami. I motioned to my receptionist with a slight nod of my head and quick flash of my eyes for her to get lost. She got the hint, but not before arguing me down with a nasty glare.

"I'm sorry this is so awkward, Matisse. I know I shouldn't be here," she said. Before Sullivan could say another word, I cut her off. I knew where she was getting ready to go, but I didn't have the time or energy to relive it.

"I saw you on TV last night." At last, I was beginning to feel like myself again. That acting like a frightened little sissy stuff was behind me. Quietly, I was starting to get kind of pissed. "What's really going on, Sullivan?"

"Matisse, I'm sorry. I know I should have at least called."

"It would have been nice!" I responded sharply.

"It's just that…." she paused and looked down at the ground before looking back up at me. Her eyes began to well up. "Well, I didn't like how things ended between us, and lately I've been thinking a lot about us. Not to mention, if you saw me on TV last night, then you know that I'm back in town working for the NBC affiliate."

"Five years is a long time to just walk back into someone's life, Sullivan." I felt like telling her to *cut the shit and get the hell out of here*, but I couldn't. I always had a weak spot for her. Weak spots—that's the kind of stuff that puts nails in brothers' coffins.

"I know, Matisse. It's not like I'm trying to make another love connection. I just wanted to stop by and say hello. You were on my mind."

Okay, it's time to take the kid gloves off, I thought to myself. *She's insulting my intelligence now*. "I was on your mind?" My voice grew louder. "Is that what you said?"

"Yes, Matisse, you've been on my mind," Sullivan said softly, almost to a whisper.

"After five years? Wow!"

"Okay, wait a minute, Matisse." The soft whisper was gone. "I can hear it your voice and I can see you're getting upset."

"You think?" My glare was piercing and she felt it.

Refusing to back down, Sullivan raised her voice. "All right, Matisse, you win. It has been five years and I shouldn't have just dropped in on you like this, but for the record, and please don't get it twisted, I'm not the sole reason for the demise of our relationship. So, get off your high horse! It takes two, and I wasn't there alone. We both know what went down, and you made mistakes too, Matisse. And, you know what?"

"No, what?"

"Your ungrateful ass should be as happy to see me as I am you!"

"Unbelievable!" I let out a laugh while shaking my head. "I don't have time for this shit! You know good and well how it went down, Sullivan, so why are you sitting in my office fronting?"

"Just saying, Matisse, we both contributed to its failure."

"Okay, well, you see it one way and I see it another. I don't want to be rude, but I have a big meeting in a few minutes here. So...."

"Of course," said Sullivan. She stood, clutching her purse. "I'm really sorry for just showing up like this. Like I said, Matisse, I just wanted to stop by and say hello. Whether you believe me or like it or not, you have been on my mind a lot lately."

"Look, I saw your ass at the airport yesterday."

She looked at me like I was crazy, "Saw who?"

"You!"

"At the airport?"

My eyes widened as I stared her in the face, "Yes! You were hiding behind those big-ass sunglasses. Say you weren't! I dare you!"

"Please! Anyway, Matisse! Why would you say some stupid shit like that? You saw me on the news last night."

"Yes, I did, but I saw you at the airport earlier."

Sullivan let out a big laugh, "Okay, if you say so, Matisse. I'm going to get out of your hair and take off now. Take care."

She walked out of my office while I just stood there. I tried not to watch her leave, but it was impossible. As I watched Sullivan make her exit, with my heart rate up and temper soaring, many thoughts, good and bad, ran through my mind. Why she didn't own up to being at the airport was beyond me. It seemed odd, but her denial wasn't my issue.

I had about an hour before Jerrell was to show up. I usually spent the time before big meetings going over my strategy, but as I sat in my office staring at the various documents scattered across my desk, it seemed useless. I started to pick up the phone and call her. However, my pride was too big for that. Plus, I no longer had her number. I meant what I had said. She couldn't just walk back into my life like nothing had happened—even if I felt she may have been the one I let get away.

A knock at the door interrupted my trip down memory lane.

"Come in," I answered. Gathering my composure, I tried my hardest to look busy. Gail, my receptionist, entered the room.

"You all right?"

"Yeah, of course." I shifted several times in my chair, feeling, and no doubt looking, foolish. "Why wouldn't I be all right?"

"I don't know. She clearly was one of your ex squeezes."

"Clearly, huh?"

"Clearly!"

"I love how you cut right to the chase, Gail. It was a long time ago," I snapped. "She had no right just showing up like that."

"She sure seemed nice. We had a pretty good conversation before you arrived."

"About what?"

"You, of course." Gail plopped down on my couch, as she often did. It'd be nice if from time to time, she'd ask. Though, I wasn't complaining this time. I wanted to hear all about this conversation.

"What was said?" I quickly asked.

"For starters, she said you always hit it properly."

"Whatever, Gail! Come on, I'm serious. What was said? How'd the conversation go? And I mean word for word. Let's not forget who signs your checks."

"All right, all right. Slow down, tiger. I don't think I've ever seen you this uptight behind a woman. A matter of fact, I know I haven't. And we've been together for a long time."

"Gail, can you save the observations and get on with what was said?"

She let out a big sigh. "Okay! All she said was that she felt uncomfortable showing up here unexpectedly, and that she was a little uneasy about how you'd react. I wasn't as inquisitive as I normally am, so I didn't get too much into her business. Like I said, it's obvious you guys had some type of hot and heavy relationship. Oh, but she did say that she recently moved back here and that she was coming out of a relationship. She had something she wanted to ask you about. Then you walked in the door and our conversation was over. There! Does that work for you? Will I still get paid this Friday?"

"Whatever! Don't you have some work to do? I know I do. Hint, hint."

Gail stood and said, "You're welcome," before storming out of my office. I didn't even look up to acknowledge her. That was our relationship in a nutshell. Though we bantered back and forth often, there was a true fondness between us; we knew that when push came to shove, we had each other's back.

8

A TRIP DOWN
MEMORY LANE

IMMEDIATELY following my meeting with Jerrell and the Knicks'
general manager, which was a complete waste of time, I took the rest
of the day off. I was meeting Miles for dinner later that night. After
Sullivan's surprise visit, I knew the prospect of having a productive
afternoon in the office was nothing but a mere pipedream. So, I went
home. What can I say? It was an excuse for me to catch up on my
soaps.

With the weather being so crisp, I figured it would be a good
opportunity to cool out in my Jacuzzi. I have one of those bathtubs
that doubles as a Jacuzzi. It's nice and I love it, but I rarely make
the time to take advantage of it. Due to my livelihood, I'm kind of
obsessive about televisions. I have them all throughout my condo,
and mind you my condo isn't all that big. Anyway, I have televisions
mounted in all of the bathrooms as well as in the kitchen. I'm almost
embarrassed to say how many are in my study, but I have ten placed
on one of the walls there. Believe it or not, that room comes in
handy when I'm trying to get a little work done and have multiple
clients playing at the same time—kudos to the inventor of flat-screen
televisions.

As I lounged in the tub trying to focus my attention

on *General Hospital*, I quickly came to the conclusion that it
was impossible. I was simply staring at the television and not
comprehending a damn thing. Sullivan had invaded every single one
of my thoughts.

I'll never forget the day we met. It was the second game of
the 1992 NBA Finals. The game was being played at the old Chicago
Stadium. I'd seen her on TV a few times covering this event and that
event, and wasn't all that impressed. I thought, *What does this silly
girl know about sports?* As far as I was concerned, she was clearly
a jock-sniffer. You know the type—around sports all of the time for
the sole purpose of landing a well-sculpted man who earns a seven-
figure annual salary.

One of my clients, Mason Brown, who at the time was
commonly referred to as "Crunch Time" due to his play late in the
games, was having a stellar playoff series. He was concluding his
third NBA season and up to that point hadn't been a media-friendly
player. It just wasn't his thing. All he cared about was balling. I had
tried to change that on a number of occasions, but he wouldn't listen.
I used to tell him that the media-friendly players were the ones who
got the big endorsement deals. You know how that goes. I was trying
to put some paper in both of our pockets, but it was to no avail until
Sullivan obnoxiously flagged me down before Game Two.

"Mr. Spencer! Mr. Spencer!" yelled Sullivan from her
courtside post. She had just finished doing a pre-game interview with
one of the players. I was on the way to my seat. My hands were full.
I had a couple dogs in one hand and a bottle of water in the other, but
nevertheless, I turned to see who was screaming out my name. By
this time she was all in my grill. I didn't have time to say anything.
"Mr. Spencer, I know you represent Mason Brown."

"Yeah, and?" I said, peeping her out on the sly. Sullivan's
look was natural. She wore hardly any makeup and didn't need it,
either. She stood around five-six, but the heels she had on elevated
her to about five-eight or five-nine. Her hair was long and wavy. It
was hard to get a body check due to the blue pantsuit she sported. I
could tell she was really thin, though. Sullivan was very stylish. If
I had to guess I would say her suit was Armani or Gucci. The thing

that stood out the most was her long eyelashes. She tried to downplay her beauty behind a pair of glasses. It worked until she stood right in front of you. At that point, Sullivan's beauty was undeniable. I wasn't going to let it get to me, though. I was determined to play hardball with her.

"Is there any way to do a ten-to fifteen-minute sit-down with him tomorrow? I know he doesn't like talking to the media, but considering the way he's playing, I just thought it was worth a try."

"That's why his team has a PR department. Why aren't you going through the proper channels?"

"Come on, Mr. Spencer, you know why."

"Actually, no, I don't. But my food's getting cold. If you don't mind, I'd like to get to my seat." I'm the type of guy who likes to watch games and eat without any distractions. I like to get the food in me first and then watch the game. I knew I was being somewhat rude, but didn't really care. What can I say? I was hungry. As I turned and began to make my way to my seat, Sullivan grabbed my arm, which forced me to turn back around.

"Excuse you!"

"Look, Mr. Spencer, I'm sorry, but this is a win-win situation. In case you don't know, my *Sports Extra* show is the highest rated in the city. The piece would be totally positive."

"The city? What city?"

"Here in Chicago." She sounded as though I should have automatically known. Of course I did know, but she didn't need to know all of that. I wasn't about to stroke an ego that was already too large.

"The highest rated in the city doesn't do much for us. Everyone knows about Mason's ambivalence towards the media, so why would his coming-out party be on such a small scale? Hell, you know as well as I do that he's having an MVP-type series, which warrants a national audience if he's going to break his silence. I mean, why should he agree to a sit-down with you and turn down Marv Albert's request?"

"In the very near future, Mr. Spencer, I'll be sitting in Marv Albert's very seat and doing a better job." I could tell she was mad, but like I said, I didn't care. I was ready to grub.

"Well, until then, the point is moot. And let me give you a little piece of advice: when you're trying to get someone to do something for you, grabbing their arm isn't the way." I turned and headed towards my seat.

I didn't have the big-baller floor seats like most super-agents did. It was still early in my career, as it was in Sullivan's. Though I was irritated by her approach, I was impressed with Sullivan's confidence.

Mason had another great game. He dropped 37 on them, including the game-winning tip-in dunk just as the buzzer sounded. You talk about a person peaking at the right time. I'd never seen anything like it. He was having the series of his career, but I'm not sure he fully understood what it all meant. I, on the other hand, knew exactly what it meant. Mason was in a contract year. He was to become a free agent as soon as the finals were over. His stock had risen considerably. I had dollar signs in my eyes while my mouth produced a continuous drool. I couldn't wait for the season to be over because I knew that I was going to go for the jugular when I negotiated his new deal. After all, in my business you have to strike while the iron is hot. I've seen players get career contracts from a good first or second half of a season, or, as in Mason's case, from a good playoff series.

After the game, Mason and I met for a late dinner at Gene and Georgetti's, a joint near the team hotel in downtown Chicago.

"You did work tonight. Way to stick it to 'em," I said, clutching a glass containing my signature Stoli on the rocks. The restaurant, known primarily for its steaks, was crowded and dimly lit.

"Thanks, man."

I could tell I didn't have Mason's full attention. I was doing most of the talking and his responses all seemed to be composed of one and two words. The bar was behind me and that was the area where Mason's eyes were fixated.

"Mason, what's up?"

"Nothing, Mat. I'm just glad we got that win."

"Tell me about it," I said. "You guys must feel a little

relieved to have a two-one lead over the defending champs."

Ignoring what I'd just said, Mason responded, "Damn, she's fine."

"Who?"

"Be cool, Mat, and turn slowly. She's sitting up at the bar in the blue. She's got a couple fly friends, too, but from where I'm sitting, she looks the best."

Upon slowly turning and focusing my attention to the bar, I witnessed Sullivan sitting with a couple of her fine-ass friends. *I'll be damned*, I thought. I turned back around and took a sip of my Stoli.

"Fine, huh?"

"Yeah, she's all right."

"All right? What! Matisse, come on. Why are you always trying to downplay?"

"I'm not trying to downplay, Crunch Time. I mean, you know, it's all subjective. I like a little thickness. She looks like one of those typical little, skinny, scrawny babes. You know who that is, right?"

"Naw, who?"

"She does sports here for the NBC affiliate."

"Here?"

"Yeah. You didn't see her covering the game tonight?"

"Naw. You know I have tunnel vision when I step on the court. All I'm thinking about is dunking on fools!"

Whatever, I thought. *This cat has a few outstanding games and now all of the sudden he's all business every time he steps on the court.*

"Well, she approached me tonight before the game about doing a short sit-down with you tomorrow. I gave her two reasons why it wouldn't fly."

"Which were?"

"Well, for starters, you don't mess with the media, and secondly, if you did decide to break your silence, it would have to be on a larger scale."

"What? Set that shit up, Mat."

"But what about your routine of not talking to the media?"

He smiled. "Hey, even I have limits. Look at her. She's fine!"

"I don't think it's a good idea, Mason."

"Oh, would you look at this. You're the one who's constantly on me about not talking to the media. Talking that endorsement deal shit all the time."

"Well, yeah, I think you should be a media-friendly player. Talking to the media on a daily basis would increase your marketability, but your coming-out party should be on a national scale."

"Mat, I don't care about any of that stuff. I just want to meet this girl. Let me make her day, bruh!"

"If that's all you want, I can introduce you to her now." I dreaded hearing his response, knowing how rude I'd been to her earlier, all behind some food, too. I was hungry then and wanted to focus on the game.

"Bet, let's go! Or, no, better yet, why don't you have her and her cute friends join us here at the table?"

Because I aim to please, especially where my clients were concerned, I hesitantly agreed. "All right, I'll be back." Though it was a short walk to the bar, I now knew how women felt the morning after a one-night stand when leaving the scene of the romp session— the infamous "Walk of Shame." This was definitely a walk of shame for me because I knew I had to eat crow.

I took a deep breath before tapping Sullivan on the shoulder. She turned, took one look at me and promptly rolled her eyes without saying a word. It was one of those times where words weren't necessary. I clearly wasn't at the top of her favorite persons list. I felt small, but this was business and I had to follow through.

"Listen, I know we got off to a bad start and I'm sorry for that." Her silence continued. "In fact, I'm having dinner with Mason as we speak and coincidentally, you've been one of our topics."

"Is that right?" Sullivan responded.

"Yeah, that's right. Mason would like to do the fifteen-minute sit-down with you tomorrow."

"What brought this on? I thought I was too smalltime for his—how'd you put it—'coming-out party'?" I had to bite my tongue on that one. Shit, truth be told, she wasn't large enough, but that's what my man wanted.

"Let me ask you this: do you want the interview or not?"

"Of course I do," she said.

"Well then, enough said. Mason would like to meet you beforehand, so why don't you and your friends join us for dinner?"

"Okay," Sullivan replied hesitantly. It was definitely one of those moments where I hated being me. It was bad enough that I had to swallow my pride by approaching her with this, but then I had to endure all of her smug responses, which were topped off by me inviting her to dine with us. Yeah, it wasn't a good time to be Matisse Spencer.

Sullivan and her friends made it over to the table, but only stuck around for just a short while. Mason laid it on pretty thick, but to Sullivan's credit, she was all business. She didn't seem the least bit interested in what he was throwing at her. However, Jasmine, one of Sullivan's girls, was clearly in awe of Mason. She should have been wearing a sign on her forehead that read, "Mason, just say the word." I knew what time it was. I'm quite sure Sullivan and her other friend knew what time it was too; Mason certainly knew because he ended up marrying her a year later.

I was impressed with Sullivan. Talk about coming full circle. After chatting with her at the table, I could tell she was serious about her profession and wasn't the jock-sniffing type I had envisioned her to be. I even peeped her out a little more. She was still a bit thin for my taste, but I could see Mason's initial attraction to her. What can I say? She was fine and there was no denying it.

Anyway, the next day Sullivan interviewed Mason. It went well, but even better for me. I had worked up enough nerve to ask her out for dinner, something that, in my mind, was totally unprofessional. I'm sure she thought so too, but for some reason agreed. From that day on, Sullivan and I were inseparable, until about five years ago when the entire relationship exploded like a firecracker. Everything was shot to shit—but that's another story.

The ringing of my phone interrupted my thoughts of Sullivan and our first encounter. It was Miles.

"We still doing dinner tonight?" he asked.

"Yeah."

"Cool, what time are you going to scoop me?"

"I'll be there around seven," I said, shifting my body in the water.

"Bet. What's all that noise? You taking a bath or something?"

"Aw, I'm cooling out in my Jacuzzi. I kind of had a stressful day."

"It wouldn't have anything to do with who we saw on TV last night would it?"

"You guessed it."

"What happened?"

"You're not going to believe this. She came into my office today. Actually, she was there waiting when I got in this morning. She and Gail were acting like they were best friends."

"What!"

"Yeah, man. Can you believe that?" I said before taking a swig of bottled water I had on ice.

"So, what's her deal?"

"I don't know, man. I told her she just couldn't walk back into my life after a five-year absence. Besides, the way it ended was way too messy."

"Why is she back here?"

"We really didn't get that far. After I got over the initial shock of actually seeing her, I started to get pissed. She knew it wasn't cool to just show up like that. She also knew I didn't appreciate it. I had to get after her a little bit. She was trying to front. Anyway, I'll tell you all about it tonight."

"All right, dog. You straight?"

"Yeah, I'm cool."

"Stay up."

"I'll see you at seven."

Hanging up the phone, I cut the television off and listened to some Coltrane on my iPad while I continued to sit and relax in the Jacuzzi. I wasn't about to let Sullivan ruin the rest of my day.

9

STEAK AND BONES

MILES and I found ourselves at Bones, one of the top steakhouses in Atlanta. The ambiance was similar to most steakhouses, dark and smoke-filled. I usually went to Bones when I knew I wasn't going to be in opposite-gender company. It was a restaurant where men could be men. Sipping on cognac and smoking cigars were almost mandatory at Bones. It was the perfect place to get full from the finest cuts of meat, get a little tipsy and engage in good conversation with your boys—or in my case, with my boy, Miles.

"I can't wait to tear into that filet," I said.

"Filet! Man, it's all about the New York. That's the best piece of meat, Matisse."

"Yeah, whatever. I see you still don't know anything about steak. You still drenching your steaks with A-1 and ketchup?"

"Oh, here you go! Man, when we were in college, I'll admit I didn't know what I was doing back then. But now, shit, Matisse, everyone knows the New York is tastier than the filet."

"Well, I beg to differ, player. Quietly, if you're talking about tasty cuts, the rib-eye beats both of them. On another front, that was weird bumping into Hunter the other day at the airport. What was even weirder was seeing you get off the plane yucking it up with her boyfriend. How do you know him?"

"Who? Jeff?"

"Yeah, I guess that's the brother's name," I said nonchalantly, trying not to sound too pressing. You know how that goes. Brothers are always trying to size up their ex's new man, hoping he's not about shit.

"I don't really know him all that well. He's one of my frat brothers. He and I met at a fraternity function about a year ago."

"Is that right?"

"Yep, but what I'm really trying to figure out is, what's the deal with Sullivan?" Miles asked, seconds before the server made it over to our table.

"Hello, how are you guys doing tonight?" asked a statuesque blond woman. She was the owner of a toothy smile.

Together we responded with, "We're doing well" in such perfect unison that it sounded like an a cappella effort by the musical group, Take 6.

"Great, can I start y'all off with something to drink?"

"What do you think, Mat? You want to start off with a bottle of vino?"

"Yeah, that's cool. We'll save the yak and cigars for afterwards."

"Right, right," Miles agreed, nodding his head before looking back up at the server. "You carry any reds by Cosentino?"

"As a matter of fact we do. We have the Zin as well as the Cigar Zin."

"No brainer," I said.

Once again, in unison, Miles and I belted out, "Cigar Zin!"

The server let out a cute chuckle before saying, "Okay! Cigar Zin it is. My name's Katie, and I'll be right back."

"Thank you, Katie," I said, trying to shoot a little game just for the sport of it.

"Oh, don't even start, Mat," Miles said playfully once she was out of earshot.

"Hey, I can still do that. I'm not the one getting married."

"You got a good point there. However, I just don't think you have the skills."

Though Miles was kidding and as we both laughed about

it, I thought for a moment before adding, "On a serious note, Miles, we both know I still have the skills. I just don't have the energy and drive to chase skirts like I once did."

"I'm hip. You're preaching to the choir right now. Why do you think I threw in the towel so soon?"

"I thought it was because you were in love and ready to settle down."

"Well, yeah, of course those are two of the reasons, but I also got tired of the game."

"That's all it is, too, huh? A game."

Our conversation was interrupted by Katie's return with the bottle of wine. I watched her perform the standard uncorking ritual and okayed the taste pour as if Miles and I were on a stupid-ass date with each other.

"Are you gentleman ready to order?"

"Yeah, I think we are. I'll go with the 23-ounce filet and all the trimmings that come with it."

Katie smiled. "Okay, excellent choice. How would you like that cooked?"

I turned to Miles and grinned before looking back up at her with my answer. "Medium rare."

"That's gross!" Miles blurted out.

"Whatever!" I said."

"Step aside, rookie, let me show you how it's done," Miles said, focusing his attention on me. "I'm not even going to look at the menu. I'll have the biggest New York you all offer and ditto what my man said about all the trimmings, cooked the only way steak should be, sweetie. Medium well!"

Miles continued to stare at me the entire time he placed his order, I guess for effect. I'll admit, it made for a few laughs.

Katie collected our menus before leaving to place the order. Silence separated Miles and me for a moment as we both surveyed the lay of the land. For the most part, it was a hard leg convention, but like I said, that's what made Bones, Bones.

I looked at Miles, smiled and gave him a pound. "My man! You're really about to do this, huh?"

"Yeah, man." A huge grin opened up Miles's face. "I'm about to go down. It's a good thing. I can't wait."

"How do you feel? I mean, marriage, if it's done right, is forever. That's the part that always scares me," I confessed before taking a sip of wine.

"Well, in that case, Mat, you should probably thank your lucky stars that I'm the one who'll be walking down that aisle and not you. No, but seriously, I think it probably scares most men. And I'm no different, bruh. I feel good, though. I'm excited."

"Glad to hear it, man. I really am." I thought for a moment about Miles and marriage. It was starting to really force me to ponder what direction my personal life was heading. "We're getting old, Miles."

"It sucks, huh?" Miles delicately placed his empty wineglass down on the table seconds before Katie reappeared.

"How are we doing on drinks? Are you guys okay with the wine?"

"Actually," I said. "We're running a little low. Let's go with another bottle of the Cigar Zin."

"Okay, I'll be right back."

I grabbed Miles's glass and filled it before giving myself a refill. "Wine," I said, looking at our two full glasses and the empty bottle in front of us. "That must be a good business to be in. I mean, think about it, Miles. One bottle is only good for three or four glasses."

Shaking his head, Miles replied, "This is true," as he glanced around.

"So, what's this guy's deal, Miles?"

"Who?"

"This Jeff cat?"

"I don't know, man. Like I said, I really don't know him all that well. Why are you so interested? If this is going where I think it's going, don't do it, Mat. Don't even think about it."

"Think about what? I'm not even tripping," I responded, shifting several times in my seat. Miles caught me slipping. Not only were my pants down, they were hitting the floor and straddling

my ankles. My poker face was non-existent. Though I refused to
let it show in Hunter's presence, it bothered me a bit that she had
already fallen in love with some peanut head. Yeah I'd run through
quite a few women post-Hunter, but they didn't mean anything. Not
that I was interested in being with Hunter again, because I wasn't.
Nevertheless, for some reason it bothered me. Typical male ego, I
guess.

"I don't know, Matisse, it seems like this brother's on your
mind quite a bit. And if he is, hey, I feel you. We've all been there.
Just don't let it get the best of you. And, by the way, you never did
respond to my question about Sullivan. What's she doing in the ATL,
man?"

"Look, Miles, I'm not trying to talk about Sullivan right now.
But, I'll be honest with you where Hunter is concerned. For some
reason it is bothering me a bit. It's funny because, had I not run into
Hunter at the airport, I wouldn't even be thinking about it. And it's
not like I miss her or want her back. Hell, I couldn't even sleep last
night because of that damn Sullivan! She's the one who's really on
my mind, but I still don't like the thought of some other cat spending
time with Hunter."

"You're starting to confuse me, Mat. Which is it? Are you
missing Hunter or are you missing Sullivan?"

"I'm not missing either one. As far as Hunter goes, I just
don't like that fact that she's moved on so soon. I figured she'd be
miserable for at least a year," I said jokingly.

"At the risk of not sounding supportive, Mat, you were back
out there with the quickness after you all broke up. I mean, you
didn't waste any time, black man! Hell, five or six women come to
mind."

"Yeah, but you know how that is—purely a guy thing. I
didn't care about any of those women. I was just trying to get over
Hunter. I take that back. There was one who was pretty special, but
you know me; the hottest, most wonderful girl could be staring me in
the face and I would still find some type of reason to run."

"Yeah, Mat, no offense, but you are that guy who looks at
that perfect statue over and over again, and sooner or later finds

cracks in it. But, hey, I've been there, too." Miles reached for his glass of wine. "Well, what's the deal with Sullivan? Why is she on your mind so much?"

"Come on, Einstein, I know you didn't just ask that. Why do you think? You know how I felt about her, and you know our history. All of the sudden she just shows up out of the blue. I mean, what is that?"

"Yeah, I'd be tripping, too."

"Enough about me. I'm tired of talking about it. Right now my social life is pitiful," I said just as Katie arrived with our second bottle of Cigar Zin.

10

PARENTS' BRUNCH

I woke up to the ringing of my phone. My mom had never obeyed my don't-call-before-ten-a.m. rule, and this Sunday was no exception.

"Matisse, you're still coming for brunch a little later, right?"

"Yeah, Mom, I'll be there. Damn, what time is it?"

"It's 8:30, Matty, and must we use such language on the *Lord*'s day?"

"What'd I say?"

"You said 'damn.'"

"Oh," I chuckled. "Is that still considered a swear word? Hell, I figured if it's used on prime-time television then the powers that be automatically eliminated it from the dirty word list."

"Yeah, yeah, yeah. You're a grown man, Matty. I can't control the words that come out of your mouth, but I would think the Lord deserves a little respect on His day."

"Okay, you're right, Mom. I know when Dad sits down to watch his beloved Bears play this afternoon he'll be watching what he says, too," I offered sarcastically.

"Matisse Spencer, don't start," my mom snapped. Though I was talking to her on the phone, I could feel her stern look.

Laughing, I replied, "I'm just playing around with you, Mom."

"You're bringing Miles too, right?"

"Yeah, I'm bringing his sorry behind."

"Oh, Matty, hush. Well, good. We haven't seen him in quite some time. I can't wait to hear all about his upcoming wedding."

"All right, well, we'll see you in a few. Bye," I said, hanging up the phone abruptly. I had to cut her off before she went any further. She loved hearing about two people coming together and tended to get long-winded on the topic of weddings. I knew it would have been just a matter of time before she started in on me, as she did every chance she got.

My parents hosted Sunday brunch every other week. It was something they had started long ago when we lived in Chicago. In addition to our family, there were usually one or two other families attending. I'll never forget how the grownups would sit at one table while all of the kids were forced to sit at another. Back then, things almost always got a little out of hand. I mean, think about it: any time you get six to ten kids under one roof for hours at a time, compounded by back-to-back NFL games on TV and a group of grownups sipping on Mimosas and Bloody Marys—mayhem, at some point during the course of the day, is bound to occur.

Since my parents relocated to Atlanta following their retirement, Sunday brunch has been toned down considerably. These days it usually consists of my parents and a couple of their friends. When I'm in town I try to make it, but usually try to steer clear from taking dates over there. Knowing my mom, she'd have us married before the end of brunch.

I had a few hours to kill before heading over to my parents' place. Though I tried to go back to sleep, I couldn't. On mornings like that I normally didn't have any problems just lying in bed watching television, but I figured I'd be productive for once. So I jumped out of bed, threw on a pair of shorts, a tee shirt and a Nike pullover windbreaker before lacing up some Air Maxes and went for a run.

Ordinarily I would have belted out three or four miles on my treadmill, especially in chilly December weather. However, my nervous energy had gotten the best of me and I had a strong hunch as to why.

At the tail end of my run I stopped off at Starbucks for a cup of coffee. The popular coffee shop was located about a block from my place, so it wasn't like I was half-stepping on my workout. I went there pretty often, but not because I'm a huge coffee drinker. I just liked the ambiance. You know how sometimes as soon as you enter a place it seems like all eyes are on you. Well, this particular Starbucks wasn't like that. Sure, it was a bit cliquish, but it allowed you much-needed quiet and alone time if that's what you desired. And I was in dire need of both.

My routine was to slowly sip on a cup of java and nibble on a scone while reading the newspaper. I often took eye-candy breaks where I'd lower the newspaper slightly and pop my head up over it to peep out the honeys. This entire process was normally done out of habit, but this was a morning where it was done out of necessity. I needed to get Sullivan off my mind. Besides, with only a few weeks until Miles's wedding, I had my work cut out for me regarding organizing the bachelor party. I was definitely behind the eight-ball at that point.

All of it was to no avail. The more I tried to peep out the honeys, the more I thought about Sullivan. It seemed like a cyclical process because it brought me right back to Miles's wedding. Though I was extremely envious of Miles and his upcoming nuptials, I wondered if I could really spend the rest of my life with one woman. I obviously hadn't found the deep connection needed to actually want to spend that amount of time with one person and be selfless all the way through. It irked me to know that my attention span was so short. Over the years, I let some pretty amazing women fall by the wayside. Hunter and Erica came to mind and, of course, Sullivan. Perhaps a little patience would have helped with Hunter, and being less superficial would have solved the problem with Erica. Sullivan, however, was a different story. When the relationship abruptly fell apart, I had very little say about the outcome and there was nothing I could do to get it back on track. She was right in that it does take two to successfully move forward together or muck things up. I played a role in the relationship's demise, but Sullivan's actions killed it for good. The taste in my mouth was still bitter, but, upon seeing her, I could feel my resolve to stay clear of her had weakened. I'm human.

By the time Miles and I made it over to my parents' place, the first game had already started. The Bears were playing San Francisco, and my dad had already assumed the position. It was known to all that his next movement wouldn't take place until halftime. His favorite oversized chair, complete with ottoman, was placed in the center of the room directly facing the television.

My mom greeted us at the door with the widest of smiles and her arms spread apart. She hugged Miles and me at once. We simultaneously pecked her cheeks.

"Well, it's about time," my mom scolded playfully, shutting the door behind us. "What took you guys so long? As you can hear and you'll soon see, your father hasn't changed a bit."

"What?" I said loudly, making light of the fact that my dad had the television volume cranked up as high as possible.

"Exactly. You see what I have to put up with, Matty. And how are you doing, Miles? I'm so glad you made it over."

"I'm doing great, Mrs. S. Thanks for having me."

"Honey, the boys are here," yelled my mom. Not bothering to turn and look, my dad motioned with his arm. The infamous "wave-while-the-game's-going-on" meant come in, sit down and shut up until halftime or a timeout. The only noises permissible in my father's house while the Bears game was going on had to be pro-Bears. Cheering for the Bears was definitely encouraged.

I gave my dad a pound while Miles patted him on the back. Seconds after sitting, my mom ordered me into the kitchen.

"Matisse, let me take a look at you. Are you taking good care of yourself?"

"Yeah, Mom. Can't you tell?"

"Are you eating okay? You're looking a little thinner than usual."

I took that as a compliment. "That's because I've been working out, Mom."

"Well, I'd like to see you with a little more meat on your bones." She handed me a mimosa before walking to the edge of the kitchen and sticking her head into the television room. "Miles, what would you like to drink? We have mimosas and Bloody Marys in the adult beverage department, and orange juice, water and soft drinks in the non-alcoholic category."

"If I remember correctly, Mrs. S, your Bloody Marys are to die for."

"Oh, you're so sweet. One Bloody Mary coming right up."

"So, what's for brunch, Mom?" I asked, surveying the kitchen. "I'm starved!"

"Omelets and French toast. Here." She handed me a sweet roll. "Eat this. That should tide you over until halftime."

"Oh, I forgot, we're still planning brunch around Dad's football game." I took a swig of my mimosa.

"I know. I know. It's ridiculous. What are you going to do? That's your father."

"No, that's your husband."

"Very funny, Matty. Can you take this down to Miles?" She handed me his drink. The Bloody Mary could have won a prize for appearance. The glass, a 16-ounce beer pint, was chilled. From just looking at it you could tell it was spicy; the cracked pepper and Tabasco were visible. A couple of green olives floated just below the surface, while a large stalk of celery leaned against the side of the glass like it was holding up a wall.

Just as I entered the television room the whistle sounded, signaling halftime. "Here." I handed Miles his drink.

"Looking good, Mrs. S," yelled Miles.

"Matisse, Miles, how you guys doing?" my dad asked, climbing out of his chair.

"Doing great, Mr. S," Miles said. "With that ten-zero lead, I'm guessing you're doing pretty well too."

"You guessed right," my dad replied before giving me a couple pats on my thigh. "You all right?"

"Yeah, I'm good. I'm hungry. You ready to eat?"

"Yep." He walked into the kitchen. "Babe, you ready?"

"Yeah, we're going to eat in the dining room."

"Let's go guys," said my dad, leading the pack. Before the

four of us sat down at the table, my dad turned to Miles. "So, I hear you're walking the plank."

"Oh, honey, stop!" my mom chastised as she sat back in her chair.

"Yeah, Mr. S. That's one way to put it, I guess."

"Aw, I'm just playing, Miles. Congratulations! Marriage is a good thing." Looking in my direction, my dad continued, "Your mother is still as fine as she was the first day I laid eyes on her many moons ago."

"Well thank you, honey." My mom leaned over and gave my dad a soft kiss on his forehead.

"Come on guys, dig in," said my mom. "God forbid this runs into the third quarter."

"Babe, this looks good," my dad responded, ignoring what she'd just said.

"I'm so excited for you, Miles. Now if we could only get this one married." She pointed at me. "Touch him, Miles. Maybe some of that will rub off on him."

"Ha ha, very funny, Mom," I said through a mouthful of food. "You're a regular Richard Pryor."

"You're not getting any younger, Matty. Don't you want to be able to play with your kids without breaking your back or damaging your knees?"

"Mom, I'm only 38. I have plenty of time. Besides, I'm not the one with a biological clock. And another thing, marriage doesn't guarantee you kids. Hell, kids are a blessing. It's not automatic. See, a lot of people have it all wrong. There are so many people out there getting married for the wrong reasons. You got people getting married because their biological clock is ticking. Or they're getting up there in age. Or because they've dated for x amount of years and feel it's time. Or they think they'll make pretty babies with this person. The list can go on and on, but in my mind, the only reason two people should get married is because they're in love. That's it! Everything else is gravy, especially kids. As a society, we're so overly concerned with producing pretty babies it's sickening. If I'm ever fortunate enough to get married and have kids, I just pray they're healthy."

"Here, here," my dad added. "Well said, Son. Sounds to me like Matisse has it all figured out, babe. It may be time to leave the boy alone."

My dad was right. I sounded like I had it all figured out. Yeah, I talked a good game, but in reality, I was clueless. Where my heart was concerned, I didn't know which way was up, let alone marriage.

"I just worry about you, Matty." She patted my hand.

"All in due time, Mom; all in due time. Everything happens for a reason."

"This is true, Mrs. S," added Miles. "It's all about timing."

"On that note," said my dad, "let me get back to this game. When you guys are finished eating, come join me. Babe, you never cease to amaze me. Another wonderful brunch." He kissed my mom on the lips and made his way back to the TV room.

11

RENEWED FRIENDSHIP

IT had been a couple of days since my parents' get-together for Sunday Brunch, and I was still reeling from the experience. Leading up to that Sunday, Sullivan had already been on my mind. But between Miles's and my parents' raving views about marriage, now she was all I thought of, despite how things had ended between us.

Seeing her and knowing that we once again lived in the same city brought back memories. Now she was a mere stone's throw away. And though it had ended badly, all I could think about were the good times we shared together. Hey, we've all had that one who we thought was the be-all-to-end-all somehow slip through our fingers. Well, Sullivan, I thought, was that one for me.

There was a time when Sullivan and Matisse went together like peanut butter and jelly, or Stockton and Malone. You couldn't think about one without thinking about the other. I just knew that we were going to ride into the sunset together, as did all who knew us.

I finished watching the Knicks game on television. With Jerrell holding out, it seemed like that's pretty much all I did now: watch the Knicks. New York was having a down year, but for some reason they saw fit to try to nickel-and-dime my client, who was clearly their best player. As a result of all of that nonsense, I had to monitor what the Knicks were doing as a team, which meant I had to watch all of their games. Believe me, at times it was pure hell.

Technology is incredible. There was a time just a short while ago when we were held hostage to our local cable companies and their programming. Those days are long gone, thanks to the NBA League Pass. But what's even crazier is being able to watch games from anywhere, compliments of iPads, computers and cell phones. We've come a long way.

Anyway, though the Knicks game had just ended, I continued to monitor the rest of my clients on all of the TVs in my study, but I wasn't into it the least bit—which was highly unusual for me. I'd reached a true dilemma, games versus real life. My livelihood was centered on athletes and games, but my personal life, especially where women were concerned, was struggling.

I took the remote and shut off each and every television one by one, leaving the room completely dark. I sat there for a moment and pondered my next move. Still feeling nostalgic, I turned on my desk light, stood and made my way over to the bookcase.

I've never been a big picture guy, but for some reason I had picture albums on top of picture albums, three of which spotlighted Sullivan and me. I sat down at my desk and began to thumb through them. Though the desk light was on, the room was still dark. My trip down memory lane was chilling.

Good times, that's all I remembered. Knowing the WXIA number by heart, which was Atlanta's NBC affiliate, I picked up the phone and dialed. I knew Sullivan wouldn't be there because it was only about 9:00 p.m. I figured she'd be out following a story or somewhere getting some grub. She wouldn't be on air until 11:00. As luck would have it, Sullivan answered the phone. All I originally wanted to do was hear her voice through her voicemail. When I realized it was Sullivan on the phone, my first instinct was to hang up, but I didn't.

"Uh, Sullivan."

"Matisse?"

"Yeah, it's me."

"Is everything all right, or did hell just freeze over?" she asked. "I'm surprised to hear your voice."

Silence filled the air.

"Don't ask me what I was thinking about because I have no idea."

"Great, that makes me feel wonderful."

"No, I didn't mean it like that. It's just that, well, you know what went on between us. I just never thought we'd ever have a need to talk again," I explained while scratching my head with one hand and clutching the phone tightly with the other. It was cold outside, but hot as hell at that moment in my study. My nerves had caused my body temperature to rise to alarming proportions.

"Yeah, I can relate. I am sorry for just showing up like that the other day. I guess I was hoping for a different response from you. A lot of times I just forget how things ended between us. We both know it was my fault, and I'm extremely sorry. Honestly. I'm also sorry I got upset and tried to place some of the blame on you the other day."

At that point I really didn't know what to say. A part of me wanted to punish her for the way things ended between us, and another part just wanted to forget the whole thing and start anew.

"Matisse, are you still there?"

I still hadn't said anything. I felt myself getting weak. As I sat there, slightly panicked, squeezing the life out of the phone in my hand, I pictured her on the other end of the line. I wondered what she was wearing. How she wore her hair. I thought of her scent. I could feel her full, succulent lips pressed against mine. I thought of her pretty hands. How soft and soothing they were, especially when she'd run them up and down my back.

"Matisse?"

"I'm still here," I said. For some reason I knew I was going to bitch up. I kept picturing the sessions we use to have. Intense is the only word to describe them—multiple orgasms for both of us. And the positions, forget about it! You name it we did it, and it usually ended in a pool of sweat. I sensed the next words to come out of my mouth would ultimately be detrimental to my future, but that didn't stop me. "Considering our past, you being back in town is kind of overwhelming. But we're both adults and that was a long time ago. What do you say we just forget the past? After all, we were friends before we became lovers. Who knows, maybe we could go back to being friends."

I knew what I had just said was like opening up the biggest flesh wound ever.

"Really? You mean that?" replied Sullivan. Though I could sense her excitement, I felt numb and weak. I was pretty sure I was thinking with the wrong head. Typical.

"Yeah, I mean it. Life's too short to hold grudges. We were once good friends, Sullivan."

"The best of friends, Matisse. Hey, I know, why don't we meet for a celebratory lunch sometime this week?"

Once again I grew silent, thinking, *Damn, she's moving kind of fast.* "Yeah, that'd be cool. Let's touch base in few days," I offered unconvincingly.

"Great, I'll talk to you soon. Matisse, thanks for calling. It really means a lot to me."

"Well, I'll talk to you later."

Afterwards, I made my way into the kitchen, grabbed the Stoli out of the freezer, poured myself a drink and returned to my study where I sat in total darkness. Completely dazed, I wondered what had just happened.

12

PIZZA AND BREW

DESPITE being met with a slight hangover when I awoke the next morning, I was determined not to let Sullivan consume my thoughts. As I lay in bed, I went over my to-do list for the day. I had already decided to work from home—one of the many pleasures of owning your own business, I guess. But my number one priority centered on putting together Miles's bachelor party. It was only a couple of weeks away and I hadn't done much of anything up until this point. Hell, I hadn't even procured the party's main ingredient—the women! This meant I had to do a little scouting. I figured about eight to ten women would suffice. I was hosting a little get-together at my place later in the evening—nothing big, just the fellas over to watch the game. It presented the perfect opportunity to get their input. I figured after the game we'd go to a few strip clubs to begin the scouting process. I know it's unbecoming, but what's a bachelor party without strippers?

I've known Miles for a long time and, if you ask me, he was handling this marriage thing a little too well. Don't get me wrong, I thought it was great and I was happy for him, but I know him, too. You know what I'm saying? We always knew he and I would be the last two to get there (which proved to be true), but damn! It was weird; I hadn't seen him come even close to flinching, which, to me, is unusual for any man about to go down. I know this cat and now he was just a little too chilly.

One of my NFL clients, Zack Owens, owns a ridiculously huge house on Lake Lanier. As luck would have it, he wasn't scheduled to return to the ATL from Boston until late February. He was the starting running back for the Patriots. Due to his enormous contract (that I recently negotiated and which made him one of the highest paid running backs in NFL history), I felt comfortable holding the keys to his digs for a few days. Zack's house was the perfect place to entertain. The twelve-bedroom house had three levels with a fully completed basement. Zack did most of his entertaining in the basement. A custom-made flat-screen television, which stretched from the floor to the ceiling, was the focal point of the room. The house was wired with surround sound throughout. The basement's bar could rival some of the bars at the nicest restaurants around. It too was enormous. The granite countertops added a special touch.

I figured we'd spend our days on the boat and nights at the house. I collected $500 from the twenty guys attending. I had the money earmarked for the food, liquor and, of course, women.

Courtney arrived about thirty minutes before the game started. I usually went a little overboard preparing the food, but this time I just didn't feel like cooking. So, I ordered a couple of pizzas from Everybody's, the best pizza place in all of Atlanta.

"What's up, Mat?" asked Courtney, still standing in the doorway.

"You," I replied. "Come on in, man."

"Here." He handed me a twelve-pack of Sam Adams.

"Oh, yeah, this is what I'm talking about," I said, grabbing the twelver out of his hand. "Let me go put this on ice. Grab a seat. The game's about to start. I got some cold ones in the fridge."

"Cool," said Courtney, making himself comfortable on a couch.

"Becks or Sierra Nevada?" I yelled from the kitchen.

"I'll go with the pale ale," Courtney responded. "Where's Jay and Miles?"

"They should be here any minute. Here you go." I handed

Courtney a Sierra Nevada in a chilled pint glass.

"Thanks. Man, I can't believe Miles is about to go down."

"Yeah, I don't know." I plopped down in my prized chair, which directly faced the television. "Sometimes, Courtney, I can believe it and sometimes I can't. I'm happy for him, though."

"Me, too. Marriage is tough, Mat. Don't get me wrong, I wouldn't trade it for the world. I love my wife and I love being married. But it's hard work. A lot of people say it should be easy and natural, but I just don't think that's being realistic. It's tough, man, and it requires a lot of time and elbow grease."

"I'm hip."

"What do you got going on these days, Mat? Do you have anything on your plate or are you trying to be a career bachelor?" Courtney took a sip of his beer. "You can't be a player forever, player!"

"Quietly, I'm trying to get there," I said, resting my feet on the ottoman. "I'd love to be married. I just can't seem to find my way to the altar. I guess finding the right person has a lot to do with it as well."

"I don't know, Mat, from what I've seen, you've had some winners."

The pizza arrived just moments before Jay and Miles, who arrived at the same time. I guess you could say I was saved by the pizza. I hate hearing people tell me that I should have held onto this woman or that woman. Everything happens for a reason and I firmly believe that. In any event, I was looking forward to the evening. It had been a while since the four of us had hung out together.

I placed both of the pizzas on the coffee table in front of Courtney. Jay and Miles entered the room directly behind me, almost as if we were reporting for boot camp.

"What's up, boy," said Jay.

"I can't call it," responded Courtney as he rose from the couch. "Same old shit just another day."

"Ain't that the truth," replied Jay. They gave each other the manly hug/pound.

"You about to join the ranks with me, huh, Miles?" Courtney

said. Still standing, he and Miles embraced the manly way as well.

"Yeah, man. I can't wait, either."

Courtney let out a loud laugh. "You say that now, Chief."

"Aw, whatever, man! I'm ready. It's time!"

"That's good, man, congrats!" said Courtney.

"I know I don't have to tell guys to dig in," I said, making myself comfortable in my chair. "You know the drill. Plus, it's game time!"

For the next ten minutes the only sounds that emanated from that room were those of four grown men eating like they hadn't eaten in years.

"Look, fellas, we need to get going on this bachelor party for my man, Miles," I said once we finally came up for air. "I mean, don't get me wrong, I know that the bulk of that responsibility is mine, being the best man. However, with you guys being the groomsmen, some of that responsibility is pointed in your direction. Quietly, Miles shouldn't even be here while we discuss this, but...."

"Whatever," Miles interjected.

"Say no more, Mat, that's why we're here, right?" Courtney asked.

"All right, cool. Let's finish watching the rest of this game and then let's go do a little shopping," I suggested.

"Hey, we don't really need to do much shopping," explained Jay with a mouthful of pizza. "Let's just use my service."

"Service?" Miles asked before taking a swig of his brew.

Jay was an investment banker who often entertained out-of-town clients. He was a couple of years younger than Miles and I. His linesman body looked like it was too much for his jockey height. He was short and stout.

"Yeah, I use an escort service for my clients."

"Your clients, huh," Courtney said, rolling his eyes. "So, do you indulge too?"

"Well, it's like this, Courtney. Would you endorse Popeye's Chicken without tasting it first?"

"My man!" Courtney chuckled, as did all of us.

"Hey, this is serious business, Jay," I said. "This could save us both time and money, but we need for you to be serious. How do they look, and are they up for anything?"

"Man, you all need to give your boy a little credit. I don't know why you'd think I'd steer you wrong. Of course they all look good and anything goes. It's all gravy, baby."

"You guys cool with it?" I asked.

"Will they give us a break on the price?" Courtney inquired.

"Yeah, man! Damn!" Jay responded. He got up out of his seat, making his way towards the kitchen. "Anyone need a brew?"

Jay was met with three simultaneous, "Yeah's!"

"So, how's the married life treating you, Courtney?" Jay asked, returning with four beers.

"It's good, man. I wouldn't trade it for the world. I love being married, but you have to understand, it takes a whole lot of work. Well, you know this, Jay, being divorced and all."

"Yeah, it's tough. It's not for everyone, though. And it certainly wasn't for me. If you can make it work, more power to you. Not to worry, Miles, I'm sure you'll revel in it," Jay stated.

Miles, sprawled out on the couch and looking as relaxed and content as I've ever seen him, responded, "Bruh, I'm not worried about a thing. I love her. She loves me. I mean, it's really that simple. We're in sync. And, I'm ready."

"I guess that's just a man thing, huh," I asked, placing my beer on top of a coaster.

"Meaning?" said Miles.

"I don't know. It just seems like we try to hold out as long as we possibly can until we decide it's time."

"I don't think it can work any other way," responded Miles.

When the game ended I wanted further assurance from Jay that we were straight where the strippers were concerned. It was late and I was tired, so it didn't really take much convincing. As crazy as it sounds, the last thing I wanted to do that night was scour tittie bars looking for the perfect strippers.

13

LINCOLN DIX

RARELY did I show up in the office before the sun rose, but up to that point I wasn't too happy about the way the negotiations had gone with the Knicks regarding Jerrell's contract. Though we had nothing planned by way of a formal call, I believed this was the perfect opportunity for a cold call. I wanted to add a little spontaneity into the picture. A lot of times going into these scheduled calls, each party has their respective notes and game plans right in front of them, and rarely do they stray from them. I liken it to being out at a bar one night and hooking up with a babe who normally wouldn't give you, or anyone else for that matter, the time of day, but on this particular night you just caught her slipping. Some of my best contracts have come by way of catching various general managers and owners slipping.

In the middle of me dialing the numbers, Gail interrupted on another line.

"Matisse, Lincoln Dix is here to see you."

"Lincoln? What's he doing here? Was he on my schedule?"

"Uh, that'd be a no, Boss."

I sighed, loudly. "Send him in a couple of minutes."

"Will do."

Lincoln Dix was my bread and butter, my top moneymaking client. He played center for the Los Angeles Kings and was the

National Hockey League's leading scorer this year, up until a few weeks ago when he was injured. Lincoln was to hockey what Tiger is to golf. He was to hockey what the Williams sisters are to tennis. Not only was he one of a few African-American players in the game, he was the absolute best the game had to offer. And, yes, I took full advantage of this.

Denzel and Taye Diggs and all those other Hollywood "pretty boys" couldn't hold a candle to Lincoln in the looks department. If you coupled his good looks with his dual J.D./M.B.A. degree from Harvard and his gift of gab, which was mired in a sea of articulate insights, you ended up with Michael Jordan times ten. Simply put, this guy was a marketing sensation. I had endorsement deals coming out of both his ass and mine at the same time.

It's hard not to like a guy who's putting that type of money in your pocket. However, Lincoln had an ego the size of the universe. I kept my disdain for his cockiness under wraps, though. My mom didn't raise any dummies. With all that said, my call to the Knicks would have to wait.

Lincoln walked through the door with his usual swagger, and this was with a banged-up knee.

"What's the word, baby," Lincoln said, still wearing his sunglasses.

"What's up, Lincoln. I didn't think you were coming to town until next week."

He made himself comfortable in one of the chairs in front of my desk. "Yeah, you know how that goes. I'm an East Coast guy. Naw, check that, I'm international—worldwide, baby!"

"Bad break, huh. Damn, you were tearing it up. You had the Kings in first place and you were scoring at will."

Lincoln stretched his legs across my desk. "Shit, Mat, nothing new since I came into the league three years ago. These fools can't touch me. Hell, they can't even see me. It's to the point now where I'm so much better than everyone else that players are taking cheap shots at me. Did you watch that game?"

"Yeah, I saw it."

"Clark's nothing but a cheap-shot artist. That was a

deliberate blow to my knee."

"It sure in the hell was," I agreed. "The league wasn't happy at all. The fine and suspension Clark received were the largest ever in NHL history."

"And that was on top of the ass-whupping he got from my teammates. It's a good thing they had my back. I figure I'm better off in the ATL rehabbing with my personal trainer than I am in LA with the team trainer."

"I don't know about that," I said, massaging my goatee.

"Please! Why not?"I think the team and its training staff have your best interests in mind and know what's best for you regarding rehabbing your knee."

"Look, Mat, Lincoln Dix knows what's best for Lincoln Dix."

"Okay, just saying," I said. "Well, I have a couple appearances lined up for you as well as a few new commercial spots."

"Let's take all of that kind of slow. Right now I just want to concentrate on getting healthy so I can get back on the ice."

"Cool. HBO keeps calling me about getting you on *Entourage*. What's up, are you still not for it?"

"Naw, that's a little rinky-dink show. I haven't seen Tiger or Jordan on there, and I'm bigger than both of them. I'm gonna have to give that one the Heisman!"

"All right, but I have to say it's a damn good show. Suit yourself."

"Listen, I have to cut out, Mat." Lincoln stood and lifted his sunglasses so that they rested on his head before giving me a pound. "I'll talk to you later."

"All right. Get that knee better." I got up and shut the door behind him.

14

TAPPAS AND SULLIVAN

As much as I hated to admit it, I was excited about my dinner plans with Sullivan. I guess it just boils down to being human and having weak spots. Everyone has weak spots and, unfortunately for me, Sullivan had always been that one person who brought me to my knees.

I picked her up at her place immediately after leaving my office. I didn't make much progress on negotiating a new deal for Jerrell with the Knicks, and desperately hoped my luck would change with Sullivan.

Though the drive to the restaurant was only about ten minutes, she talked the entire time. Sullivan seemed to be in an upbeat mood, which I viewed as a good thing. I picked the restaurant without running it by her. After all, I didn't just fall off the turnip truck. I know women hate indecisive men, and I also knew Sullivan and her eating likes and dislikes. I didn't want it to seem like I was trying to woo her with a night of fine dining. This dinner date was designed to help rebuild the friendship we once shared; it wasn't supposed to be this big romantic thing. So, I went for a light, casual, fun atmosphere. Bistro Peachtree was the perfect place.

The restaurant is located in the heart of Buckhead, one of the most affluent neighborhoods in Atlanta. It is known primarily for its appetizers. In fact, I think appetizers are the only things on the menu, which is why I liked it.

The hostess seated us at a table in the back where it wasn't as loud as the rest of the restaurant. This was good because we'd have little trouble hearing each other talk.

"This place seems cool, Matisse," Sullivan offered, looking around. "Do you come here often?"

"Uh…." I thought about it for a moment before replying, "It's in the rotation." I marveled at how good she looked, which caused my mind to wander. Yeah, I was undressing the hell out of her with my eyes. She kept smiling at me, but all I could think about was what type of thong made the cut underneath the tight black leather skirt she had on, or maybe she was really bringing it these days and going straight commando. Sullivan, as I remember, always wore a skimpy thong/bra set that was to die for. It was sexy, but classy. And that was right up my alley.

"In your rotation, huh?" She smiled devilishly and shook her head. "You must eat out a lot."

I smiled like a cat that just swallowed the canary. I could hear myself saying, *Slow down, tiger. Get your mind out of the gutter.* "When I'm in town, I guess I do," I responded, refocusing my attention. "It's hard. I mean, you know how it is. Your schedule's busy, too."

"This is true," Sullivan agreed. "Matisse, I just wanted to thank you again. I'm so glad we're trying to be friends all over. When I think about our time together, we were really good, huh?"

I smiled and, though I wanted to resist, nodded my head. I knew I had to shift the focus of the conversation, even if I didn't necessarily want to. After all, the weak spot I had for her hadn't faded one bit. Her natural beauty was undeniable. If she asked me to roll over and bark like a dog, I probably would have. That's how bad it was. Yeah, I was feeling like an awestruck little sissy. "So, you hungry?"

"I'm starved," Sullivan replied. "I love this menu, Matisse. With all of the different appetizers, we can try a little bit of everything."

There was a brief moment of silence after ordering our

drinks as we perused the menu. Really, Sullivan was the only one
looking over the menu. I pretended like I was, but I knew that thing
like the back of my hand. I wasn't one who liked trying new things,
especially where restaurants were concerned. Once I found a place I
liked I usually stuck with it for awhile.

"So, what's good here, Matisse?" she asked, breaking the
silence.

"Uh, I keep it kind of simple." I sat back in my chair and
drew my fingers through my goatee. "I usually do stuff like the
buffalo fingers and shrimp. However, don't sleep on the filet mignon
kabobs. That's probably my favorite. It's ridiculous!"

"In that case, I'm sold," Sullivan said just as our drinks
arrived. "Still drinking Stoli on the rocks, huh, Matisse?"

"That's right. I see you've gone from a dry martini to the oh-
so-trendy Cosmopolitan."

"I know, I know. I'm such a follower."

"Naw, that's not what I meant." Before I started to explain, I
felt a hand on my shoulder.

"What's up, baby?"

I turned and looked up, but I already knew who it was.
Lincoln Dix loved using the word "baby." He stood over me, wearing
a huge grin.

"Lincoln," I said. "What's going on? Twice in the same day.
Are you following me?"

He laughed. "If I wanted to be bored, I'd go home and go to
sleep."

"Oh, whatever," I responded with a fake laugh. "Lincoln, let
me introduce Sullivan to you. Sullivan, meet Lincoln."

Sullivan held out her hand for the usual business shake.
Lincoln grabbed it and instead of giving it a shake, pulled it to
his lips and kissed it before saying, "It's a pleasure to meet you,
Sullivan."

Sullivan withdrew her hand so fast it made Speedy Gonzalez
look slow. There seemed to be an uneasiness about her as she shifted
in her chair several times. "Hello," Sullivan replied softly.

"I didn't know you had it in you, Matisse," Lincoln said, not bothering to take his eyes off Sullivan.

"Oh, please," I said, adding another fake laugh. The truth of the matter was I really didn't appreciate him interrupting our dinner. It's one thing to say hello, but it's another to try to hit on my date right in front of me. As usual, where Lincoln was concerned, I held my tongue. He was lining my pockets with too much cheddar. As annoying as he sometimes was, it still didn't stop me from doing the unthinkable. "I'm hosting a brunch this Sunday at my place. If you're not doing anything, why don't you stop by?"

"Alright, Mat, cool, count me in."

"Who you here with, Lincoln?" I asked as I wondered what the hell I was thinking about when I invited him to my brunch.

"Just some friends. You know how that goes, baby. As a matter of fact, I need to get back over there. Matisse, I'll see you later. And Sullivan, I certainly hope I see you later." Sullivan made a few more movements in her chair, responding only with a smile.

"You all right?" I asked after Lincoln finally left.

"Yeah, I'm fine. Why?"

"I don't know. It just seemed like you were kind of uncomfortable in his presence. I mean, come to think of it, if you were I can surely understand. He's one of my clients, but he's cocky as hell."

"Matisse, everyone knows who Lincoln Dix is. He's the best hockey player in the world. But, no, I wasn't uncomfortable around him. Well, maybe I was a little uncomfortable when he slobbered all over my hand. What was that all about?"

"I just hope the rehab goes well so he can hurry up and get back on the ice and out of my hair. He's very high-maintenance."

"Yeah, he seems like the type. But, then again, he's all over the place. Everywhere you turn, there he is. You must have gotten him a lot of endorsement deals."

"That's why I can sit here and continue to smile, even after seeing him twice in the same day." Sullivan laughed and placed her hand on top of mine for a moment. While I was kind of taken aback, I acted like it was nothing. But, her touch immediately took me back to a dark time in my life after the passing of my sister. Sullivan was there for me. Her selfless acts of kindness, being there and having my back, meant the world to me then. I wouldn't have gotten through it without her. It wasn't until her warm hand rested on top of mine that I remembered some of the truly good qualities Sullivan possessed that had been overshadowed by my shallow gawking at her physical beauty. She was about much more and it took her touch to remind me.

***

The next morning, Miles violated my don't-call-before-ten-a.m.-on-the-weekends rule, putting him in the same category as my mom. It was Saturday morning and I had planned on sleeping in for a bit. In all honesty, though, I was already awake when he called. My date with Sullivan had gone well and it was still very much on my mind. I tried my best not to get too much into her business, and I could tell the same went for her. We mostly kept the conversation to our jobs and how much we were enjoying the food.

"So, how'd it go?" Miles asked.

"Miles, didn't I tell you about my ten a.m. rule?"

"Oh, man, please! Really, how was the dinner date with Sullivan? Is she still fine?"

"You saw her that night on TV. What'd you think?" I sat up in my bed, grabbed the remote and turned on the television.

"I think she looked pretty damn good."

"Well, nothing's changed. I was having a hard time concentrating, she looked so good."

"Did everything go all right, player? I can see now I'm going to start having to call you player again. It looks like you're back."

"Whatever, man. Yeah, it went surprisingly well." I turned off the television. "I don't know, Miles. All those feelings I once had for her are starting to come back. Am I crazy or what?"

"Hey, it's like that sometimes, Matisse. Follow your heart. However, where Sullivan is concerned, you might want to proceed with caution."

"True that. Good advice, Miles. It's about time," I said, laughing.

15

BRUNCH WITH A TWIST

IT took me a good hour to tidy up my place Sunday morning as I prepared for the brunch I was hosting. I thought about doing it all out by the pool, but that would have meant even more work. I have one of those huge decks that wraps halfway around the condo, so I wasn't overly concerned about having a lack of space. To ensure we didn't miss any of the Sunday NFL action, I mounted a couple of flat-screens out there. At the risk of sounding as cocky as Lincoln, the setup was banging!

My brunches were usually more of an intimate affair, but considering the large number of people I had invited, I called in a favor. I wasn't about to slave over a stove, especially while football was being played. I always hooked up this cat who owns a restaurant I frequent with tickets to various sporting events. In return, he almost always offered his services. "If you need anything, anything at all, don't hesitate to ask," he would say. Well, needless to say, I hit him up this time.

He has one of the most successful catering businesses in Atlanta and breakfast is their specialty. It was great. All I had to do was tell them what I wanted and it was done.

There were five stations set up on the deck. One was for pancakes, waffles and French toast; the second was for made-to-order omelets; the third station had scrambled eggs, bacon, sausage and grits; the fourth had fruits and desserts, and the last had a full bar. Like most brunches, mimosas and Bloody Marys were the preferred adult beverages. The televisions were mounted at each end of the deck.

Miles and his fiancée, Shelby, were the first to show up. Hand in hand, they walked in giddy as hell, with the widest of smiles. It was my first time seeing Shelby since Miles had been in town.

"Hey, you," I said, "congratulations!" I gave her a hug and a peck on the lips.

"Thank you, Matisse. Can you believe it? Finally! I was about to give up on your friend here."

"Oh, babe," Miles said. He gave her a quick kiss. "I'm like that nicely-aged wine. It gets better with time. Good things come to those who wait—you know that, right?"

"Oh, anyway!" Shelby nudged me. "Matisse, are you listening to this? Honey, are you carrying around a book of clichés?"

Miles laughed. "The important thing is I got there. We got there! And we're getting married in a couple of weeks."

"I love you, baby," Shelby said before kissing Miles.

"If I remember correctly, Shelby, I know you want a mimosa. And, Miles, I don't even have to ask."

"That is correct, Matisse," Shelby confirmed. "Are we the first ones here?"

"Yep," I replied, leading them out onto the deck.

"Daaaamn! I see you, but then again, I wouldn't expect anything less. This is a tight setup, Matisse. You must be expecting a lot of people," Miles said, looking around. "I'm used to you being in the kitchen, flipping omelets and flapjacks, and, you know, doing your thing!"

"Yeah, I called in a favor this time. Here you go." I handed Shelby a mimosa and gave Miles a Bloody Mary, his standard brunch drink.

"Miles said he got the okay from you for my girlfriends to come."

"Yes he did. That's cool. The more the merrier."

Courtney and Jay showed up with a few more of our buddies, followed by a gang of Shelby's fine-ass friends. Lincoln appeared with the perfect ten on his arm. All the women were checking him out, while all of the guys were checking her out. I couldn't blame him. Hell, when you're a bona fide superstar making millions, it makes no sense to have anything less than a perfect ten on your arm—at all times.

The eye-opener of the day came when Sullivan showed up with Hunter and Hunter's boyfriend, Jeff. What were two of my exes doing socializing and walking around in my house, looking like partners in crime?

"Hey," Sullivan said.

"Welcome," I slowly responded, looking more than startled.

"Hello, Matisse," Hunter said stiffly. Her greeting dropped the temperature considerably, and it was a nice December day in the ATL. The brisk air, coupled with the bright sun, made for a perfect day to eat, drink and watch football. "You remember my boyfriend, Jeff, don't you?"

"Yeah. Hey, man, what's up? Y'all come on in. Make yourselves comfortable."

I spent the remainder of the day mingling and playing host. You know how that goes, a five-minute conversation here, a five-minute conversation there, none of which are of much substance. At one point, I just kind of sat back and observed. It was interesting to see the various people conversing with one another. I watched Miles and Sullivan from afar. It seemed they were getting reacquainted. Obviously their association went back to the days when she and I dated. Shelby and her girlfriends, it seemed, were having the time of their lives. I sensed they got great satisfaction from clowning my single friends who tried to talk to them. Isn't that something? We're constantly hearing about women and their desires to meet bright, intelligent, good-looking men, which is what all of my boys are, and they have the nerve to play them. Go figure. I guess that's just women though, one big puzzle. I found the fact that Hunter and Lincoln were engaged in a conversation especially funny.

"I can stay and help you clean up," Sullivan whispered into

my ear.

"You don't mind?" I whispered back into hers.

"No, not at all. In fact, I'd love to."

"All right, thanks. You need anything? I'm on my way to the bar."

"Twist my arm, why don't you? I'll take a Cosmo."

"I'll be right back."

***

Once the party ended and we finally shut the door on the last two people, who happened to be Miles and Shelby, I had one question to ask Sullivan. I couldn't get it out fast enough, as it had been on my mind all day long.

"I didn't know you knew Hunter." I tried to sound like I wasn't pressing and that it was just a question while we passed the time.

"Oh? Yeah, I know her. Is that a problem?"

"No, do your thing. I just thought it was kind of strange when you guys showed up together."

"Why, because you guys dated?" Sullivan asked before handing me one of the many dirty plates that filled the sink. We had a pretty good program going. She rinsed and I placed the plates in the dishwasher.

"Well, it sounds like you guys really do know each other. Did you compare notes?"

"Come on, Matisse, you know good girls never kiss and tell," she laughed.

"Is that so?" I said, smirking. "I don't know about that. Really, though, how do you guys know each other?"

"We met through a mutual friend some years ago." I could tell Sullivan was purposely being vague. I could also tell she was enjoying watching me try to mask my frustration about being kept in the dark. *There's more to it*, I thought.

"Matisse, you're looking kind of tense," Sullivan said, walking towards me. She positioned herself behind me and started massaging my shoulders. It felt good. "We had some great times, huh? This is all too familiar. That's the one thing we were always good at as a team—entertaining."

"Yeah, our dinner parties were legendary."

Still massaging my shoulders, she whispered into my ear, "I miss that."

Suddenly, my pants were fitting a little tighter than usual. My excitement was beginning to show. Luckily for me, Sullivan was standing behind me. I couldn't take it any longer. I turned and faced her and applied a couple of soft kisses to her lips. She automatically pulled me closer to her. We kissed at a frantic pace.

Though I wanted to proceed slowly, this time it just wasn't in me. I wanted her and she wanted me. Clearly visible through her shirt, Sullivan's nipples were so erect they could cut glass. For a minute there, I could have sworn one said, "Matisse" while the other said, "Spencer." Yeah, they had my name written all over them. I didn't waste any time. I lifted her shirt and undid her bra before circling each hard nipple with my tongue. I didn't discriminate one bit. I made sure each received the same amount of love.

"Oh, baby," Sullivan moaned.

'*Oh, baby' is right!* I thought, just before I peeled her pants off. Sullivan looked incredible, standing there wearing nothing but a thong. I dropped to my knees and used only my teeth to peel it off.

"Baby, taste me," she said. I lifted her up onto the island in my kitchen and buried my head between her legs. Before I knew it my pants and boxers were straddling my ankles, while Sullivan was completely naked. Her clothes formed a pile in the middle of the kitchen floor, and yes, Sullivan's signature sexy and classy thong and bra set were among them.

"Wait," I said, grabbing her hand. "Let's go into the bedroom."

"No, climb on top of me right here and now. I want you, Matisse, and it can't wait."

"It's going to have to wait for a minute," I said, reaching for my wallet. I know grown men shouldn't be walking around with condoms in their wallets, but I was a nerd like that, and it finally paid dividends. I don't think I've ever truly been to the Promised Land, but being inside of her surely was the next best thing, if not better.

"Shit! Baby, you feel so good!" Sullivan yelled.

"Is it still mine?" I whispered into her ear.

"It's still yours, baby. Yes!" she yelled. "It's still yours. It's always been yours, baby."

When we made it to the bedroom about thirty minutes later, both of us were drenched with sweat and out of breath.

"What do we do now?" I said, curling around her in the spoons position we had long-ago established beneath the covers.

"What do you mean what do we do?" She turned and faced me. "We move forward. Maybe this time we'll get it right."

I didn't respond. Though I was excited about the possibility of a future with Sullivan, I saw nothing but many *Proceed With Caution* signs, just as Miles had warned me. Despite being incredibly stoked, I thought to myself, *Yeah, maybe?*

16

SHORTLIVED RECONNECTION

SULLIVAN left my place first thing in morning. It was 5:30 and still dark outside when I walked her to her car.

Climbing back into bed, I was giddy inside. The spot where she had lain was still warm. The room was immersed in her scent. At one point, I rolled over to her side of the bed and just smelled the pillow. It was one of the best aromas I had smelled in a long time. She had been gone only five minutes and I missed her already. Though this was exactly what I didn't want, I was quickly coming to the realization that this could be one of those situations where my falling back in love with Sullivan was inevitable.

For someone who had been in the game as long as I had, I was feeling like I was back in high school, pumped and excited after a first date. My energy level was high when it should have been low, especially after the many sessions Sullivan and I had just had.

As much as I tried, I couldn't go back to sleep. Instead, I jumped out of bed, threw on my workout clothes and went to the gym. I figured a 45-minute run and a little lifting wouldn't hurt me.

On my way there, I called Sullivan from the car. Judging by the way she answered, I could tell she didn't have any problem getting back to sleep.

"Did I wake you?"

"Yeah, but it's all right, Matisse," Sullivan whispered.

"Well, I'll let you get back to sleep. I just wanted to make sure you got home okay."

"You're so sweet. I'll call you later."

"Okay, bye." I hung up the phone thinking, *I wish I was next to her.*

Quietly, I was tripping. I had gone down this road a time before with Sullivan and the result wasn't pretty. Was I a glutton for punishment? Because surely I was headed in that same direction. The fact that I couldn't get her out of my head, coupled with the upbeat feeling I was experiencing, must have meant something.

I made it to the office long before Gail. I don't recall a time when I had been in there so early. I felt like a million bucks, though. The power of a good morning workout is amazing. Add a night of great companionship and unbelievable sex to the mix and you have the makings for a potentially great Monday.

Gail's night before must have been as good as mine. I could hear her whistling as she made her way through the office's front door. It continued as she put on a pot of coffee.

"What in the world are you doing here so early?" Gail asked, peeking her head in my office.

"What? I'm not allowed to come into the office early? I mean, this is my business, right?"

Gail's lips smacked. "Pleeeeze, Matisse! What's really going on?"

"Whatever, Gail." I stood and made my way toward her. "Bye," I said, practically slamming the door on her face.

Gail buzzed me on the intercom moments later. "Matisse, Ms. Sullivan is on line one."

Though Sullivan was her first name, people in the south have a habit of attaching Mr. or Ms. to first names. Judging from Gail's sarcastic tone, I could tell she was having fun teasing me.

"Thanks," I responded as I pressed line one. "Glad to see you're finally awake."

"Barely," Sullivan said. "I'm still laying here in bed."

"I see. It must be nice."

"Believe me, it is. I had a wonderful time last night, Matisse. I just wanted to thank you."

"That makes two of us. I had a great time, too." I tried to keep my voice down because, knowing Gail, she probably had a glass to the door.

"I'd love to see you again tonight." The sexy manner in which she said that awoke the lumberyard. My *boy* was growing by the second.

"I'll second that. Let's make it happen."

"Okay, but tonight I'm playing host."

"Cool, that's even better," I replied, smiling from ear to ear.

"Great. Can you be at my place by six?"

"Yeah. What should I bring?"

"Just yourself, Matisse."

"Okay, I'll see you then." I hung up the phone, beaming with joy. Maybe in order for us to get where it seemed we were headed, we had to go through all of that other stuff from back in the day.

***

I arrived at Sullivan's place with two bottles of wine, one red and one white, and a dozen red roses. I know she said not to bring anything, but I just wasn't that type of brother. It was something embedded in me by my old man from the time I was a little shorty. "Never show up empty-handed," he would say.

Sullivan answered the door wearing a number that was breathtaking. It was kind of chilly outside, but man was it warm inside. And her outfit reflected just how warm and cozy it really was. One feature I thoroughly enjoyed about Sullivan was her long, toned, mocha-chocolate legs. She knew this, too, which was probably why she chose to wear the tight-fitting dress that stopped well above her knees. Her pretty feet were exposed through the open-toe heels she wore. I always liked that French thing women do with their fingernails and toenails. Sullivan's feet looked like she had just come from a pedicure.

"Matisse, I told you not to bring anything," Sullivan said, smiling.

"I know, but you know me."

Sullivan's eyes rolled. "Yes, I do. Well, that's sweet, Matisse. Come in," she said, grabbing the wine and flowers out of my hand before shutting the door behind me. I don't know what she had going on in the kitchen, but whatever it was, the place smelled good. And I was hungry.

I noticed how immaculate her place was as she led me to the kitchen.

"Do you mind hanging out in here with me while I put the final touches on our meal?"

"No, not at all." I settled onto one of the barstools in the kitchen.

"This is good wine, Matisse," Sullivan noted, uncorking the bottle of red. "I love this Zinfandel. Here you go."

"Thanks," I said, taking the filled glass from her. "I love your place. It's nice."

"That's right, this is your first time here, huh?"

"Yep."

"Well, thanks! Yeah, I like it, too." Sullivan held her glass high. "Here's to us. Cheers."

Our glasses touched, making that clinking sound, and we each took a sip.

For a second, there was an uncomfortable silence. Sullivan looked into my eyes as I looked into hers.

"I don't want to scare you, Matisse, but I'm really happy we're spending time together. Last night was amazing." Sullivan leaned across the countertop and kissed me. I made sure it wasn't just a peck, either. I kissed her back, which made for a passionate, heartfelt kiss.

"I guess I'll come clean, too. I'm really beginning to enjoy this as well. I just don't want it to end up like last time," I said, sounding like a little wimp.

"That's understandable, Matisse. Neither do I, but hold that thought. I'll be right back. I have to go to the little girl's room."

As she made her way to the bathroom, I marveled at how well she was put together. I mean, along with her great legs came an outstanding ass. Sullivan's cell phone vibrated nosily while she was in the bathroom. It was lying on the countertop right in front of me. I didn't want to answer it, nor did I want to yell for her while she handled her business in the bathroom. So I just let it vibrate. I glanced down at the number. For some reason it seemed familiar to me. My mind must have been playing a trick on me. Was I already jealous? I looked away from the phone, trying to stay out of her business.

"Did you hold the fort down in my five-minute absence?"

"Oh, yeah, of course. What do you got going on in here? It smells awesome."

"It's a surprise. Just wait and see."

My intuition, or should I say nose, was right. In fact, the meal tasted even better than it smelled. I especially liked the fact that she remembered what I liked most when it came to food. Yeah, I was a steak and potatoes man, which was precisely what she prepared. I felt like I was in an upscale restaurant, based on Sullivan's presentation. Her homemade mashed potatoes were topped by asparagus, which was topped by one of the tastiest fillets I've ever eaten.

Sullivan's phone vibrated a few more times throughout the course of dinner. Each time she ignored it. At one point I asked her if she was going to answer it and she responded by saying, "Are you kidding me? We've been apart far too long. I'm not letting anyone ruin our time together. Besides, that's why voicemail was invented."

Sullivan's answer gave me goosebumps. I liked knowing that I was the absolute center of her attention. Needless to say, I spent the night at Sullivan's. Hell, it would have taken an entire army to get me to leave after such a perfect night. Though we turned in early, we did not sleep much. I could tell that our intimacy had progressed from that of the night before. The sex we experienced 24 hours prior had elevated to genuine lovemaking. Each session, and there were plenty that night, grew more intense, which was a direct result of how strongly we felt for one another. It was official. We had reconnected.

After that wonderful night with Sullivan, I felt like I was

walking on air the entire day. It's amazing what the right person can do for your psyche. It was definitely a Tuesday to remember. I was so pumped and high on life that my production level soared to new heights. Finally, I got the Knicks to agree on a deal in principle for Jerrell. Additionally, I inked two more endorsement deals for Lincoln. I was rolling, but the hard part was getting Lincoln to commit.

Sullivan and I had agreed to get together again for dinner, but I found it odd that I hadn't heard from her at all throughout the day. That just shouldn't happen, especially if you took care of business the night before. I had left her a couple of messages, but was sensing I was beginning to look like a sissy. I also sent her several texts and got back nothing. Nevertheless, it didn't stop me from racing over to her house as soon as I left the office.

My knocks on the door and ringing of the bell fell on deaf ears. No answer, but I could hear the television going, so I took it upon myself to see my way in, especially knowing that she wasn't a stickler about locking the door.

I was stunned and momentarily paralyzed by what I saw. "Oh, shit!" I yelled, "Sullivan!" Sullivan was sprawled out on the floor in what appeared to be a pool of her own blood. I rushed to her and tried to shake her to life, giving her a couple of hard tugs. Nothing. Then I put my index finger to her throat to check for a pulse. Nothing. Her skin was cold. It was too late. Sullivan was dead.

17

THE CRIME SCENE

SEEING Sullivan lying there helpless and lifeless, drenched in her own blood, I felt like someone had just ripped my heart out. I panicked. I immediately ran out the door and stopped a couple of yards from my car. Seconds later, I found myself running back inside. I was both dumbfounded and delirious. I didn't know what to do. I had seen enough television shows and movies to know better than to touch anything—but obviously I had flunked that lesson, seeing how her blood was all over me. I immediately called 911. They made me identify myself and asked where I was calling from, which I provided. Barely! My body was shaking, my hands trembling, and I was having trouble talking.

While I waited for the police and paramedics to arrive, I sat on the floor with my head buried between my legs, crying like a baby.

I could hear the sirens from at least a couple of blocks away, but it didn't change a thing. I continued to sit and cry, not moving one bit. I was expecting a bunch of police officers and paramedics to show up all at once, which wasn't the case. One police officer arrived first and went straight to Sullivan. He closely observed her and then quickly glanced around before immediately making a call.

"This is Reporting Officer Leary. I need backup and medical assistance at 615 Lennox Road," he said while continuing to assess the situation. He then walked over to me and asked, "Who are you and what are you doing here?"

"I'm a friend of Sullivan's."

"Who is Sullivan?"

I couldn't talk. All I could do is point down to Sullivan's body.

"We're going to have to get a statement from you in a bit. But, right now I have to secure this area, which means you'll have to wait outside. This is a crime scene and we can't have anyone in it," Officer Leary demanded as he walked me to an area outside of the house that wasn't deemed a part of the crime scene. His face was round and red. I'm not sure if the extreme redness was a result of years of heavy drinking or just a strong case of rosacea. "Wait here and don't go anywhere. I'll be back for your statement shortly."

Within minutes, two more police officers had shown up. They were both wearing suits and walked in unison over to Officer Leary.

"Detectives Miller and Jackson," Officer Leary said, void of emotion and not bothering to shake hands. Though I was outside of the crime scene area, I could still see inside the house. The door was open and Sullivan's body was in clear view from where I was sitting outside.

"What do we got here?" Detective Miller asked.

"Not sure."

"We see you've secured the scene," Detective Jackson said. He turned and pointed in my direction. "Who's that?"

"He said he's a friend of hers."

As I watched Detective Miller walk back out of the house and towards me, the EMT-paramedics showed up, bursting through the door like the US Cavalry must have done back in the day. Two men and a woman huddled around Sullivan's naked, lifeless body. Her hair was saturated in blood. From what I could tell, they checked various things like pulses and whatnot.

"Don't go anywhere," Detective Miller barked. Having already been told that once, I simply nodded and continued to sob before he turned and rejoined the crime scene inside. By this time,

I really didn't know who was who. The Crime Scene Unit team had grown in numbers. Pictures were being taken. Samples of Sullivan's blood that rested on the floor around her were being collected and the room was being dusted for fingerprints. Those were the obvious things I saw. I'm sure it was more involved than that. I just cried and looked on from outside of the house, near the front door where they had me contained.

"Doesn't appear to be a forced entry," Detective Miller noted, closely examining the front door.

"Nothing on this door and door frame," Detective Jackson agreed. "We'll have to check the rest of the doors."

"I'll do that. Why don't you search the area for a possible weapon?" Detective Miller suggested.

"I'm on it," Detective Jackson responded.

As I continued to sit and sob, I wondered why this was happening. It had taken me years to get over Sullivan, and then she comes back into my life only to be taken away in a matter of days. I felt horrible for her but, in all honesty, at that moment I felt worse for myself. Obviously, it was a selfish thought. Life is funny sometimes. I'm a firm believer in second chances, but I'm well aware of the fact that very few people get them. At that very moment, I realized that people who do get second chances in life are beyond lucky.

When Detectives Miller and Jackson finished their respective thorough checks, they reconvened not far from where I was sitting.

"I didn't come up with anything that resembled a possible weapon," Detective Jackson said. "Any forced entries?"

"Nope," responded Detective Miller. "It's beginning to look like we may have our work cut out for us on this one. Let's go talk with the coroner's inspector."

Coincidentally, just as the detectives walked over to the coroner inspector, it looked like she had finished whatever she had to do.

"We need to quit meeting like this," Inspector Lee said, grinning.

"Tell me about it," agreed Detective Miller. "What are we looking at here, Beth? Oops, I mean, *Inspector Lee*."

"That's more like it. Let's keep it professional here," she said with a quick wink. "It looks like the victim has been dead for approximately eight to eleven hours."

Detective Jackson scratched his head, "So, you're saying it went down this morning?"

"That's what I'm saying, Jackson. We'll be able to tighten the timeline once we get her out of here and onto the table."

"No gunshot wounds. No knife marks. We have a busted skull and bloody carpet. The blow to the head did it, right?" Detective Jackson inquired.

"The apparent cause of death was a penetrating head wound. You guys know the drill. We'll have more accurate information in the official autopsy report."

Detective Miller sighed. "That's too bad. You recognize her?"

"Looks like the new newscaster at Channel Eleven," Inspector Lee said, shaking her head and frowning in a way that suggested she shared Detective Miller's sentiments. "You guys come up with anything on your end?"

"Nothing glaring," Detective Miller said. He head-motioned in my direction. "Hopefully this guy has some information."

"Well, seems like time's a-wasting, boys. Looks like you have some more work ahead of you. He seems to be pretty shaken."

Detective Miller, who was now staring at me, said, "Yeah, he does, but you know as well as we do that these cases usually involve a shit-load of smoke and mirrors."

Inspector Lee nodded her head. "All right, guys, as always, let's talk later."

"Come up with some good stuff for us in that report," Detective Jackson added.

Inspector Lee smacked her lips, chuckled and said, "Don't I always?" as the detectives walked away from her. Finally, Detectives Jackson and Miller were standing before me, or should I say, over me.

Looking down at me, Detective Jackson asked, "Who are you?"

"Matisse Spencer," I replied, wiping the tears from eyes.

"What's your relationship with the deceased?"

"We were friends."

"Did you see what happened here?"

"No," I said, wondering, *Who could do such a thing?*

"We know you've been waiting here for a while, but we're going to have to ask you a few questions," Detective Miller said, looking down at his notepad and repeatedly tapping it with a pencil. It was annoying as hell.

I stood. "Certainly," I said before blowing into a handkerchief retrieved from my pocket.

"Let's step over here." We moved farther away from the house. I leaned against a tree and looked down at the ground.

"Why are you here?" Detective Miller asked.

"Sullivan and I had a planned dinner date."

"I see." Detective Jackson said, pausing before his next question. "Did you see her this morning or last night?"

"Yes, both."

"Did you guys have an argument?"

"No, I told you she and I were friends."

"Friends are certainly capable of arguing," Detective Miller said, looking over at Detective Jackson. "Isn't that right, Jackson?"

"That's right. By the way, we're going to have to take that shirt when we're finished here."

I knew what these two clowns were getting at, but I really wasn't in the mood. "Look," I said, "you guys must have shit for brains if you think I did this. How simpleminded are you? First off, I'm the only person here who knew her and, like you said, I'm covered in blood, yet still here. Secondly, I'm the one who called you guys. Thirdly, if I killed Sullivan, accident or not, I'm not stupid enough to sit around and wait for you guys to put two and two together. I'd be in Mexico or Canada by now. Lastly, am I under arrest? If not, I'd like to get out of here and properly mourn the death of a friend."

"For now, Mr. Spencer, no." responded Detective Jackson. "Seeing as though you claim to be a friend of the deceased and didn't witness the crime, we aren't going to force you to come in right now. But, we are going to have to have you come in and give a formal statement in the next 24 hours. So, you're free to go for now. Just don't leave town anytime soon."

"Whatever," I said. "Why don't you guys forgo a few donut breaks and find whoever did this?"

I took off my shirt and tossed it to them on my way out, but as I did, I looked back and saw a zipped body bag being rolled out on a gurney. The finality and reality of Sullivan never taking another breath overwhelmed me as I exited the courtyard and encountered a sudden sea of news cameras, lights, media trucks and vans, police cars and various onlookers. I wondered what would be made of the shirtless, tear-streaked man they captured leaving a heinous crime scene where a beautiful TV celebrity had just been found dead.

18

THE STOLI AFTERMATH

I had never thought of myself as being a very emotional person. Sure, I had a heart. I mean, I felt things. As grown and masculine as I prided myself for being, I occasionally shed a tear or two at movies and whatnot. I had lost friends and family members before, causing me to cry at their funerals. But never had I witnessed, firsthand, someone with whom I'd shared a very intimate history, and who seemed destined to be in my future, lying dead in her own blood.

It was a blow to the mind, and I took it hard. I didn't leave the house for two days or have contact with a single person. Prior to that, I'd prided myself on being an upbeat person. What could I say? I was depressed. Extremely depressed. Two bottles of Stoli a day depressed.

Finally, on the third day of my depressed, secluded existence, I heard hard knocks at the door, followed by the loud ringing of the doorbell.

"Matisse, you in there?" yelled my dad as he pounded on the door. "Open up!"

"Come on, Matisse, open the door," Miles insisted. "We're worried about you."

I didn't budge. I figured in time they'd go away. However, what I didn't count on was my dad using the key I had given my parents for emergencies. Given the amount of time it took for him to use it, I was comforted to know that it was used purely as a last resort.

They found me sitting in the dark on the floor in the front room surrounded by empty bottles of Stoli, and clutching one full bottle.

"It's been all over the news for the past two days, Son." My dad stood over me, looking around my place. "You kind of put a hurting on this place."

"She's gone, man," I said, not bothering to look up.

"Yeah, I'm sorry about that, Son. But you have to go on. I know it sounds cold, but you have to move on."

"Damn, Mat, this place is a mess," Miles offered. "Hey, man, I feel you. I liked Sullivan, too, but Mr. S is right. You have to move on—as harsh as that sounds and as hard as it will be."

My dad sat down beside me and put his arm around me. "It's going to be all right, Son. It's going to be all right."

"I know," I responded as tears rolled down my face.

Miles had gone into the kitchen and re-entered the room with three glasses of ice. He grabbed the bottle of Stoli out of my hand and filled each glass. "Here," he said, handing one to me and one to my dad before copping a squat on the floor beside us. "Here's to Sullivan." Miles tapped each of our glasses, and the three of us took a swig at once.

"I just don't get it," I said. "Why would anyone want Sullivan dead? I really thought there was a reason why she walked back into my life. I'd always thought she was the one that got away. When she reappeared, I just automatically assumed it was for a reason."

"Life's funny like that sometimes, Son. The damnedest things occur without rhyme or reason. In the end, though, I think God has a plan for everything and everyone. Obviously, *He* needs her now."

"It's just not right."

"At 38, Son, I'd say you're relatively young in life. Unfortunately, you're going to find out that a lot of things in life aren't right, nor are they fair."

"I know, Pop, but damn!" I slammed my fist down onto the floor. "I don't know, maybe I'm being selfish. Maybe I'm thinking more about what could have been between the two of us than about her."

"Maybe. Chalk it up as being human. Sullivan was a sweet girl, Son. Your mother and I liked her, though we hadn't seen her in about five years. You guys seemed to have had a good run years ago. Why you stopped seeing each other is none of my business, but it was always something that your mother and I wondered about."

Miles didn't say much. He just sat there with us and refreshed our glasses whenever they appeared to get light. Come to think of it, none of us were really in the mood to talk. When it was all said and done, we'd gone through two bottles. Luckily, after the first one, my dad called my mom to tell her he was staying the night and Miles did the same with Shelby.

19

A VISIT FROM
THE DETECTIVES

I wallowed in my own self-pity for a couple more days before I finally cleaned up and forced myself to be semi-productive. Needless to say, I took Sullivan's death pretty hard. But my dad and Miles were right; I had to move on.

After I showered, I spent the first part of the morning cleaning my place. Ordinarily, I would have called my cleaning service, but I was too embarrassed. My place looked like an Alcoholics Anonymous meeting gone awry. I mean, it was downright despicable. It's a wonder I was still alive. How one man could consume so much alcohol is beyond me. There were empty Stoli bottles everywhere I turned. Though I'd showered, I could still smell it in my pores. It was gross and sickening. As good as it felt at the time, it certainly wasn't the best way to handle my grief. The only good thing that came out of it was the fact that it was all behind me now, and I had completed the first step in moving on. Though showering and cleaning my place was hardly a reason to celebrate, I felt like I'd accomplished something major.

During those dark days, my diet was purely liquid, and it showed. I'd lost close to 10 pounds. Unfortunately, my appetite still wasn't up to par. The only thing I managed to get down was a couple pieces of toast.

I knew I needed to give Gail a call at the office, but as I sat at my kitchen table, slowly eating toast and devouring orange juice like it was going out of style, I thought it was best to wait until it was close to lunchtime before I made any calls. It was nice having a few sober minutes to myself. Besides, I needed to catch up on current events.

In reading the paper and flipping through the various local television news stations, I was quickly reminded that Sullivan, being a local newscaster, was a public figure. The news of her death was all over the place: print, television, radio, the Internet, even social media sites.

After I'd had my fill of news, I picked up the phone and dialed Gail's number at the office. She answered on the first ring.

"Hey, it's me," I said, void of emotion.

"Are you all right?" She sounded concerned in a motherly way.

"Yeah, I'm all right. It sucks, but I'm all right."

"It's awful, Matisse. Who would do such a thing?"

"That's the million-dollar question, I guess."

"Do you need anything? I hope you don't think I was being insensitive by not calling, but the morning after it happened I got a call from your parents. They said you'd probably go into hiding for a few days, like you did when things bothered you as a kid."

"I guess they really know me, huh?"

"Your dad called the office after he spent the night with you. He said you were going to be all right, but he said it would probably be best to wait until you reached out to us."

"Gail, it's all right. I knew you'd be there if I needed you." I stood and made my way out of the kitchen and into my study. "What's going on there?"

"The Knicks GM has called a few times. I explained the situation to him, but he didn't seem to care. I think you should probably call him soon."

"Yeah, he's been texting the shit out of me. I'll hit him back."

"Oh, and Lincoln came by a couple times as well. Come to think of it, he didn't look so well. I'm no genius, but he seemed troubled. He wasn't nearly as talkative and cocky as he normally is."

"Hmm," I said, turning on my computer. "Another problem with Lincoln doesn't sound too unusual. Well, I'm going to work from home today. My first call will be to the Knicks. We have a deal in principle. I hope that's still the case."

"Oh, I almost forgot, Jerrell's been calling everyday, too."

"I'll call him as well."

"Keep your head up, Matisse, and call if you need anything."

"I will. Thanks."

While I surfed the many sports sites on the Internet, it was hard escaping Sullivan's death due to her being a former sportscaster. I turned on one of the TVs and immediately clicked the channel to *ESPN News*. There was no need to have all of the televisions on because it was early enough in the day that there weren't any games being played. I was amazed to find out how much one can miss in the world of sports by being out of pocket for a few days. What was even more astounding was the fact that most of the sports news had little to do with sports itself. I was just trying to see if my clients, who were in season, had had a good couple of days in my absence, but it seemed like most of the news reports were off-the-field and -court theatrics, such as bar-fights, paternity suits and child custody battles involving various players. Though I grew tired of it quickly, I also wanted to make sure nothing fishy was going on regarding the Knicks before I placed a call to Billy Baxter.

Baxter had been the Knicks GM for about five years, which is a good run in the NBA at that level with the same team. The life span of most coaches and GMs in the NBA is much shorter. So it goes without saying that he'd done a good job with the team in the toughest media market around. Baxter had a reputation as being a hard-ass when it came to negotiating player contracts, but he and I developed a pretty good rapport throughout the years. In my business, much like most businesses, I imagine, developing good relationships is what it's all about. It's half the battle. With that said, I still had to make sure everything was on the up and up before

I placed that call. A deal in principle meant that we had a verbal agreement, but nothing had been signed yet. Deals in principle are always subject to change or even fall apart altogether. Unfortunately, especially early on in my career, I'd been bent over a time or two behind verbal agreements while we waited for all of the parties to sign the contract.

The more I thought about it, the more I thought I should give Jerrell a call first to see if this was still what he wanted. For some reason, I always had trouble contacting him, so I called Gail to get him on the line for me. A few minutes later, Jerrell's high-pitched voice was on the other end of the phone.

"It's about time, Matisse!" Jerrell yelled, sounding like he'd just inhaled a bottle of helium. His woman-like voice definitely didn't fit his tall, thick frame. "Where the hell you been?"

"It's a long story, Jerrell."

"Yeah, yeah, I know all about her, Matisse, but I don't give a shit! I'm trying to get paid and I'm trying to get back on the court all at the same time. And just when we have a good deal on the table, you pull this disappearing act. It's unacceptable, man! You're my agent! Shit! Listen, don't get me wrong, it's terrible what happened to her. And yeah, I heard through the grapevine that y'all had a little history together, but business is business, Matisse! Handle it, man! Get Billy Bax on the line and let's do the damn thing!"

"You're absolutely right, Jerrell. I owe you an apology. I'm sorry I was so unprofessional."

"Apology accepted, Matisse. Let's just get it done."

"So, you're all right with what we agreed upon a few days ago?"

"You're kidding, right? Hell yeah! I'm ready to sign today!"

"All right I'll call him," I said, grabbing a bottle of water from the mini-fridge that sat alongside my desk. "Get your bags packed. We're probably going to have to catch a flight up there either tonight or tomorrow morning."

"My man! That's what I'm talking about."

Just as I hung up the phone, my doorbell rang. As I walked to the front door I just knew it had to be one of three people: my mom, Dad or Miles. If it were a baseball game, I'd have just whiffed on all three swings.

Two of Atlanta's finest greeted me with stone faces.

"Detective Miller and Jackson," I said. "What can I do for you?"

"We have the results of the autopsy, Mr. Spencer," Detective Jackson said. He looked like Carlton from *The Fresh Prince*—old buster-ass. "May we come in? We'd like to ask you a few more questions."

I sighed loudly. "Sure."

I walked them to the living room where the three of us took seats. They sat on one of the sofas and I sat in an oversized chair facing them. A rectangular coffee table separated us.

"Well, Mr. Spencer," Detective Miller started, "based on the autopsy, we know that her death resulted from a hard blow to the head. There were also marks around her neck. We have a strong hunch that it was the result of some type of altercation with someone, which caused her to fall back. She cracked her head open on the corner of the coffee table in the front room and fell near the door where you found her. And lastly, we know that it happened around nine in the morning."

"Man, you guys are geniuses," I said, scratching my head. "Let me get this straight. The autopsy showed marks around her neck and you guys have only a *strong hunch* that Sullivan's death was the result of some type of altercation with someone? Brilliant work there, guys," I said while thinking, *What a bunch of idiots!* "Okay, so, what does this have to do with me? Why aren't you guys out there looking for the killer?"

"Where were you that morning around nine?" Detective Jackson asked.

"Really?" I said, shaking my head. "Come on, guys! This a bitch! Look, we've been through this. You guys still think I had something to do with Sullivan's death?"

"We're just trying to do our jobs," Detective Miller stated. "Nothing unusual about this line of questioning."

I stood. "I don't believe this shit! I was home in bed."

"Was anyone else with you, Mr. Spencer?" Detective Jackson inquired.

"Nope, not a soul. I spent the evening at Sullivan's place, but left around two in the morning," I said in a matter-of-fact way. I probably shouldn't have been so forthcoming with that information, but I figured, hell, I'm tired of them wasting their time with me when there was a real killer at large.

"So, you all were involved?" Detective Miller fished.

"No. Like I told you the other day, we were just friends. One thing led to another that night, and we just kind of went there. Not that it's really any of your business. Truth be told, we were involved years back and had just reconnected as friends."

"So, you don't have anyone to corroborate this story?" Detective Jackson asked. He smirked as if I was lying.

"Once again, I was home in bed alone. Look, am I under arrest? Because if not, I have some pressing matters to attend to."

"No, but like we said the other day, don't leave town anytime soon."

20

RAINMAKER CALL

DESPITE all that nonsense the police were talking about me not leaving town, the very next day Jerrell and I left for New York. I wasn't all that talkative on the way up, for obvious reasons. I knew I didn't need to give Jerrell an explanation. He knew what time it was. Hell, anyone who lived in Atlanta and could read knew what time it was due to the five-page exposé the *Atlanta Journal-Constitution* did on Sullivan. And yes, my name was mentioned as being romantically involved with hers years ago.

Uncharacteristic of Billy Baxter, we were in and out of there in no time. The deal we signed was the deal we agreed upon in principle. Not a single word or figure was changed, which is pretty uncommon in this business. To put the icing on the cake, instead of having to sit around there for an extra day for the press conference, we had the presser a couple hours after the i's were dotted and t's were crossed.

Ordinarily, after inking a multi-million-dollar deal like that, I usually went straight home and popped open a bottle of champagne. I made it home alright, but wasn't in the mood for champagne, especially after consuming all those bottles of Stoli. My appetite was slowly beginning to resurface so I ordered takeout: a filet from Bones to go along with my usual side dishes. As I washed the meal of champions down with a bottle of water, I was interrupted by a phone call.

Miles's name and number lit up the screen. I debated whether to answer it or not. I was having another one of those nights where I reveled in being alone. I gave in, though.

"Matisse, you doing alright?"

"Yeah, I'm fine. What's up?"

"Shelby and I talked it over. Considering all that's gone on the past few days, we'd like to postpone the wedding for a few weeks. I don't think anyone feels too good about Sullivan's death."

I was silent for a moment.

"Matisse, you there?"

"Alright," I said. "Don't do it on my account."

"We aren't. Shit, no one's even thinking about your water-jug head," Miles said, chuckling.

We chopped it up for a few more minutes talking about a lot of nothing before I finally brought it to an end, "Alright, bruh, I'll talk to you later," I said, hanging up the phone before hearing Miles sign off.

I finished eating in complete silence. It probably was the first time ever that I didn't sit down and eat and watch television at the same time. There were all kinds of games on, too, but none of that seemed to matter.

Knowing that Coltrane was already in my CD player, I plopped down on my couch and pressed play. The loss of Sullivan was beginning to sink in. There was nothing I could do to bring her back, and no way to know for sure if we would have ended up together. But something else was bothering me. I thought about Detectives Miller and Jackson, and felt my body temperature rise. Those guys irked me. I mean, I knew they had a job to do and obviously questioning people is a large part of that. How many times, though, did I have to tell them that I didn't kill Sullivan? If they were so hell-bent on me being the killer, then why didn't they just arrest me? Why all of this three-questions-here and four-questions-there, followed by *don't leave town*? They must have gone to the Barney Fife School of Detectives.

Forget that! I wasn't having it. I decided right then and there that I was no longer going to sit around and wait for those two fools to find the real killer, or worse yet, frame me as the killer. It was time for me to be proactive. I knew I was a sports agent and didn't have any experience in that type of work. But, hell, I figured if those two clowns were out tracking criminals down, I surely could do a little sniffing around and come up with something. I knew a couple of Atlanta policemen, and figured I'd start out by having them give me a few tips on what to look for and how to go about doing this.

Falling asleep on the couch to the smooth sounds of Coltrane, I was abruptly awakened by the ringing of my phone.

"Hello," I whispered with one eye open.

A muffled voice offered, "Where was your rainmaking client Lincoln Dix on the morning of Sullivan's death?"

I immediately popped up from the couch. It was like someone had poured ice water on me. "Who is this?" All I heard next was a dial tone.

21

SULLIVAN DRESSED IN WHITE

I received more anonymous, vague, insinuating calls regarding Lincoln over the next couple of days. I didn't quite know what to make of it. Obviously someone was trying to tell me that Lincoln was somehow involved in Sullivan's death. But why tell me? Why not make those calls to the police department? Who knows? Maybe whoever was calling me also made the same calls to the APD.

 I really didn't know what to do. If Lincoln was involved with Sullivan's death, talk about a Catch-22. He was my top moneymaking client, one who, most of the time, depended on me to get him out of messes. On the other hand, this could be one of those cases of survival of the fittest. After all, the way the police had been on me lately, I was without a doubt one of the leading suspects in her murder.

 Upon seeing Sullivan's reaction to Lincoln stopping by our table that night at dinner, maybe my original hunch was right about them knowing one another. Thinking about it was giving me a headache. I had to talk to someone about it before I acted on it. I called Miles and told him to meet me at my place.

***

 "What's up, man, you sounded like you had something on

your mind," Miles said on his way in.

"Yeah, well, I have a lot on my mind," I responded, closing the door behind him. "Here, let's go into my study."

I took a seat behind my desk, while Miles settled in on my couch.

"Want a water or brew or something?"

"Uh, I'll take a water." Miles leaned towards me. "So, talk to me, man. What was so urgent?"

"Here," I said, handing Miles a bottle of water from my mini-fridge. "All right, here it goes. I told you how the police have been on me lately, right?"

"Right."

"Well, I'm obviously a suspect."

"Yeah, but I think it's just a formality. After all, you were the first person on the scene, right?"

Without saying anything, I nodded my head.

"I think they're just messing with you right now."

"Messing with me? That's not cool. Shit! Anyway, for some reason, I've been getting these anonymous phone calls from someone suggesting that Lincoln had something to do with Sullivan's death."

"What?"

"Yeah, it's a trip. I mean, why are they calling me? Why aren't they calling the police?"

"How do you know they haven't called the police?"

"That's just it. I don't."

"This shit is crazy." Miles scratched his head. "What?"

"I don't know, man. I mean, it's crazy that I'm getting calls like that. But what's even crazier is that they're insinuating Lincoln had something to do with her death. And if that's the case, what do I do? I didn't even know they knew each other. Mind you, I had a hunch, but I didn't know for sure. I know I'm being kind of selfish here, but that guy puts a lot of money in my pocket. We're talking about Lincoln Dix. You know, the same cat who used to skate circles around Gretzky. Yeah, that guy. From a marketing and endorsement standpoint, he's an agent's dream. Am I about to drop a dime on him based on some wacky anonymous phone calls?"

"Hell yeah, Matisse. You said it yourself—the police think you had something to do with Sullivan's death. You have to look out for yourself, even if someone is just messing with you. Who knows, there could be something to those calls."

"But if I implicate Lincoln without any real proof, do you know how much damage that could do to his career? It could end it all, especially with such a high profile case."

"Well, it's better than sitting in a prison cell for a crime you didn't commit, wouldn't you say?"

"Good point." I leaned back in the chair and folded my arms behind my head.

"Let me ask you this. What's been said when they call?"

"It's a muffled voice, and it's a man. And the person says the same thing every time: 'Where was your rainmaking client Lincoln Dix on the morning of Sullivan's death?'"

"Sounds like this person knows you, or at the very least knows of your association with Lincoln and Sullivan. Mat, you have to go to the police with this information."

"Yeah, you're probably right."

"Probably? Shiiiit! I know I'm right!"

"Whatever!" I said, looking him dead in the eye.

"Whatever? Yeah, okay, Matisse." Miles shook his head as if to say I sounded like a fool. "Just as long as you're not saying, 'whatever' from a jail cell."

"All right, Miles, I got your point. I'll go down to the precinct tomorrow morning, but first I'm going to have a talk with Lincoln."

Before I could get Lincoln's name out of my mouth the ringing of my doorbell sounded once again. At this point, my mind was swirling in every direction. Miles definitely made some good points, and even though I agreed to go to the police with that information, I still felt a little leery about it. After all, the phone calls were anonymous and weren't altogether convincing. If there's one thing I've learned during my 38 years on this earth, it's that there are all kinds of crazy people out there.

I walked to the door with an I-don't-give-a-damn attitude

because I didn't. I mean, I did, but I didn't—if you can understand that. Surely, I didn't want to go to prison, but I was at the end of my rope with the entire thing. I was tired of the police hounding me. I was tired of receiving the calls regarding Lincoln. And I was bummed about the fact that Sullivan was gone.

"What do you know," I said upon opening the door and finding Detectives Miller and Jackson standing side by side.

"We have a warrant to search your place," Detective Jackson said, displaying it proudly.

"Oh, here we go," I responded. "I've seen enough movies and cop shows to know that this is where you guys come in, don't find shit, but royally jack my place up, right? Hey, have at it, Barney one and Barney two."

They didn't waste much time at all. My place was a complete pigsty in a matter of minutes. I knew I had nothing to hide, but I was concerned about them planting some type of evidence connecting me with Sullivan's death.

"Uh, I think this would be a good time to mention those calls about Lincoln, don't you think?" Miles urged as he and I stood and watched Frick and Frack wreck my place. I didn't respond. I was pissed. Hell, they could have been civil about it. They could have gone through my shit without totally ruining everything. I mean, damn! I felt like I was in LA dealing with those crooked, rotten-ass cops.

Many things went through my mind while I stood and watched them go through my place and my belongings in a tornado-like fashion. My anger was eased by the thought of Sullivan. Where was she now? What was she doing at this very moment? I thought of her dressed in all white, sitting up there in Heaven without a care in the world.

"What?" Miles asked.

"Huh? What do you mean, 'what'?"

"You're standing here smiling while these fools are tearing up your place," Miles said.

"Am I?"

"Yeah, what's that all about?"

"Nothing," I said, picturing Sullivan smiling right back at me from up above.

When they finally came up for air, Detective Jackson approached me. Detective Miller closely followed him. Their affinity with one another made me wonder if they held each other's johnson while taking leaks. I mean, their closeness was freaking me out.

"Can you tell me who these belong to?" Detective Jackson asked. He was holding a pair of thong underwear that he undoubtedly found in my clothes hamper. I'm sorry, but there was just something about him that I didn't like. He was a buster. And I resented the fact that they had a little formula working. In cases that involved black people, Detective Jackson was the lead detective. And in cases that involved white people, Detective Miller was the lead guy. This was my theory, anyways. I didn't know this for a fact, but it sure seemed that way.

"Yeah," I said. "They were Sullivan's. Wait, let me guess, that makes me a killer, right?"

"What were they doing in your clothes hamper?"

"Do I have to spell it out for you? Like I've said over and over again, we were friends. Friends with benefits, mind you. I mean, granted, we went there a few times, but the last time I checked, that wasn't a crime. Is there anything else? Because, honestly, I just want you guys out of my house. You guys jacked up my place for no reason, and on top of that your detective skills are suspect. No, I'll take that back. They suck! You guys are here, asking some bullshit-ass questions, while whoever killed Sullivan is out there kicking it. I mean, damn! Am I under arrest or what?"

"No, Mr. Spencer, but we have to take you down to the station for additional questioning," Detective Miller said, finally standing straight. Clearly his back was tired from bending over.

"Take me down to the station?" I replied. "For what? I've answered all of your questions. What now?" I raised my voice intentionally. Though I didn't let on, I was taken aback a bit when those two clowns produced Sullivan's thong from my clothes hamper. I didn't realize she'd left it behind. We obviously had gotten close—at least close enough for me to wash her skivvies.

"You know what? I'll go down to the station with you guys. Hell, I'm tired of this shit."

"What?" Miles looked at me like I was crazy.

"Yeah," I said, turning to Detective Jackson. "I haven't done anything wrong. You guys know I'm an attorney, right?"

Neither responded.

"Well, you better come up with something that puts me away for a long time because when this is all said and done, I'm gonna sue the shit out of the both of you personally, and then the entire APD. Bet on that," I said in a hard, Shaft-like fashion. The only thing missing at that moment was Isaac Hayes's song from the movie.

22

INTERROGATION AND DUPED

ONCE in the interrogation room, it became clear to me that shows like *Law and Order* had really done their homework. The two-way glass was in full-effect. I sat behind the table, facing the glass, while the two punk-ass detectives stood with their backs to the window.

"You guys are detectives, right?" I said, looking up at the two of them.

"That's right," Detective Jackson confirmed.

"You mind if I call you guys dicks?"

Neither seemed amused.

"Look, let's cut to the chase here, Mr. Spencer," Detective Miller said firmly. *Ain't this a bitch,* I thought, *now he wants to play the head honcho? In the field, the brother was doing all the work.* "While you find a need to make jokes about the situation, the reason why we hauled your ass down here is because your fingerprints were found all over Ms. Williams' place."

"Is that all you have?" I asked, wondering how those fools got their jobs. "Okay, I see I'm going to have to spell it out for you. I thought I was being tasteful, subtle and even tactful. And I thought you all, especially being dicks and all, could read between the lines, but obviously that's not the case. Sullivan invited me over for dinner the night before she died. Dinner was outstanding, the ambiance was outstanding, and we spent the rest of the night butt-ass naked. I got up and left early in the morning, long before the sun came up. Get the picture? I mean, how would I not have fingerprints all over that place?"

"We're just covering all of our bases here, Mr. Spencer," Detective Miller said. "I think you should know we're also holding one of your clients, Lincoln Dix, in a cell down the hall."

"What?" I sat up in my chair. "Why?"

"His fingerprints were also found all over her house, not to mention his semen inside of her."

I sat back in my chair. "Bullshit!" I said, wondering how they had our fingerprints on file. Then it dawned on me that Georgia was one of the states that mandated fingerprints at the DMV. So, they definitely had our prints in a database.

"Bullshit?" Detective Jackson blurted. "Why are you acting surprised, Matisse? You knew this. We aren't telling you anything you didn't already know."

"Oh, we're on a first-name basis now, huh?" I said, buying time as I tried to digest what they had just told me. As much as I didn't want to believe them, the more I thought about it the more it made sense. I thought about how uncomfortable Sullivan seemed the night we ran into Lincoln at dinner. Was that Lincoln's number on her caller-I.D. that night? You'd think I'd know, as many times as I'd dialed it in the past, but my mind was drawing a blank. I was a little nervous. "So, you want me to believe Lincoln and I were doing the same woman at the same time? Is that what this is all about?"

"I'm afraid it's about a little more than that, Mr. Spencer," Detective Miller said. He took a seat across from me at the table. He leaned forward. "So, what happened? Obviously, both of you guys were banging her. My guess is you found Lincoln in bed with her, became enraged, went ballistic and killed her."

"Yeah, right, dick!"

"Or maybe you simply found out about the two of them, then went ballistic and killed her."

Leaning forward to where my nose almost touched Detective

Miller's, I said, "You guys must have shit for brains. I mean, that doesn't even make sense. If that was the case, why would I just kill her? If I found my girl in bed with another man, they'd both have hell to pay by way of an ass-whoopin. But there's no way I'd ever kill anyone over a piece of ass."

My palms were sweaty. At that moment, I didn't care what those dickheads thought. All the hurt I'd felt since I found Sullivan that morning had become anger. She had done it to me again. She had betrayed me one last time.

Detectives Miller and Jackson continued to talk, but I no longer listened to what they said. I thought about the past couple of days and how Sullivan and I had gotten closer than close. I had fallen back in love with her, and I had assumed she felt the same. She had said that we'd move forward together. Give it another shot. And all the while, she was boning my man, Lincoln. How does the same woman dupe me twice? She and Lincoln must have had some really good laughs at my expense.

23

ANOTHER NIGHT
IN THE POKEY

THOSE two bone-headed detectives put me the through the ringer in a textbook-like fashion, but they knew they had nothing on me. They informed me about Lincoln's fingerprints and semen, and then I was free to go.

As much as I didn't want to believe them, I knew it was true. I knew Lincoln and his player ways and, unfortunately, I knew Sullivan and her trifling ways. Don't get me wrong, I was blindsided all right. I felt like a Mack truck had just run over me. But more than that, I was embarrassed.

I didn't get much sleep that night as I ran various scenarios involving Sullivan through my head. The next day I was content just casually lounging around at home. I had already told myself that I wasn't going to do any work from my home or the office.

Sullivan was still on my mind; I couldn't help it. Our first time around, I was to blame. My stupid actions led to Sullivan's actions, which ultimately led to our demise. I strayed a time or two early on in the relationship, thinking at the time that my relationship with Sullivan was to be like all of the other relationships I had had—meaningless and shallow. I never bargained on falling in love with her. Once I realized it was love that I was experiencing, I was a one-woman man where Sullivan was concerned. Things were good between the two of us for about a three-year period. That was the best time of my life. It wasn't until Sullivan inadvertently found out about one of the two women I had been with years before that things changed for the worse.

Maybe her recent actions were part of a master plan of payback. In any event, I knew I was at fault as much as anyone. No one said I had to fall head-over-heels for a woman with whom I shared a bad history, especially after only three dates. I mean, I should have known better. I've been in the game way too long for that. It was a rookie move on my behalf.

I sat in complete silence, looking out my window down at the busy streets of Atlanta's midtown section. It was a cold, gray day. Most of the cars had their headlights on, and this was early afternoon.

My quiet, peaceful afternoon was interrupted by a phone call from Lincoln.

"Matisse, get me out of here." Lincoln's voice cracked. He had lost all of his cool points. No longer was he ending every sentence with *baby*. "You have to believe me, I didn't do it."

"I figured you'd be out by now. Why didn't you post bond, Lincoln?"

"They're trying to make an example out of me, Matisse. I'm sure it's all over the news by now," Lincoln said, raising his voice.

I turned on the television. Sure enough, it was all over the news.

"You need a criminal lawyer, Lincoln, this is a serious matter."

"Oh, that's why I've been sitting in a cell without any chance of bail all night long, huh? Don't you think I know this, Matisse? You're the best agent I've ever had, and I know you're a good lawyer. I need your help, man! Will you represent me? You're the only person I trust."

"Did you say 'trust'?" I asked, thinking, *I should hang up on this clown right now.*

"You have to get me out of here, Matisse!"

"Let's say you didn't kill her, Lincoln. You were still boning my girl. Look, from a business standpoint, we both make each other a lot of money, but what kind of shit is that, Lincoln?"

"Aw, come on, Matisse. That girl was a freak. The night I bumped into you guys, I just figured you were getting some, too. I didn't know it was like that between the two of you. I mean, I didn't see you guys all hugged up at your brunch."

"Whatever, Lincoln! You knew I'd started seeing her again."

"All right, Matisse, maybe it was messed up on my part. You know me when it comes to women. I can't keep it in the pants, but Matisse, my life is on the line. I swear to you on my mother, and you know how much I love my moms, I didn't do it. The only thing I'm guilty of is waxing that ass that morning."

"You're pushing it, Lincoln."

"Okay, maybe that was below the belt, but seriously, Mat, do you think I would let them do a DNA swab if I was guilty?"

"Why'd you do that?"

"I don't have shit to hide. I took Sullivan for a ride, which, the last time I checked, isn't a crime."

"Look, Lincoln, I never liked you. You've always been cocky and arrogant," I yelled into the receiver. "Our relationship has always been strictly business, and I intend on keeping it that way. I'll think about it and let you know in the morning."

"What! In the morning! Come on, Matisse, I can't stay another night in here. You have to get me out of here, and now!" Lincoln's voice cracked so much he sounded like a little girl who was afraid to leave her mom on the first day of school. When it became clear to him that I meant what I had said, he then tried to man-up. "Matisse, don't forget you work for me. You are my agent, and I need you, man!"

At that point, I couldn't have cared less. "I'll call you in the morning." I could hear Lincoln saying something before I cut him off with the loud sound of the dial tone in his ear. It sounded like he said I was fired. Like I said, I didn't care. This was one time where he needed me a lot more than I needed him. I thought one more night in the pokey would do Lincoln some good. It definitely lifted my

Darrin May

spirits.

I was in a tough situation. No matter how gratifying it was at the moment to know that Lincoln was behind bars and no matter how much I wanted to take him behind a shed and beat the hell out of him, he was still my top client. Financially, we had a mutually beneficial business relationship. And he was right, I was on his payroll. Though I was determined to let Lincoln spend the night in jail, I knew I had to act fast in the morning regarding his release. Considering his celebrity, it was just a matter of time before the media got their hands on him. It's amazing how the media salivates over the bad stories and, in most cases, lets the good stories fall by the wayside. As self-absorbed as Lincoln is, he's given hundreds of thousands of dollars to various charities over the years, but it has never been mentioned by the media. However, when the media got wind of him getting arrested, rest assured, it would be the top story.

24

AL'S AND REVELATIONS

I sat around my place for another couple hours after talking to Lincoln. Eventually though, I was tired of being cooped up inside. I needed to get out. I called Miles to see if he wanted to meet me down at Al's for a bite to eat and a few drinks.

Seeing as Al's was a stone's throw away from my place, I left immediately, knowing full well I'd be there for at least half an hour before Miles made his appearance. I didn't care.

Like always, I took a seat at the bar.

"How goes it, Matisse?" Al asked as he handed me a Stoli on the rocks.

"What's up, Al?" I took the drink and downed it in one gulp.

Al looked at me in a concerned way. "You all right, Matisse?"

"Yeah, I'm fine, Al. You got another coming for me?"

"Of course I do." He began to make another one. "What's with the long face?"

"Nothing," I snapped, not bothering to look up at him. My eyes were fixated on the television.

"Here you go." He placed the Stoli on the rocks in front of me. "Pace yourself, Matisse."

"I will," I said, again slamming it in one gulp. Al just looked at me and shook his head in a disapproving way. This time he didn't even bother using a new glass. In light of me devouring the vodka, the glass was still full of ice. Al simply refreshed it.

"Hey, isn't Lincoln Dix one of your clients?"

I nodded before responding, "Yeah."

"That's some mess he's gotten himself into. Have you talked to him?"

"He's one of my clients, Al. What do you think?" I knew I wasn't being very pleasant, but the whole thing left a bad taste in my mouth. Lincoln wasn't exactly at the top of my list of favorable subjects.

"What do you think? Did he do it?" Al stood in front of me. Only the countertop separated us. With one towel draped over his shoulder, he wiped the surface of the bar down with a rag.

"Honestly, Al, I don't know what to believe."

"Didn't you know her, too, Matisse?"

"Yeah."

"She sure was nice-looking. That was the only news show I watched with any regularity—and all because of her. Well, whatever the case may be, it's a shame, if you ask me."

"Yep!" I said, feeling the effects of the two drinks I had slammed moments before. I lifted my glass up in the air before taking a swig.

"You haven't been around here lately, Matisse, but do you know who's been here a few times in the past week or so?"

"Who?"

"Your ex-girl, Hunter."

"What?"

"Yeah!" Al lifted my glass and wiped the area below. The toothpick he was gnawing on looked like it had been through a war.

"Who she been in here with? Her boyfriend?"

"The times I saw her she was alone."

Then I felt a hand on my shoulder.

"What's up, bruh?" Miles said while taking a seat next to me.

"It's about time. Damn! You get lost?"

Ignoring me, Miles extended his hand to Al. "How you

doing, Al?"

"I'm doing fine, Miles. I got one cold brew coming right up for you."

"Thanks, Al."

Miles turned to me. "You alright?"

"I'm alright I guess. I'm just trying to figure shit out right now."

"Well, what went on at the police station?"

"I think they know I had nothing to do with Sullivan's death. They were just trying to pump me for information."

"Wow!" Miles responded. "So, your boy caught a case, huh?"

"Yep!"

"That's what I don't understand. If they have this overwhelming evidence against Lincoln, which is obviously enough to lock him up, what the hell did they need with you?"

"Good question. Like I said, I think they were just pumping me for information."

"Well, damn, they wrecked your place. What's up with that?"

"I don't know, man. A lot of things just aren't making much sense right now," I said, motioning to Al to hit me with another one.

"Have you talked to Lincoln? What's your take on all of this? Do you think he did it? It's a small world isn't it? Hell, I didn't even know he knew Sullivan. Did you?"

"Which question do you want me to answer first?" I said sarcastically just as Al arrived with my fourth Stoli on the rocks.

Miles looked at me like I was crazy. "Whatever, man."

"No, I didn't know they knew each other, though I had a strong hunch."

"What? How so?"

"Well, one night when Sullivan and I were out to dinner we ran into Lincoln. There was just something about her body language that suggested they knew each other. I mean, she seemed really uncomfortable around him. I asked her about it, but I didn't want to make too big of an issue over it."

"What'd she say?"

"She said no."

"I'll be damned. He was banging her, huh?" Miles couldn't care less about my feelings. It was like he'd forgotten all about the five years I'd spent with her, and he certainly wasn't tripping over the fact that I had fallen back in love with her. It was classic Miles. He was never one of those guys who was big on compassion, and he certainly wasn't tactful in his approach to anything.

"According to the police, he was going there," I said, staring at the television above.

"How do they know?"

"They said they found his semen inside of her."

"Damn, bruh, that's foul. Sullivan was a freak, huh?"

"I guess so."

"Women! That's exactly why I'm about to be out of the game. Marriage is going to be good, bruh! Shelby would never do any shit like that. She knows better."

I just looked down at the bar, waiting for Al to fill me up again.

"So you talked to him, right? I know how much he relies on you. I bet you were his first call from the joint."

"Yeah, I talked to that fool. I shouldn't have. I should have whooped his ass. He knew what the deal was between Sullivan and me. He tried to say he was clueless. Shit, apparently, I was the only one who was clueless about what our deal was. We obviously weren't as into each other as I thought."

"Hey, man, win some, lose some. Tomorrow's another day."

"Yeah, easy for you to say. I seriously thought she was the one. Why else would she come back into my life like that?"

"Yeah, I know what you mean. All of this is kind of bizarre." Miles stood and flagged Al down. He was obviously ready for another brew. "Speaking of bizarre, I overheard Hunter talking about Sullivan in a jacked-up way at your brunch. There's two more people I had no clue they knew each other."

"That makes two of us," I said. "What'd she say?"

He sat back down in the stool next to me, tightly clutching his full pint of beer. "Well, I had to run out to my car for a minute to get something. My car was parked behind hers. She was sitting in her car talking on the phone, and her window was slightly cracked open. All I heard was, 'Sullivan's a ho. But that's okay because I like to keep my friends close and my enemies closer.' At that point, I kind of ducked because I didn't want her to see me."

"Come on, Miles. Are you sure?"

"Bruh, that's exactly what I heard. Unfortunately, that's all I heard."

I sat back and thought about it for a moment. "And you're just now telling me about it? What kind of shit is that?"

"I don't know. I didn't really think much of it at the time."

"What! Didn't think much of it? Come on, man! Damn!"

"I mean, I did, but I didn't. You know how it is, Matisse. In case you forgot, I am about to get married. Hell, sue me. I had other things on my mind. I'm about to go down. That's a scary thing don't you think?"

"Oh, now it's scary? Man, anyway! Please! Just the other day you were talking about how you couldn't wait, and how Shelby was the best thing that ever happened to you."

Miles stood and took a lengthy gulp of his beer. "I can't wait, and Shelby is the best thing that ever happened to me."

"That didn't sound too convincing, Miles. What gives?"

"Nothing gives, Matisse. It's just…." He paused and sat back down in the stool beside me. Miles then lunged toward me. "I think I'm getting cold feet."

"Come on, man, that's natural. You said it best. You're about to go down—one woman for the rest of your life. Hey, don't get me wrong, I envy the hell out of you. I wish I was in your shoes, but there is a finality to it all. We have been looking for our respective Misses from day one."

"I hope you're right, Matisse. Come to think about it, I guess you're still taking applications, huh? Oops, my bad. I shouldn't have said that, considering all that's gone on in the past few days with Sullivan and all." Miles administered a couple of pats to my back. "I'm sorry, Matisse."

"Whatever, man, I'm over her." I waved my arm in the air

to get Al's attention again, even though I was starting to really feel the vodka. I was trying my best to act like I was a tough guy void of feelings and emotion, but deep down inside I was both hurt and mad. *How she gonna bone Lincoln and me at the same time? That's foul*, I thought.

Not bothering to ask what I needed, Al walked over and placed another one of my signature drinks in front of me. "Remember what I said, Matisse, pace yourself."

"Don't worry, Al," Miles said. "I got it. It's been one of those weeks. You know how it is."

"Unfortunately, Miles, I do," Al responded as he placed another beer in front of Miles.

"Finish your story about Hunter and Sullivan, Miles," I said, slightly slurring my words.

"That's it. That's all I heard."

"I wonder what's going on. Al said she's been in here a time or two in the past couple of weeks, and now you're telling me she had something against Sullivan? What gives?"

"I don't know," Miles replied.

"I thought it was more than weird that they showed up together at the brunch."

Though I had a little heater going, all of this got me to thinking. There was some outlandish stuff happening in my world. First Sullivan's death, then I find out she and Lincoln had a thing going while she and I had something going on, and now the whole Hunter-Sullivan connection. Yeah, my pride was a bit wounded, but it didn't stop me from thinking about Lincoln sitting in that jail cell for a crime he possibly didn't commit. Who knows? Maybe he did do it. My gut said something fishy was going on, and I wanted to get to the bottom of it. I decided right then and there that I'd represent Lincoln. I had absolutely no experience in the courtroom, but Lincoln was right, I was a damn good agent and lawyer. Hell, come to think of it, Lincoln too had his J.D., and together maybe we could present a good case.

25

REAL TALK
WITH LINCOLN

I found myself sitting at Starbucks the next morning hoping the large cup of coffee I was about to consume would cure my hangover. Ordinarily I'd get it to go, but for once I was on my time. Lincoln had no idea I'd decided to represent him. Though I was on my way over to the station to post bail and give him the news of my decision, I kind of liked picturing him in that cell, which caused me to move even slower.

Staring at the newspaper in front of me, I read a couple of lines but they didn't register. Thinking about Lincoln, I automatically thought about Sullivan and Hunter, which caused me to think about Erica. I'd come to the conclusion that most women couldn't be trusted. Sullivan was shady. She burned me twice. Hunter, it seemed, had some type of hidden agenda, which, in my book, put her in the shady column. Hell, I could go down my entire list of lifetime exes and it would probably amount to one big shade tree, with the exception of Erica. Now there was a woman who really loved me for me. She would have run through brick walls and walked over hot coals for me. For some reason, sitting in that coffee shop, it all became crystal clear to me. Yeah, the grass always seems greener, but at the end of the day you need someone in your corner who truly has your back. Don't get me wrong, they have to be easy on the eyes as well. I had that with Erica, but all I could ever think of when we were together was other women. When it was all said and done, I hurt her. I hurt her bad. Why didn't I just tell her I loved her? When she asked, I couldn't bring myself to say the words. I was so full of myself, I thought that there would be plenty of women around the corner who possessed all of the great qualities that Erica had, but ranked a notch higher on my self-imposed scale of perfection. What a fool I was. When she walked out the door for good that night, I remember thinking that I was the dumbest man on earth.

Perfection! What a joke. A lot of us spend a great portion of our lives looking for that flawless, perfect person who doesn't exist, when all the while that person who is perfect for us has been right there all the time, staring us in the face. You know that person I'm talking about; the one who ends your sentences and the one who fits you like a glove and the one who is flawed, as we all are, but nonetheless, is simply perfect for you. It's amazing that we rarely see who they are in a timely manner. All too often by the time we wake up and smell the coffee, it's too late.

I grabbed a lid for my coffee and a couple of napkins on the way out of Starbucks before making my way over to the police station. At this point, even I thought Lincoln had waited long enough. The process of posting bail for Lincoln took about an hour. On the way out of the station, neither of us said a word.

"So, does this mean you'll represent me?" Lincoln asked as he strapped the seat belt across his body.

I started the car, turned to him and said, "You look like shit. Rough night, huh?"

"You know, I should fire your ass! What kind of agent leaves his number one client, and you know I am, in a damn jail cell for that amount of time?" he screamed. "Hell, Matisse, you've made incredible amounts of money off of me, and this is the thanks I get? You know I didn't have anything to do with that girl's death."

"Oh, don't mind me. I'm just the one who negotiated all of those multi-million-dollar contracts and endorsement deals for you. You probably could have done it on your own, or used a different agent," I said sarcastically.

"Whatever, Matisse. You still shouldn't have left me in that damn cell for as long as you did. Shit, you work for me, dammit! Are you representing me or what?"

"I'll represent you, but we're going to have to sit down and have a serious talk once we get to your place, Lincoln. You have a lot of explaining to do. This shit just doesn't make any sense."

"Bet. But first, can you stop off at Gladys Knight's Chicken and Waffles? I'm starving. I'll get it to go."

"How can you think about food at a time like this?"

"I have to eat, Matisse. Damn! I've been locked up in a cold, stinky jail cell all night long. Can a brother get some breakfast? I see you found time to stop off at Starbucks this morning," Lincoln pointed out, looking down at my half-full cup of coffee sitting in the cup holder. "Do you see me sweating you?"

Rather than respond, I just drove to the restaurant. I pulled up to the front and kept the car running. Lincoln jumped out of the car and made his way inside. Before he got to the door, he turned and came back to the car. I acted like I wasn't paying attention and looked straight ahead. He knocked on the window while motioning with his hand to roll it down. I hit the button to my left, and stopped the window at the halfway mark. Lincoln leaned forward and stuck his head inside the car.

"Do you want anything?"

"No, I'm good, thanks," I responded, reaching for my cup of coffee.

"All right." He turned and went in.

Lincoln lived only a couple blocks away from the chicken and waffle spot, but that short drive to his place was tough because the food smelled ridiculously good. I used to go there all of the time, and the chicken and waffles were off the chain!

The moment we stepped inside Lincoln's house, I waited for him to put his food down before hauling off and hitting him squarely on the jaw. He stumbled backwards a few steps, but didn't fall.

"What the hell was that about!" Lincoln yelled, holding his jaw. I didn't say a word. I just stood there looking at him sternly, hoping I wouldn't have to spell it out for him. He knew good and well why I stole on him. "All right, man, maybe I deserved that. Maybe."

"Maybe, huh," I said. "You know damn well you deserved that and then some. You knew Sullivan and I were involved."

"Involved? Matisse, like I said on the phone yesterday, I just thought you were doing her. Sullivan was a freak, dog. Since when was she a one-man woman? Plus, how involved could you have been? She hadn't been back in town that long."

I was crushed to hear that, and tried my best not to let on that this was news to me. I mean, don't get me wrong, I knew she'd played me by sleeping with both Lincoln and me at the same time. But freak sounded a little harsh. However, after taking a moment to think about it, I concluded that Lincoln was right. She was doing two guys at the same time. As far as I was concerned, that pretty much put her in my freak category. And, last time I checked, two or three dates rarely solidified a relationship with genuine legs.

"I guess everyone knew she was a freak except me," I conceded.

"My bad, Matisse. I thought you knew, man."

"Win some, lose some, I guess," I said, shrugging my shoulders. "Let's talk about that morning. It looks like the police department has a hard-on for you. And, why not? You're about as high profile as they come."

"But, Matisse, I didn't do it. I don't care how it looks. Here, let's go in here."

I followed Lincoln into the kitchen where we each took a seat at a large rectangular table. He immediately tore into his food. "Can you get me out of this mess?" Lincoln asked with a mouthful of food.

"If I didn't think so, Lincoln, I wouldn't be here. I know it's easier said than done, but you just have to trust me and remain patient. I have to be honest with you, though. All of my work as a lawyer has been contractual. I have little experience in the courtroom."

"That's all right, baby, you're the best agent I've ever had.

I know you have mad skills as a lawyer. It's time to put that J.D. to use." He swallowed, and then reached for the glass of water in front of him. "But I feel you, it is easier said than done. My life's on the line, Matisse. You can do this. I trust you."

"Okay," I responded. "We have a lot of work ahead of us. Let's not forget you have a J.D. as well."

"Yeah, but come on, Mat, I'm a hockey player! And, you know this." Lincoln pushed his plate away from him and only five minutes had passed. It was empty with the exception of the bones from the chicken. "Cool, let's get started right now."

I placed a pocket tape recorder on the table and took a notebook and pen out of my briefcase. "Well, let's start from the top," I said, turning the tape recorder on. "I was over at her house the night before, and when I left she was alive and well. What time did you make it over there? Was it in the morning or right after I left?"

I almost didn't want to hear what he was going to say, but after thinking about it for a moment, considering the way she dogged me, hell, I was over her.

Lincoln cleared his throat before saying anything. I could tell he was perplexed about how to begin. "Well," he started, "I, uh, I had gone to the Thrashers game that night to see my boy, Zack Darby, play. He's the starting center for the Rangers. I don't know if you remember, but he and I played at Harvard together."

"I remember," I said. "That front line was unreal. He was your right-winger, though, because you were the center."

"Yeah, well, afterwards, he and I and a few other cats went over to Magic City to check out some dancers. You know how it goes, Mat. That game was hard for me to watch and it kind of bummed me out," Lincoln said, looking down at his knee, "knowing that it would be awhile before I hit the ice again. And, before you say anything, I know what you're thinking. Yeah, I said Magic City. Those white boys love some sisters. Believe me, I tried to get them to go to the Cheetah. They weren't having it."

"Hmmm, I know that's right," I said, thinking about the abundance of beautiful women of color Magic City had to offer.

Lincoln stood and made his way over to the refrigerator.

"You want anything to drink?"

"No, I'm good right now."

He opened the door, grabbed a bottle of water and returned to his seat across from me at the kitchen table. "I figured a couple lap-dances and a trip to the champagne room might have helped my mood. You know how that goes. Being around a few big-tittied women usually puts a smile on a brother's face. As it did that night."

Lincoln paused and looked at me, probably expecting some type of chuckle. I didn't respond. I just sat there waiting for him to continue.

"Anyway, after a few hours and a couple-thousand dollars later, we bounced. I dropped those guys off at their hotel and started to make my way home. It was about two in the morning. At that very moment, my phone started to blow up. It was Sullivan. 'Hey, baby, why don't you come over?'

"'What are you doing up so late?'

"'Thinking about you' she said in that sexy voice, causing instant wood. And, I know you know what I'm talking about, Matisse.

"'Oh, I see, this is a booty call,' I said. You know me, Mat, I was trying to play a little hardball. So, then, I just ran with it. 'You want me to come over and tighten you up, huh?'

"She responded with some shit like, 'And you know this!' and hung up the phone before I could say anything else. Needless to say, I drove my black ass over there."

I couldn't help but think about the night Sullivan and I had shared only hours before Lincoln's arrival at her place. I thought we'd made passionate love. Apparently, it was just sex for her. Life's funny. Just when you think you know a person is usually when it all goes to shit. I really thought I knew her. I mean, truth be told, I'd never had sex like that before. I'll call it sex now, but at the time I damn sure thought it was love. How could it not have been? There was intense passion on both of our behalves, but mine was charged by my strong feelings for her. I guess that was the difference. Some people get passionate about having sex, while others are passionate about making love.

"When I got over there," Lincoln continued, "she answered the door in a skimpy red and black lace teddy, holding a bottle of champagne. Never mind the fact that it was past two in the morning...."

"Do you know the exact time?" I interrupted.

"No, but I'm fairly certain it was somewhere between two and three in the morning."

"So what happened next?"

"Well, as soon as I shut the door behind me, I took one long look at Sullivan, and her fine ass." Lincoln paused and shook his head in an approving way as if he was taking a trip down memory lane. "I then grabbed the bottle of champagne out of her hand before lifting her off the ground and carrying her up the stairs to her bedroom. I mean, what can I say, Matisse? There wasn't a whole lot of talking going on in those wee hours of the night. I tapped that ass and left before the sun came up. And, like you, she was alive and well when I bounced.

What a dickhead, I thought. *He's so full of himself. And Sullivan, well, she was clearly a ho, and he probably did tap that ass.* Why it still kind of bothered me, I didn't know. But it did, and I didn't like it.

I left Lincoln's place thinking, *What have I gotten myself into?* But I was quickly reminded that it would behoove me to do whatever I could to help find the real killer because I wasn't yet completely off of their list of suspects.

Though Lincoln didn't supply me a whole lot of pertinent information other than the fact that he hit it right after I hit it, I nevertheless rushed home to get started.

26

THE FUNERAL

I woke up the following morning in my study, still sitting in my chair, hunched across my desk. I'd spent most of the night going over various scenarios regarding the case. Though a lot of what was going on in my head a few hours ago made sense to me at the time, now it all seemed a bit far-fetched. I looked down at my desk, examining the long night's work. Lincoln's and Hunter's names were written in caps and highlighted in bold, along with one big question mark. Frankly, knowing Lincoln and Hunter the way I did, I just couldn't see them doing any such thing to Sullivan, or anyone else for that matter. I thought it best to focus my energy on the question mark. However, the more I thought about it, the more a voice kept saying to me, *You never know*. Hell, we see it on the news every night. Our next-door neighbors, our best friends, our colleagues at work—people whom we think we know, but who prove to have dark sides. I've said it before and I'll say it again, there are some crazy-ass people out there and you just never know.

I couldn't spend any more time brainstorming because I had to get showered and dressed. Sullivan's funeral was to start in an hour. I dreaded going, but even though she dogged the shit out of me, I had to pay my respects, for more reasons than one.

My five-minute shower shattered my record for the fastest ever. It was a game that I usually played when I was in a hurry. There were stringent rules. You couldn't just jump in the shower, get wet and get out. No, you had to hit all of the vital spots with ample soap and water.

Ordinarily, either the television or radio would have been blaring during this time, but it just didn't seem right. I got dressed in complete silence. I know she played me, but this wasn't about me; it was about her, Sullivan. As I picked out a suit and tie, I thought about her and me and the time we shared together. It's funny how a lot of times when we take those trips down memory lane, we tend to spend the majority of our time focusing on the good times shared. For the most part, the bad times always seem to fall by the wayside.

I am a pretty traditional guy when it comes to suits. I picked out a black suit by Jones of New York, and accessorized it with a patterned shirt with shades of blue and a silver tie. The shirt and tie were my way of jazzing things up a bit.

Miles had called earlier and said that he and Shelby wanted me to go with them. I kind of felt like a charity case, but the truth of the matter was I really wasn't tripping anymore. Sure, I took my trip down memory lane, highlighting the good things. But there were a couple very bad incidents that didn't, and will never, sit well with me regarding Sullivan. So, life goes on.

I heard a couple loud honks of a car horn, and immediately knew it was Miles and Shelby. That was Miles's trademark. Talk about being lazy. Man, just park the car, get out and ring the doorbell. Anyway, I was glad they finally made it because we were running a little late.

"Come on, man, let's go," Miles shouted as I approached the car. "We're late."

"And, whose fault is that?" I asked, climbing into the back seat. "Shit, I was waiting on you all."

Miles turned and looked at Shelby.

"Sorry," she replied, followed by a loud sigh and the folding of her arms. Shelby then turned to me. "How are you doing, Matisse?"

"I'm all right, Shel. Thank you. You're looking lovely, as usual." She was, too. But, you know, I really wasn't supposed to be peeping my boy's girl out like that. I mean, hell, it was a known fact that Shelby was fine. She'd always been the cream of the crop.

"Well, thank you, Matisse. That's so sweet. Unfortunately, after all of these years, you haven't rubbed off on my husband-to-be."

Miles didn't respond, but gave Shelby one of those "whatever" looks.

"This is just awful, Matisse," Shelby continued, ignoring Miles's rude look.

"Yeah, it is," I said, only to be interrupted by Miles.

"Man, sorry we were late. Shelby was half-stepping. You know how women are. She changed clothes about three times, and applied different makeup a couple of times. I mean, damn, what happened to showering, getting dressed and bouncing?"

Shelby nudged Miles. "Don't start."

"Oh, anyway," said Miles before looking at me in the rearview mirror. "You alright, dog?"

"Yeah, I'm cool," I said.

"You sure you're going to be able to handle this?"

"Miles, I said I'm cool."

Still looking at me in the rearview mirror, Miles said, "All right," and began driving. Moments later, Shelby turned and looked back at me and smiled warmly. I gave her a fake smile in return, wondering what that was all about. I assumed she was trying to subtly comfort me. Unfortunately, we all know what usually happens when one assumes.

A large media contingent, ranging from television, print, radio and the dreaded irritating bloggers, congregated just outside of the gates of the funeral home. I counted six television trucks lined up in a row as we drove through the gates.

"What a zoo," Miles commented.

"I'm just glad they aren't allowed on the funeral grounds," I said.

"That's just wrong," Shelby added. "They shouldn't be allowed anywhere near here. Talk about classless."

"That word best describes most of those people," I said,

opening the door before I made my way out of the back seat. "Well, here we go. Let's go say our goodbyes."

Judging from the lack of empty seats, the funeral home had to be near capacity. The three of us found seats near the back just as the service began. Though Miles and Shelby seemed concerned about my well-being, I knew I was all right—I wasn't about to shed any tears over Sullivan. Don't get me wrong, had I not known about Lincoln and her, in all likelihood I would have been a complete mess. Sullivan and I shared a history together and I wanted to pay my respects, but, at the risk of sounding cold and shallow, I had bigger fish to fry.

I listened to what the priest had to say in the beginning. Yeah, Sullivan was Catholic. But, about halfway through I focused my attention on Hunter, who was seated about two rows in front of us, just off to our right.

Hunter had always been an emotional person. I knew she couldn't go to a funeral without shedding some tears. However, as I watched her cry uncontrollably with Jeff's arm around her, it seemed to me that Hunter had gone Hollywood on us. I mean, the more I watched, and the louder she cried, the more I called bullshit. The conversation Miles had overheard was now ringing loud and clear. Hell, I didn't even know Hunter and Sullivan knew each other, let alone knew each other that well.

I studied people in attendance closely for the remainder of the service. I advised Lincoln to attend the funeral because I thought we might get some positive publicity out of it. As I perused the room, though, I didn't see him.

At one point, I looked over at Miles and Shelby. Shelby periodically ended sniffles here and there with a slight tap to her nose with a handkerchief. I was, however, a bit surprised to see tears rolling down Miles's face.

Is the killer here, I wondered? It's funny, in a 24-hour time span I had gone from super sports agent to some kind of lawyer/crackpot detective who really had no idea what he was doing. Going over a to-do list in my head, the one thing that stood out the most was the fact that I knew I had to get in touch with the few friends I had in the police business. I needed some serious pointers on how to go about this, coupled with their advice on knowing when and where to start the process.

The service concluded with a very moving song. I could tell the song touched Shelby, judging by the way she sobbed and how tightly she clutched my hand. Though Miles already had his arm around her, I applied a couple of soft pats to her back in an attempt to console her. I sat there completely void of emotion, which was a strong indication that I was indeed over Sullivan.

On our way out of the church following the service, I thought about approaching Hunter and Jeff, but quickly decided against it. I had to keep in mind that I was a complete novice in all of this, and one wrong move could prove to be fatal in more ways than one. We did, however, run into Lincoln just before we exited the church.

"Hey," I said. The three of us stopped. Lincoln was propped up against the wall a couple of inches from the doorway. "I didn't think you were going to make it. Were you here the entire time?"

"I walked in just as you guys were sitting down," Lincoln replied nonchalantly. He was wearing dark sunglasses that hid his eyes. As dark as it was in the church, it was a wonder he could see at all. "I just watched while I stood back here. So, what's next? Where do we go from here?"

"Well, I think you should go back to your place and sit tight. I have a couple of friends who happen to be police officers. I'm going to hook up with those guys to pick their brains in about an hour or two."

Lincoln chuckled sarcastically. "Sit tight, huh." He chuckled again. "Easy for you to say, Matisse. You're not the one they're trying to pin this on."

I started to say, *N-word, please! They questioned my ass on several occasions, and let's not forget how they ransacked the hell out of my place. Quietly, I'm still not over that one. And if those crooked-ass cops think for one minute that I'm going to let that incident fall by the wayside, they have another thing coming. Oh, yeah, when this is all said and done, I'm going to sue the shit out of the two detectives individually, the entire APD and the city of Atlanta*, but I bit my tongue. He didn't need to know all of that, but I sure wanted to let him know he wasn't the only brother they were messing with. Shiiiit!

27

CLARITY!
LEGAL DREAM TEAM

AFTER Miles and Shelby dropped me off at my house, I went inside for a moment and reflected. All the drama had a brother's stomach growling. I needed to get a bite to eat. While I grubbed on a stack of French toast, which, by the way, was dripping with much butter and syrup, I was a bit taken aback by the ride home from Sullivan's funeral. I couldn't quite put my finger on it, but something wasn't right. It was just weird. I mean, of the three of us, I was the one who knew her the best and yet it seemed like Miles and Shelby took her death kind of hard.

After finishing my breakfast, I sat there not quite knowing how to proceed. Yeah, the plan was to pay my two police friends a visit, but the longer I sat and continued to think about the case and my role in it, the more I thought about how foolish Lincoln and I were being. We were way out of our league. I immediately reached for the phone. Lincoln answered on the first ring.

"What'd you find out?" Lincoln said, as though he was in a contest to see how fast he could get the words out.

"I haven't found out anything, but I've been thinking."

"I'm assuming that's good news. After all, I'm not paying you to sit around and not think."

"This isn't going to work, Lincoln."

"What's not going to work?" he said, cutting me off before I could continue.

"Me representing you in the courtroom."

"Oh, for crying out loud, Matisse, haven't we already gone through this? You're my man, baby! Look, we've been together for a while now. Am I right?"

"Yeah," I said reluctantly.

"In all of those years, you've never let me down, Matisse. I value you. Hell, I need you…and now more than ever."

"I realize that, Lincoln, but hear me out."

"Hear you out? Matisse, I don't have time to hear you out. While I'm hearing you out, the actual cat who killed Sullivan is out there breathing the air he's not worthy of." Lincoln's voice rose. "Hear you out? This a *bitch*! Come on, baby."

"Well, you're going to have to hear me out this time!" I yelled.

Lincoln sighed, "Okay, come with it. Give me your best shot."

"I'm your agent, man. And you're right, I'm good at it. But I negotiate contracts, Lincoln. I'm not a trial lawyer. Hell, I don't even know where to begin with this shit!"

"Oh, that's a crock!"

"No it's not, Lincoln. Think about it. We're in a good situation here."

"Good situation? They're trying to lock me up, Matisse! We're talking murder, dammit!" Lincoln screamed at the top of his lungs.

"Lincoln, calm down."

"Calm down? What kind of shit is that? Calm down!"

"Can I finish?" I didn't hear a response from Lincoln. "Thank you," I said with an obvious attitude. "Now, our good situation is the fact that you're loaded. You have all the money in the world."

"And? That doesn't mean dick! I'm still a black man in America, Matisse."

Ignoring his last comment, I continued. "Here's what needs to be done. Let's go out and get a team of highly experienced professionals, spearheaded by me. Let's get the best trial lawyer in the nation. Let's also get a police expert or someone who knows how to come up with key evidence that would be beneficial to our cause. And, let's not forget, I'll be right there the entire time. You see where I'm going with this, Lincoln?" I could feel the wheels spinning in his head. He was thinking about it.

"You'll be there the entire time?"

"I'll be a part of the legal team. I mean, think about it, Lincoln. If we're going to do this, and like you said, your life's on the line, we may as well do it right. I think we're better off getting someone who really knows his or her way around the courtroom and a case like this. And I think we're definitely better off with me riding shotgun on this one. Let's not forget that once upon a time a guy by the name of Lincoln Dix earned a dual J.D./M.B.A. You have legal skills, too. Or did you forget?"

"All right, it's starting to make sense. But promise me that you'll truly ride shotgun the entire time. By the way, unlike you, Matisse, I never passed the bar. Those are just degrees. I'm a hockey player!"

"I hear you. It's a done deal then. Remember, Lincoln, you line my pockets well. I can't have you in prison, either. The way I see it, we have about two more big-time contracts to ink before your playing days are over."

"So, who do you have in mind?"

"Right now, I'm not sure. Whoever we get, though, will be top-notch. You have my word on that."

"Yeah, I hear you. Your word and my money."

"Unfortunately, that's how this one's gonna have to play out. We also have to remember how that O.J. case went. I think the public felt ripped off on the outcome. I know I didn't feel particularly good about it. And here comes another case where a high profile athlete, who happens to be black, is being accused of murder. See what I'm saying? It's tricky and we need to get the absolute best."

"Well, do your thing, man," Lincoln responded.

I hung up the phone wondering how I pulled that off in just a matter of minutes. In addition to feeling a huge sense of relief, I was extremely confident in my decision to employ a team of highly skilled legal professionals. And though Lincoln would never completely admit it, I knew deep down inside that he also knew this was the best way for us to proceed.

28

ENTER ANDY WEINBERG

I slept like a baby that night. It was beyond a doubt the best night's sleep I'd had since Sullivan's death. As a result of our coming to the conclusion to go in a different direction regarding Lincoln's case, I canceled the meeting I had scheduled with my two police friends. I figured now that we were going to assemble this team, whoever we chose as the lead trial lawyer would, in all likelihood, have certain people to serve that purpose. So, I waited.

Feeling like a huge weight had just been lifted off my shoulders, I hurried to my office.

Gail must have read my mind because a large cup of coffee and a box of Krispy Kreme donuts were sitting atop my desk when I got there.

"Damn, you're good," I said, talking into the speakerphone as I settled into the chair behind my desk.

"Just don't forget it when it comes time for a raise," she responded from her desk just outside of my office. "On a serious note, how you doing, Matisse?"

"Much better, Gail. Much better."

"Good. Do you need anything?"

"As a matter of fact, I do," I said before biting into a donut. "Can you come into my office when you get a chance?"

"I'm on my way."

Gail, not bothering to knock, entered my office holding a pen and pad. As always, her work attire was impeccable. She was one of those women who looked sexy in a business suit.

"Why don't you turn around and go grab your cup of coffee?"

Gail looked at me like she was on *Candid Camera*. I could tell she didn't know what was going on. She said hesitantly, "Okay," and returned seconds later holding her cup of coffee.

"Have a seat," I said, polishing off my third donut. I don't care what anyone else says, Krispy Kreme donuts and a hot cup of coffee are the best way to start a day off. Gail gingerly settled into one of the two seats that faced my desk. She set her cup of coffee on a coaster on my desk before reaching for her pen and pad. "For now, why don't you relax on the pen and pad and help me enjoy these donuts?"

"Uh, okay." Gail placed her pen and pad in her lap, and slowly reached for her cup of coffee. "What's going on, Matisse?"

"I'll tell you after you do work on a couple of these donuts."

"Hey, enough said," Gail replied, reaching for one. "Thank you."

"Have we gotten any other calls from Jerrell?"

"Not a one," Gail responded, applying a napkin to her mouth.

"Well, that's a good sign. Let's face it, he and the Knicks are a great fit."

"It certainly seems that way."

"Well, here it is, Gail. I'm sure you already know this, seeing as how it's been all over the news, but it appears our boy, Lincoln, has gotten himself into a quite a pickle."

"Yeah, it's all over the Internet. I've been reading about it and watching all of those annoying news reports. It's not looking too good for him right now, is it?"

"Not at all. I've spoken to him a few times on the matter, and call me crazy, but I believe in his innocence. You?"

"All I know is what I've read and seen on television, Matisse. Knowing Lincoln, and yeah, he's a cocky bastard, but I just don't see it."

"Neither do I."

"He's our biggest client," Gail noted in between bites.

"That he is, and with that said, here's what were going to do. We're going to assemble the best legal team money can buy—and when I say we, I mean you and I. Lincoln, understandably, is freaked out to the point that he actually wanted me to represent him solely."

Gail laughed, "No. Really?"

"Yeah. Funny, huh?" I replied, shifting in my chair. "You know what's even funnier is the fact that my fool-ass almost did. In fact, I originally agreed to it. For some reason, though, last night I came to my senses."

"Thank God for that." Gail laughed some more. "You're a great agent, Matisse. I know you have your law degree, but negotiating contracts and trying a case in court are two different beasts. Can you walk on air, too?"

"Very funny."

"In any event, I'm just glad you came to your senses," Gail said, still cackling. "What do you need me to do?"

"I need you to compile a list of the top trial lawyers in the country, keeping in mind Lincoln's celebrity. In other words, I want someone who's been to the dance before with high profile types."

"Too bad Johnny's not around anymore, rest his soul."

"Yeah, it is too bad. He may have been our first call. That brother did a lot for a lot people through the legal system."

Gail shook her head and said, "You're right about that, Matisse. But O.J. was guilty as hell!"

"It sure seems that way now, huh?"

"Puh, it seemed that way then, too. In any event, I'll get on that right away, Matisse."

"Yeah, that's the other thing I was going to tell you. We need to move on all of this quickly."

Gail stood and threw her used napkin into the empty box of donuts before removing the box from my desk. "Do you want any more coffee, Matisse?"

"Naw, I'm good, thanks."

She grabbed my empty cup along with hers and made her way out of my office. As soon as the door closed, I reached for the remote and turned on the television. While I watched the many reports, ranging from ESPN to CNN to all of the local stations, the one thing that stood out the most, which was comforting, was the fact that Lincoln hadn't yet been charged. This was something that I think both he and I failed to remember. Having never gone through anything like it, Lincoln was scared to death and automatically thought the worst. However, with him being the lead suspect, we had to treat it as the highest priority. Hell, technically I was still a suspect, according to those two rent-a-cop detectives. In any event, by us putting this top-notch legal team together, we were definitely ahead of the game at this juncture.

I knew Gail would have that list for me in a matter of hours, which enabled me to focus my immediate attention on Lincoln. All of my clients were programmed in the speed dial component on my phone. I pressed the number one and moments later found Lincoln's voice on the other end. I had one major request for him.

"What's up," Lincoln said, void of emotion and any type of inflection.

"Good, you're still there."

"Where am I gonna go? Have you been watching the news? I'm all over the damn place," Lincoln replied angrily.

"That's the reason why I'm calling. Do me a favor. Don't go anywhere. Stay in. I know it sucks, but I wouldn't be surprised if television crews and whatnot were staked out in front of your place."

"You think?" Lincoln responded sarcastically. "Hey, you and I both know I'm the shit, but this is foul in a big way. Hell, these fools are even starting to take shots at me on Twitter! Not cool. What the hell is going on? I thought I was everyone's favorite."

"Perceptions change quickly in this simple-minded society in which we live. If it's in print, people automatically tend to believe it's true and valid."

"True. That's some bullshit!"

"Bullshit is right. I didn't make the rules. Look, just stay in and stay off Twitter too. I'll get someone over there to run errands for you. Cool?"

"Cool? Did you just say cool? Man, none of this is cool, Matisse. It's like I'm under house arrest for some shit I didn't do. From now on I'm going to think twice before I wax some ass."

"There isn't a humble bone in your body, huh?"

"Humble? There's no time for that, Mat. You're the shit or you aren't. I'm the shit! Larger than large! Is the legal team in place yet?"

Ignoring his dumbass, egotistical-yet-truthful comment, I responded, "Not yet, but we're working on it as we speak. We should be set by the end of the day. Hang in there, man. Remember, we, as Americans, have short attention spans. This should all blow over in a couple of days, so the house arrest thing should be short-lived."

"Any word on whether or not they're going to officially charge me?"

"Not yet, but expect it within the next few days."

"All right. Later." Lincoln hung up the phone without allowing me an opportunity to say goodbye.

As soon as I hung up, the phone buzzed, which was accompanied by the flashing of a red light. It was Gail. Seeing as how I knew exactly who it was before even answering it, I decided to take a page out of Lincoln's book.

"What's up?" I said, smirking.

"Miles is here to see you, Matisse."

"Miles?" I looked down at my watch to see what time it was. Technically, it was still in the a.m. *This is kind of early for Miles*, I thought. "Okay, send him in please, Gail."

"Will do."

Miles entered the room wearing a sweat-suit, baseball hat and sneakers. All Nike, of course. He plopped down on the couch without saying anything.

"What are you doing here, man?" I asked.

Miles rose from the couch and sat in the very seat Gail had sat in moments before.

"Shelby and I wanted to know if you wanted to go out to dinner with us tonight. What do you say?"

"Oh, I don't know, man," I responded. I folded my hands behind my head and leaned back in my chair. "I still want to know what you're doing here so early. You mean to tell me you couldn't have called to ask me that?"

"I suppose I could have. Is there some new law that I don't know about, saying a brother can't get out for a little fresh air in the morning? Why are you tripping? It's not even that early."

"Miles, how many times have you been to my office at this hour?" Before he could answer, I said, "Uh, none!"

"Damn, Matisse, it's a simple question. Yes or no? Why you busting my balls?"

"I'm just wondering what's going on, bruh. This isn't like you," I said as I watched Miles roll his eyes. "I'd like to, but I don't know if I'll have a chance tonight. I'm up to my ears with Lincoln."

"How's that coming?"

"If they charge him, I think we'll be ready."

"Who's *we*? The last time I talked to you it was you and only you."

"Yeah, well, I woke up."

"Meaning?" Miles pried.

"Meaning I was crazy to think I could pull off something like that alone. We're calling in the troops as we speak." I came from behind my desk and started throwing darts at the board that hung to the left of my chair. I often did that when I had company in the office. "Why don't I give you a call sometime this afternoon? I should have a better gauge on the situation by then."

"Cool," Miles said. He paused for a moment. "That was a sad funeral, wasn't it?"

"Yeah. I think most funerals are pretty sad." There was an uncomfortable silence. "You and Shelby seemed to take it kind of hard. At least much harder than I anticipated."

"It was sad, Matisse; plus we both liked her."

"Yeah," I responded, opting to take the high road. I wasn't going to bash her for being a ho. "You guys still going to push the wedding back a week or so?"

"It's a done deal."

"Well, that's good, I guess. Like I said, don't do it on my behalf. That reminds me, I need to get going on your bachelor party," I noted, sitting back down in my seat.

"Don't even worry about it, Matisse."

"What? Please! Everyone thinks I'm all broken up over Sullivan. I'm over it. Yeah, I was acting like a little lovesick sissy for a while, but that was before I learned a few pertinent facts about her." Miles didn't respond.

"Well, hey, let me get out of your hair, man. If you can make it, that would be cool." Miles stood and held out his fist for a pound. I arose from my seat and dapped him before he turned and headed for the door.

I worked for a couple more hours before heading for lunch at The Tavern in Phipps Plaza. When I returned to the office, Gail was waiting at her desk, wearing a huge smile.

"What?" I asked on the way to my office.

"Two words," Gail said, holding up two fingers.

"Okay, bring it!" I replied as I stood over her in front of her desk.

"Andy Weinberg."

"Ooooh! That's a good one." I thought about it for a moment longer. "Yeah, Gail, that could work. He has a great track record representing celebrities, and his reputation speaks for itself. Isn't he based out of Boston?"

"Yep. I wanted to run it by you first before I tried contacting him. Well, what do you think?"

A smile appeared across my face. "I think we should go for it."

"Great! I'll see what his availability is."

"Cool," I said, then made my way into my office, shutting the door behind me.

Gail did good work with that one. Andy Weinberg was a legal giant. In addition to successfully trying high-profile cases, he also taught law at his *alma mater*, Harvard University. One of the required textbooks in most law schools is one that was written by him. I, in fact, had to read it when I was in law school.

Out of excitement, I immediately called Lincoln.

"How does Andy Weinberg sound?" I yelled through the speakerphone.

"Who's that?" Lincoln responded, still void of emotion.

"Who's that? What? Let's just say he's probably one of, if not *the*, best trial lawyer in America."

"Yeah?"

"Yeah," I replied. "What in the hell were you doing in school?"

"Huh? What do you mean?"

"Lincoln, you should know full-well who Andy Weinberg is. He's one of your fellow Harvard alums and you had to have read his book when you were there. It was mandatory reading for any graduate student trying to obtain a J.D."

Lincoln ignored me. "Have we locked him down?"

"We're working on it. Gail's checking his availability right now."

"Now, that's what I'm talking about, baby!" Lincoln's excitement was obvious. "Let's lock him down."

"Hopefully, he'll be free." I paused. "And, hopefully, he'll agree to represent you."

Lincoln giggled. "I'm the best hockey player in the world, Matisse. How could he possibly say no? Plus, as you duly noted, we're both Harvard alums."

"Let's not get the big head yet. I know with you it's hard because it's a twenty-four/seven thing. On that note, I'm going to get off this phone and try to get this guy on our team. Peace!" I hung up the phone and walked over to Gail's desk.

"Well?" I said. She was still on the phone. Gail looked up and hushed me with her index finger. I continued to stand in front of her desk.

Moments later, she hung up the phone. "He'll be on the first flight down here tomorrow morning."

"All right!" I yelled, sticking my hand in the air for a high-five. "Good work, Gail. Good work!"

Gail reciprocated with a high-five. I pulled a hundred-dollar bill out of my wallet. "Here, go have a nice dinner on me tonight."

"Thank you, Matisse," Gail said, grabbing it with the quickness.

After I broke the good news to Lincoln, I called Miles and told him I was on board for dinner.

29

TWIST

I arrived at Twist, a trendy restaurant in Buckhead known primarily for its sushi, about thirty minutes early. I waited at the bar for Miles and Shelby. I decided to take a departure from my signature Stoli on the rocks due to the celebratory mood I was experiencing, and instead ordered a glass of champagne. I kept it simple and went with the relatively inexpensive Korbel. I've always been one of those guys who couldn't tell the difference between a five-dollar bottle of champagne and hundred-dollar bottle. It all pretty much tasted the same to me.

While I sat at the bar, I did what I do best: people-watch. It was crowded, and the beautiful people were out. I couldn't help but think about Lincoln. He and Twist were synonymous. Lincoln loved sushi and he loved dining there. He was also in my thoughts because of the major coups we scored earlier by acquiring the services of Andy Weinberg. I was giddy, but a lot of that, and I'm not embarrassed to admit it, had to do with the fact that all of the pressure was now off of me. If this thing went where we all felt it was inevitably going, it was up to Andy and his team of legal eagles to save the day. This was the one time I actually jumped at the possibility of playing second fiddle.

Miles and Shelby arrived just as my second glass of champagne was placed in front of me.

"It's packed up in here, huh," Miles noted, resting his hand on the back of my stool.

"Yep," I agreed. "What's up?"

"Hey, Matisse," Shelby said, holding her arms apart. I stood and gave her a hug.

"Hey, girl," I said into her ear. I applied a friendly peck onto her forehead before reaching for my glass of champagne. "Is our table ready?"

"Yeah," responded Miles. "Let's go."

We were seated at a table I thought was desirable because, though it was kind of in the back of the restaurant, all three of us were still able to do plenty of people-watching. With every passing minute, I was feeling more and more like my old self. However, I'm not so sure that was a good thing. I found myself doing a lot of skirt-watching, believe it or not, in the middle of December.

"Things turn out the way you wanted today, Matisse?" Miles inquired.

"Better! Andy Weinberg is going to represent Lincoln!"

"*The* Andy Weinberg?" Miles asked.

"Yep, that Andy Weinberg," I responded.

"Yeah? Wow!" Shelby added. "You must be stoked. How's Lincoln holding up?"

"He's doing all right. He was a little bitter because he swears up and down that he's not the one who committed the crime, and yet he's the lead suspect. And to add injury to insult, I told him to not go anywhere until this whole thing blows over. So he's locked up at his place, probably bored out of his mind."

"I feel so bad for him," Shelby said. "That's scary. So, do you really think this is going to just blow over, Matisse?"

"Blow over? No. But we have to keep in mind that they haven't even officially charged him yet. So, until that happens, and remember, it may not happen, we have to play it safe."

"Do you think he did it, Matisse?" Shelby asked.

"No, I don't. Lincoln's cocky and he's the biggest jerk sometimes, but he's no killer."

"Yeah, I can't see him doing it, either," Miles added. "Now,

Hunter, she's a different story. Did you ever look into what I told you
I overheard?"

"What'd you overhear, Miles?" Shelby asked at the speed of
light. Her look was unsettled.

"I'll tell you later, babe," Miles said, and turned his attention
towards me.

"I don't think so, Miles. You'll tell me now."

"No, I haven't looked into it yet," I said, interrupting a fight
in progress. Miles and Shelby's bickering immediately ceased. I
had the floor. "It's something that I definitely plan on looking into.
I just haven't had the time. But now that Andy Weinberg has signed
on, I'm quite sure he'll have a top-notch legal team I can pass this
information along to."

I looked at Shelby and could tell by the way she was sitting,
coupled with the frown on her face, that she wasn't about to let this
die, let alone wait until they got home. Just as she began to open her
mouth, our server showed up to take our orders.

"Good evening," he said as he placed menus in front of
each of us. His nametag read "Reggie." He was tall and slender. His
hair was shaved close to his head, and his skin was milk-chocolate
brown. Reggie's voice was mousy. "I see you're working on that
glass of champagne. Can I get anyone else a drink?"

"I'll take a dry martini with three olives," Shelby said, still
not looking too happy.

"Do you have Anchor Steam on tap?" Miles inquired.

"We sure do," Reggie replied.

"I'll go with that, then."

"Great, my name's Reggie and I'll be your server tonight. I'll
be back shortly with your drinks, and take your order."

"Spill it, Miles," Shelby said as soon as Reggie left the table.
"What did you overhear Hunter say?"

"Shelby, why are you making such a big deal out of this? It
doesn't concern you. But if you must know, and I can tell you must,
here it goes," Miles said, looking at me as his eyes rolled. "I went
out to my car for a moment during the brunch Matisse had at his
place. While I was milling around in the car, Hunter was in the next

car over talking on her cell phone. Well, her windows were down, as were mine, and I overheard her talking about how she didn't like Sullivan, but always kept her friends close and enemies even closer. I know, it's such a cliché, but that's what she said."

"And from that little piece of information, you think she's the one who did Sullivan in?" Shelby said, like, *Get real!*

"Hey, you never know. There's some crazy people out there."

"This is true, Shel," I added.

"Anything's possible, I guess. Since when did you two become detectives?" Shelby replied, jokingly.

I didn't respond, but wanted to change the conversation. I was up to my eyeballs with Sullivan's death. I was ready to have a nice dinner and talk about normal, everyday stuff.

"So, you excited about the big day, Shel?" I asked.

"Don't ask me why, Matisse," Shelby replied, smirking and looking in Miles's direction, "but yes, I'm very excited. I can't wait."

"You better say that," Miles chimed in before leaning over and giving her a kiss.

Reggie returned with our drinks seconds later. "Here you go," he said, placing a martini in front of Shelby and an Anchor Steam in front of Miles. "Have you had a chance to look over the menu?"

All three of us replied, "No" at the same time.

"Okay, I'll come back a little later. Would you like another glass of champagne?" Reggie asked, looking at me.

"I'm okay right now. Actually, I wouldn't mind another glass of water."

"Coming right up." Reggie turned and walked away. His walk was a little light in the pants, if you asked me. If I had to guess, I'd say he had a little sugar in his tank.

"Well, Shelby, I've had plenty of talks with Miles about your upcoming nuptials, and for the record, he can't wait, either."

"Yeah, ball and chain time," Miles said, laughing.

"Quit it," Shelby responded, elbow-nudging Miles in his side.

"Aw, baby, I'm just joking."

"Yeah, you better be. And you, Matisse, you better not have a bunch of nekkid hoes running around Miles's bachelor party. If I hear of any wrongdoing, I'm personally holding you responsible. So, spill it. What do you have planned for my husband-to-be?"

I applied a couple of soft pats to the top of Shelby's hand where it rested on the table. "A gentleman never tells, Shel. This is man stuff. But I will say this: you have absolutely no need to worry."

Yeah, I lied out of my ass because, rest assured, there was going to be gang of naked big-tittied hoes running around at my boy's bachelor party. It was my duty. But she didn't need to know that. Like I said, this was man stuff. However, I was being honest when I said she didn't have a thing to worry about. It was all in good fun. I was going to make sure Miles only looked and didn't touch.

"Yeah, right! Whatever, Matisse."

"No, I'm serious, Shel."

"You better not be serious, Matisse," Miles said, laughing loudly. "There better be a boatload of butt-ass naked freaks running around the place that night. The lap-dances better be in abundance. I plan on smacking a lot of asses."

Shelby gave Miles a scathing stare. "Keep bumping your gums, Miles, and I guarantee you'll be going home alone tonight."

Miles's incessant laughing came to an abrupt halt, which was followed by him sitting up straight in his chair. Silence filled the air for a few moments while we perused the menu. When Reggie came back a couple minutes later, we ordered. All three of us went with different types of rolls. Mine had a combination of shrimp tempura, salmon, cream cheese, crabmeat and cucumbers. I'd had it many times before, and knew from experience that it was good as hell.

"So, you gonna be able to move on, Matisse?" Shelby wondered aloud. At first, I didn't know what she was talking about, but then it hit me.

"Oh, you're talking about Sullivan?"

"Yeah. I know you guys had kind of started seeing one another again. So, it has to be hard on you."

"You know, Shel, at first it was. But, I'm finding out now that she wasn't the person I thought she was. It's sad she lost her life, but I'm fine. I'm over it. I know it sounds mean, and I know I shouldn't bash a person after they're gone, but she was into some bad stuff. And that's all I'll say. Honestly, I'm ready to find love. I want to be right where you and Miles are. And soon."

Miles and Shelby looked at each other at the same time, then looked at me and said, "Yeah, right!"

For the rest of the night we laughed, talked, and ate great sushi. Though we enjoyed ourselves immensely, from the moment I talked about my desire to find a mate for life, I couldn't get Erica out of my mind. For some reason I had a history of going to the barrel a couple of times. And it always seemed like two times too many.

30

WEINBERG
IN THE FLESH

THE next morning I drove to work bright and early, just as I had the day before. Only this time I picked Lincoln up at his house on my way in. It was important for all of us to be there when Andy arrived.

When we got to the office, Gail was in the conference room putting the final touches on what appeared to be a wonderful power breakfast. That conference room, I had a strong hunch, would later become our war room. I didn't use the room too often because most of my business was done in my office or at incognito locations. Most of the GMs I dealt with rarely liked to meet in their offices. I normally spent most of the time negotiating with them over the phone, and once a deal was close to coming to fruition, we'd come up with a meeting place. So, I was stoked to finally put this state-of-the-art conference room to good use. I'll be honest, I kind of went overboard with the room. Three of the four walls boasted 70-inch flat screen televisions. Even though it was just one big room, it had a full service kitchen, complete with stainless steel Viking appliances and a circular bar that separated that area from the rest of the room. The floors were hardwood. The oversized conference table, which was long and rounded at the ends, was made from the same cherrywood that topped the bar.

"Damn, this is tight, Matisse," Lincoln said as he looked around the conference room. "How come you and I never do business in here?"

"Opportunity hasn't presented itself, Lincoln."

"Aw, that's some old bullshit, baby. Anyway, Matisse, you come in this early all of the time?" Lincoln took a bottle of water out of an exposed ice bin, quickly broke the seal and took a big swig.

"Not always. I try to, but fall short a lot of the time. It all depends on what's going on"

"What time is Old Boy coming?"

"He should be here pretty soon," I responded.

"Man, I'm exhausted. I haven't been sleeping too well lately, as you can imagine."

"I can imagine."

"You mind if I go lay down on the couch in your office?"

"No, knock yourself out," I said, grabbing a piece of bacon out of the warmer. "I'll come grab you when he gets here."

"Cool."

I walked over to Gail to see if there was anything I could do. She seemed to have everything under control, but I didn't want her to think she was in this alone. I occasionally had a tendency to big-time people, and wanted to make sure this wasn't one of those times.

"We good?" I said, pouring a cup of coffee and handing it to her.

"Yeah, I think so," Gail replied, taking the filled cup out of my hand. "Thanks."

"Is there anything I can do? It looks great. The food looks awesome, too. If he doesn't get here soon, I might have to say, 'Forget it,' and throw down. I'm hungry!"

"You're the boss," Gail said as she hurried out of the room. I followed her to her workspace.

"What's that supposed to mean?"

"It means, you're the boss, Matisse. You can do anything you want. If you're hungry and you want to eat, then knock yourself out."

"You all right, Gail? You seem to be a little short, like you're on edge or something."

"Yeah, I'm fine. I've been working like a dog behind this the past couple of days. I'm just a little tired, that's all."

"Well, you're doing a great job and I appreciate it very much. Here," I said, handing her another hundred-dollar bill.

"I wasn't complaining, Matisse, and I certainly wasn't trying to get another hundred dollars out of you. I was just letting you know that I'm a little rundown. That's all."

"I know. Use it to get a massage or something tonight after work. Hell, do whatever you want with it."

"Thanks, Matisse."

"I'm going to be in my office for a bit. Call me when he gets here."

"Will do."

It had been only a few minutes since Lincoln first sprawled out on my couch. However, it didn't take him long at all to get acquainted with it. From the way he was snoring, my couch was obviously comfortable. I took a seat behind my desk and jotted down some notes. Though Lincoln's snoring was obnoxious, I figured just this one time I'd overlook it, considering all he'd gone through to that point. Believe me, I was being really nice. I didn't even turn on the television in an attempt to keep it quiet. That act alone was so not me. Ordinarily, I didn't care who was in my office. Nothing, and I mean nothing, would have stopped me from going through my normal routine, especially in my own office. But I cut him some slack.

As I continued to jot down various notes and thoughts, it dawned on me that I didn't really know what to expect going forward.

"Matisse." Gail lightly tapped on my door before slowly entering. Immediately spotting Lincoln on the couch, she whispered, "They're here."

"They are?"

"Yeah, they're waiting for you all in the conference room."

I could feel my heart racing and the butterflies swarming. Why I was nervous I didn't know. After all, being in pressure situations was my thing. I had ice in my veins, and anyone who ever did business with me knew that. But it was different this time because of the unknown. The world I was about to enter, I could honestly say, I knew very little about.

I rose from behind my desk and made a beeline for the bathroom, which was located inside my office. Momentarily, I thought about taking a quick shower, but knew the time wasn't there. I quickly brushed my teeth and gargled with mouthwash before waking Lincoln up.

"Hey," I said, shaking Lincoln a couple of times. "It's showtime."

"Huh?" Lincoln said slowly with only one eye open. He quickly came to and abruptly sat up. "He's here?"

"Yeah," I replied. "You ready to do this?"

Lincoln stood. "Let's do the damn thing."

I walked out of my office and Lincoln followed. We were in the conference room in a matter of seconds.

Just as I expected, Andy arrived with a team of people. I presumed each had a specific specialty. Well, I hoped, anyway. Andy stood as we entered the room. He was shorter than I expected. I guess television not only adds pounds, but inches as well. Yeah, he was a little guy. He seemed cooler than I had originally thought. I mean, don't get me wrong, he still had nerd qualities, but for some reason it didn't seem as bad as I'd anticipated. I think the fact that he was an above-average dresser had a something to do with me giving him some cool points. His long, thick, curly hair overshadowed his fashionable prescription glasses. He was one of those Jewish cats with an afro. I've always said black folks and Jewish folks have more in common than what most people want to let on, especially the two groups.

"Andy," I said, extending my hand for the standard shake. "Matisse Spencer, and this is Lincoln Dix. I take it you've already met my assistant, Gail."

"I have. Gail's made us feel comfortable. It's nice to meet you guys. I'm familiar with your work as a sports agent, Matisse. And I'm a big fan of yours, Lincoln. We have to get you back out on the ice."

"Here here to that," Lincoln agreed, just as he and Andy finished shaking hands.

"Glad to have you aboard," I said.

"We're glad to be here," Andy responded. "We definitely have our work cut out for us. Let me introduce you to my team, as we'll all be working together. I don't take on any cases without these guys."

"Okay, great!" I said.

His team of four stood. "Stuart Collins is a partner in the firm, and my lead council. Angela Jackson is on her way to making partner, but for now she's a senior associate and the best damn researcher out there. Tom DeMarco and Jason Biggs, better known as Big Jay, are detectives in our firm."

After all of the pleasantries were exchanged, I wasted no time in inquiring about the detectives in Andy's firm.

"So, do most law firms employ in-house detectives?"

"No, not normally," Andy explained. "It's something I started doing a long time ago. They're an invaluable resource for us, and I think it's a better gig for them because the money's a lot better. I snagged Tom and Big Jay from the New York PD."

"Interesting," I said. "Well, Gail has gone above and beyond the call of duty by arranging this beautiful breakfast. So, why don't we start off by grabbing a bite to eat, and we'll go from there. Sound okay?"

"Great," Andy replied. He turned to Gail. "Matisse is right, Gail. It looks outstanding. Even though the flight was only a couple hours, I think we're all pretty hungry. The airlines these days are nickel-and-diming the shit out of the consumer, serving us trail mix and peanuts. And we were sitting in first class. I hear it's gotten so bad in coach that they've actually started charging for food."

"Yeah, I've heard that, too," I responded. "It's a damn shame."

After each of us piled a heap of food onto our plates, the eight of us took seats around the conference table. Andy was the last to sit. I watched as he settled into one of the oversized black leather office chairs that surrounded the table. He seemed less interested in his food and more interested in his surroundings.

"This is a very nice conference room, Matisse," Andy noted, looking around. "Did you design it?"

"Yeah, I did. I'll be honest, it's one of my babies."

"You did a hell of a job. When we put all of this to rest, I'll probably be calling you. It's time for our conference room to get a facelift. And believe me," Andy said, turning to look at Lincoln, who was sitting next to him, "this will all be behind us in no time. Rest assured. I don't lose."

Lincoln cracked a smile. "I'm liking you more with every passing second. I'll tell you what, though, in all honesty, I didn't do it."

"And that's exactly what we'll prove if you're charged, which, by the way, is a decision that should come any day now." While breaking a biscuit in half, Andy focused his attention on me. I was sitting directly across from him. "I hear you may also need my services, Matisse."

"Yeah, it's possible. Two flunky APD detectives have been seriously harassing me. They don't have a damn thing on me. Hell, the timeline doesn't even match. That's why I just view the whole thing as harassment."

"It certainly sounds like it," Andy agreed. "I don't want to get into too much right now. Let's enjoy this breakfast, but afterwards we're really going to have to delve right into it. Just so you know, we'll need to know everything. And I do mean everything. Deal?"

"Of course," I replied.

"Bet," Lincoln responded.

Not much was said for the remainder of breakfast. While I marveled at just how nice my conference room was, giving myself invisible pats on the back, I caught Lincoln constantly eyeing Angela. I just shook my head. That guy is like a puzzle sometimes. He just got done telling me how he was having trouble sleeping at night behind all this madness, yet here he is peeping Angela out. I don't know. I'm probably being too hard on him. After all, they didn't cut his balls off. I mean, he is a man. And that's what we do.

We see a good-looking woman and we look. And we look, and we look some more.

The more I thought about it, the more I started checking her out. I soon felt Lincoln. What could I say? She had it going on, hands down. There was nothing suspect about her. She was straight, at least physically. Her petite body came with the womanly curves most men desire. She wore her hair in cornrows. Her skin color was auburn. But the one thing that stood out most about her was the fact that she always seemed to be smiling. And believe me, her teeth were very white and very straight. Okay, I'll go ahead and say it. They were perfect. A woman who seems to be happy by nature is always a plus in my book. To further illustrate how curvaceous her body was, she wore a business pantsuit. Those joints usually aren't that revealing. Granted, it was tight fitting, but I have to believe the lack of extra room was a direct result of all of that body.

31

GAME ON!

As soon we finished breakfast, we rolled up our sleeves, put our game faces on and got to work. It was good for me because this was Andy's show, and I was content to let him run it however he saw fit.

"Let's take it from the top, Lincoln," Andy began. Lincoln was now sitting across from Andy along with me. Angela and Stuart book-ended Andy. "What was your relationship with Sullivan?"

Lincoln shifted in his chair for a couple of seconds before speaking. "I met Sullivan a few years back. At the time, she was a sportscaster. We were playing on the road somewhere, the city escapes me at the moment. I normally don't talk to the media on game days, but for some reason I granted her an interview after our morning skate. I didn't think much of her at the time, outside of the fact that she was about as fine as they come, and the fine ones came at me pretty often. But, other than that, I just figured she was the usual jock-sniffing woman sportscaster. And,"—Lincoln paused, turned and looked at me—"sorry, Matisse, she proved me right. She was a jock-sniffing freak. So, I put her on my roster."

Andy interrupted. "Roster?"

"Yeah. At the time, I had about an eight-woman roster of freaks I rotated in as many different cities. Being a professional athlete, it's hard maintaining a monogamous relationship with our demanding traveling schedule. And, I'm not going to lie, it's also hard when you have an abundance of beautiful women throwing themselves at you everywhere you go. I figure now is not the time to be a one-woman man. When my playing days are over, I'll start moving in that direction. But as long as I can put the puck in the net, hockey is the most important thing in my life.

"Anyway, Sullivan became a part of my stable of freaks. Whenever we were in the same city, we usually did the damn thing."

"Did the damn thing?" Andy interrupted again, clearly puzzled.

"Yeah, you know, the relationship was purely sexual. Whenever we saw each other, I'd tap it. Man, I used to knock the bottom out."

Is this guy an idiot or what? I thought. *Talk about no tact.* It was embarrassing, and I felt really embarrassed for Angela, who was the only woman in the room. Gail had gone back to her desk.

To Angela's credit, she didn't seem to be too fazed by Lincoln's comments. However, I did catch her rolling her eyes a time or two while he reminisced about his Mandingo/Superfly days with Sullivan. I guess the business Angela was in required a thick skin.

"So, you didn't have any emotional ties with Sullivan?" Andy said as he took notes on a small pad of personalized paper.

"No, not at all," Lincoln replied.

"Your relationship with her was about sex only?"

"Absolutely!"

Though everything said was being recorded on the small yet seemingly advanced and expensive tape recorder in the middle of the table, Stuart and Angela joined Andy in the note-taking process. The two detectives, Tom and Big Jay, just sat there and listened, as did I.

"Okay. Well, that's good to know," said Andy.

"Why is that?" Lincoln asked, looking perplexed.

Andy removed his glasses and took a deep breath. "Well, Lincoln, in a case like this, at this point we don't know what or who caused Sullivan to fall to her death. But, when the authorities try to pin it on a former lover, the emotional state of the relationship is seriously questioned. And, you're saying that your relationship with Sullivan was based solely on sex. For our purposes, that's a good thing.

"Okay, let's fast forward to the early hours of December 15th, the morning of her death." Andy paused, directing his attention to me. "In looking over the police report, Matisse, I know you were at Sullivan's that night as well. So, just sit tight. What I want to do right now is get Lincoln's take on that night/morning and then I'd like to hear your perspective. All right?"

"Yeah, of course," I responded.

Andy continued. "What we're attempting to do here is establish a timeline. So, what exactly happened, Lincoln? And try to remember times, if you can."

"To be honest, Andy, it's really simple," Lincoln explained. "The Rangers were in town that night playing the Thrashers. I had taken a couple of buddies who play for the Rangers out after the game for some drinks. As usual, we ended up at a strip bar. After I dropped those guys off at their hotel, which was roughly around 2 or 2:30 a.m., my phone started blowing up. After the fourth or fifth ring, I picked up. It was Sullivan inviting me over. You know how that goes—it was a booty call, which, after spending a few hours in a tittie bar…"—Lincoln stopped momentarily and looked at Angela—"…excuse my language, darling, was right on time."

Angela, in textbook fashion, didn't blink, nor did she respond. She just kept jotting down notes. Lincoln, who liked to hear himself talk, was oblivious to her non-reaction.

"What time did you get to her house?" Andy inquired.

"Sometime between 2:30 and 3 a.m."

"Okay. Then what?" Andy asked.

"I did my thing for about an hour or two and then bounced."

"Did your thing? What was your thing? And, bounced?"

"I tossed it for an hour or two, and then got up out of there."

"Okay," Andy smiled and nodded his head like the light bulb had just gone on. "Okay, so you bounced and got up out of there, meaning you left?"

"Yep! Left and went straight home."

"So, you're saying you left her place roughly around 4 or 5 a.m.?" Andy said.

"That's right."

"And, Sullivan was still alive?"

"Yeah, she was still alive! Shit, as loud as she was yelling and screaming, all of Atlanta should have been awake."

Man, this guy loves himself, I thought, wondering if he knew how foolish he sounded.

"Did you notice anything out of the ordinary that night?" Andy quizzed. "Can you remember anything?"

"Not really. It was pretty much business as usual with her and me. I went over to her place late night, hit it and left. That was the extent of it."

"Did you guys talk at all after you left her place?"

"No, not that I can remember."

"No phone calls to let her know you made it home safely? No texts?"

"Naw, it was never that type of party."

"No calls from her saying how good you were or how much she enjoyed your company?"

"Nope. Though I'm sure she thought both of those to be true."

"So, that's it? No contact with Sullivan after you left her place."

"That's it. Nothing."

"Okay, well, Lincoln, I can tell you now that we're really going to have to get more precise with our times," Andy cautioned. "Right now we're dealing with too many ballparks. We need to tighten it up. One of the first things we'll need to do is get in touch with your buddies who you dropped off at the hotel. Maybe they'll have a better sense of time regarding the drop-off. The good thing is I can't see the DA's office supplying a sufficient motive. Unless they say the sex was horrible and you went ballistic as a result."

"Yeah, right," said Lincoln.

"My thoughts exactly: yeah, right." Andy chuckled. He stopped the tape recorder. "I think this is a good place for us to stop and take a break."

It was about 11 a.m. when we took our first break. I looked

around the room, saw this high-priced trial attorney, whom I had seen on television numerous times, including his team of legal professionals, and thought, *Am I dreaming, or is this a nightmare?* I mean, truth be told, I had been in the limelight on many occasions. The whole world of glitz and glamour was nothing new to me. Hell, my number one client was the top sports figure in the world. But, for some reason, I never really looked at the sports world as being as worldly as it really is. All eyes were on Lincoln.

The experience was quickly beginning to open my eyes. Though I was a complete novice in the world of criminal law, I pretty much knew it was a foregone conclusion that the hammer was going to drop on Lincoln at any minute and he would be formally charged with murder. I certainly didn't want that to happen, but with that came my being crossed off the suspect list.

As Andy and his team huddled closely around one another, comparing notes, Lincoln sat there emotionless. Looking at him and his body language, it was obvious he had a lot on his mind. He had to be wondering what his future had in store. I could tell he was scared—as anyone in his situation would be. I stood and slowly made my way over to the window, opened the blinds and looked down at the city. I had one of the best views Buckhead had to offer. The street below was the ever-so-popular Peachtree Street, which always seemed overcrowded with cars at all hours of the day. At night, due to the many upscale restaurants and bars that Buckhead had to offer, that same strip of Peachtree Street was overpopulated with an abundance of foot traffic. It was also nice to be able to see the skyline of three vital areas of Atlanta from that very same conference room window. In addition to being privy to breathtaking views of Buckhead's skyline, I had a direct shot of the Colony Square/Midtown area as well as Atlanta's downtown. It was really something to see at night when all of the buildings were lit. Lincoln joined me moments later.

"You alright?" I asked.

Lincoln shrugged his shoulders. "Yeah, I'm cool."

"If this thing goes to court, rest assured, justice will prevail!" I turned and pointed to Andy and the rest of the team. "Besides, look at who we have working for us. It's going to be all right, man. No worries."

"I'm going to hold you to those words," Lincoln said before walking over to the bin where all of the drinks were heavily packed in ice. He reached in, grabbed a bottle of water and returned to his seat.

Andy, who had his back to me, turned and said, "Are you ready to start back up, Matisse?"

"Yep," I responded and returned to my seat next to Lincoln. As Andy began talking, I looked down at my notes and saw Hunter's name boldly scribbled, reminding me that I had to supply Andy with that information. Not that I put a whole lot of stock in her having something to do with Sullivan's death, but you never knew.

"I'd like to hear how your night went with Sullivan, Matisse," Andy said, turning the tape recorder back on.

"I guess you could say Sullivan and I had rekindled an old flame. We had gone out on a few dates, and things seemed to be moving in a direction that we both were familiar with, having dated years before." I looked across the table at Andy and his team of four. I knew by their blank stares that they'd done their homework. The information that I'd just given wasn't new to anyone in the room. I continued. "Sullivan invited me over for dinner that night. Dinner was outstanding. When we finished eating, we retired to her bedroom where we soon became intimate."

Andy interrupted. "By intimate you mean the two of you had sex?"

"Yes, sex," I replied.

"What time did you leave?" Andy asked.

"I think it was around 2 a.m."

"Okay. Hold up for a moment, Matisse." Andy looked at Lincoln. "See this is why the timeline has to be tight, Lincoln. You said you got to Sullivan's place sometime between 2:30 and 3 a.m. Matisse is saying he left her place somewhere around 2 a.m. This is an area where I'm asking both of you to come up with more definitive times. I know it's hard, but we really need exact times."

"I don't know, Andy," I said. "I could have left Sullivan's

place a little earlier. It's all become somewhat of a blur."

"How about you, Lincoln? Could your timeline be off by an hour or two?" Andy asked, removing his glasses. He rubbed his eyes, which looked bloodshot red.

Lincoln twisted open the top from his bottle of water, and took a large gulp. "At this point, Andy, anything's possible. In realistically thinking about it, I'm normally one of the last cats to leave the tittie, I mean, *strip* bars. And that's normally around 4 a.m. So, who knows? It could have been later."

"Well, that's what we're going to have to find out. Same goes for you, Matisse. We're going to have to dig deep here. I suggest both of you check your cell phones. Hopefully, if you talked to her on the phone, it's still logged. Unfortunately, if your phones are anything like mine, it only stores the last ten calls made and received. I'm long overdue for an iPhone, but I'm attached to this one. It's one of my many quirks."

Angela and the rest of the legal team chuckled. It seemed like it was one of those moments where I didn't get the feel they thought what Andy had said was all that funny, but recognized he was their boss and acknowledged his attempt at trying to be kind of funny.

"Let's pick up where we left off, Matisse," Andy said before putting his glasses back on.

"Well, that's basically about it. I left her place, went home and went to bed. Sullivan was alive and well when I left."

Silence filled the air for a moment. I listened to the traffic on the streets below, never really noticing just how loud it could get at times.

"So, I guess Matisse left Sullivan just as you did, Lincoln. Alive and well," Andy said, breaking the silence. Lincoln didn't respond with words. He simply moved his head up and down.

Angela stood, "If I may interrupt briefly, I have some information supporting a reliable timeline."

"By all means, do tell," Andy responded.

"We were able to access Matisse and Lincoln's phone records with Gail's assistance. Lincoln, you must have left the club around 4 a.m. because your first call with Sullivan took place at 4:15 a.m. So, it's probably safe to say you arrived at her house somewhere between 4:30 and 5 a.m. And, based on what you said regarding being there for approximately two hours, you probably left no later than 7 a.m."

"Great work, Angela," Andy said. "That's the information we needed."

Just as Angela returned to her seat, I took it upon myself to have the floor. I stood and addressed the room. "I have a couple pieces of information surrounding Sullivan's death that could be helpful to the case."

"We're all ears, Matisse," Andy responded.

"Well, a buddy of mine overheard a woman who I used to date saying that she disliked Sullivan."

"What exactly was said?"

"My friend, Miles, overheard Hunter, that's the woman, saying that Sullivan was a ho. But that it was all right because she liked to keep her friends close and her enemies even closer. Now what that meant, I couldn't tell you. I will say, though, that our breakup was a messy one. Despite the fact that Sullivan and I had gone out on only three or four dates in our attempt to rekindle, maybe Hunter somehow found out about it and was bothered. I know I'm sounding kind of egotistical like my man here," I said, playfully nudging Lincoln in his side, which generated a smile from Angela, "but, who knows?"

"You're right, who knows? But that's definitely an area you guys should look into," Andy replied, looking past Angela at Tom and Big Jay.

"What's Hunter's last name and where can we find her?" Big Jay asked, clutching a pen to write down his first set of notes of the day.

"Her last name is DePasse. D. E., capital P. A. S. S. E. When we're through here I'll get the rest of that information for you."

"You said you had two pieces of information," Andy said.

"Well, the other thing was the day after Sullivan died, I began getting anonymous phone calls from some joker implying that

Lincoln had something to do with her death."

Lincoln turned to me and said sarcastically, accompanied with a sore look on his face, "Thanks. That should help me get out of this mess, Matisse."

"In all likelihood, Lincoln, it probably will. I certainly wouldn't have taken on this case if I didn't believe in your innocence, regardless of what my reputation suggests. A couple of things could be going on there. One, it could be a scorned ex-lover who wants to see you get the chair. Or, it could be someone making sure the path doesn't lead to them."

I didn't say anything, but when I turned and gave Lincoln one of those, *Punk-ass, so, there*, looks, he knew it said it all. In my moment of gloating, Gail, who rushed in like a hurricane, interrupted our meeting.

"The District Attorney's office is on the line for you, Matisse. Would you like me to send the call in here or would you rather take it in your office?"

"I'll take it in here, Gail. Thanks."

She hurried out, and sent the call in seconds later. It was kind of an uncomfortable moment because they obviously weren't aware of the fact that we had hired Andy to represent Lincoln. Andy seemed a bit put off by it all. As I listened to what the DA's office had to say, I didn't say much in return, other than, "Okay and thanks."

All eyes were on me during the brief conversation and as soon as I hung up, Andy said, "Well."

"Well," I started. "A few things. First off, they've decided to press charges against Lincoln. Secondly, they're holding a press conference in about an hour to inform the world of this decision. And, finally, I am no longer a suspect."

"This news is exactly what we expected," Andy replied. "None of this comes as a surprise."

Before he could go on, I cut him off and turned to Gail, who was standing over me. "Can you have our PR staff prepare a press release saying that we have hired Andy to represent Lincoln?"

"Sure thing," Gail responded.

"And that needs to get done as soon as possible, preferably

in the next twenty minutes or so. Oh, and make sure they call us for a couple of quotes before they send it out."

"Okay," Gail replied, scurrying out of the room.

"There you have it," Andy said. "And, so it officially begins, people. We are at war. Let's all put on our hard hats and get this done. Let's prove Lincoln's innocence beyond a shadow of a doubt. None of that O.J. shit. We want the world going away from this knowing that Lincoln had absolutely nothing to do with the death of Sullivan Williams."

"Should we hold some type of press conference?" I asked naively.

"No. A lot of times, Matisse, the DAs love the publicity. They eat it up, thinking it's going to further their careers. A lot of times it does. These high profile cases don't come around too often, and in most instances the cases make celebrities out of them. At this point, the key for us is to just sit tight and see what they've got. How are you feeling, Lincoln? You all right?"

"I'm feeling like I'm about to get sick. I'll be in your bathroom, Matisse." Lincoln rose to his feet, holding his stomach. Making his way out of the conference room, he parted with one last shot: "One wrong move and it's my ass. Remember that."

"Let's see if this room can back up its lovely looks, Matisse. Let's utilize those flat screens and see what the talking heads are saying."

"Good idea," I responded, reaching for the remote. I turned on all of the screens. Sure enough, every news station, including ESPN, was reporting on the upcoming press conference, all the while speculating on what it was about. Each station was right, too. It amazes me sometimes how they get their information. Don't get me wrong, I've seen them come up short on many occasions. But this time they were money, no doubt leaked by the DA's office.

"We should probably get Lincoln out of here. There's really no need for him to stick around at this point," Andy suggested.

I called Gail at her desk. "Can you have the company that handles Lincoln's security place two more guards outside of his house?"

"Sure," Gail replied. "What time do you want them over there?"

"Now. And have two others meet us here, pronto."

"Okay."

I got up and went into my office to see how Lincoln was doing. Poor guy. I have to admit, I was extremely relieved to finally have my name dropped from the list of suspects. *Punk-ass detectives.*

When I arrived inside my office, Lincoln was nowhere to be found. However, I could hear him in the bathroom, doing a number on my toilet, undoubtedly ralphing up his entire breakfast. I knocked on the door, which was locked.

"Lincoln! You all right?"

He made a couple more loud noises before offering, "Do I sound alright, genius?"

I ignored his comment. "Well, hurry up. We're going to get you out of here. I've arranged to have a couple more security guards outside your house. And I have a couple more on their way over here to take you home."

The unruly noises that emanated from Lincoln earlier finally ceased. I heard water running, followed by the sound of mouthwash swishing and swirling inside of his mouth. He opened the door moments later. Lincoln looked like a strung-out crack addict.

"Whew!" The smell was unbearable. "Damn!"

"Oh, anyway! Let's see how you'd react after finding out you might have to spend the rest of your life in the pokey," Lincoln replied, plopping down on my couch. "Man, stay on these fools. Like I said, one slip-up and I'm toast. Make sure they're all on top of their games. We both have a lot at stake here, and don't forget it."

"Yeah, yeah, yeah. Come on and gather your belongings. Your security guards are in the waiting area waiting to take you home. We have to go before the media shows up here."

Lincoln stood and walked out without saying anything. I followed him.

"Gail, I'm going to ride with these guys over to Lincoln's place. I don't have time to say bye to Andy and the rest of them. Can you tell Andy I'll give him a call a little later? Where'd you guys park?" I asked the two security guards, who each looked like poster boys for steroid abuse.

"We're parked in front."

"Go get the car and bring it around to the back. I have a secret way out using the back entrance."

The car and the two guards were waiting for us when we arrived at the back entrance. Surprisingly, there wasn't a member of the media in sight until we passed the front of the building. Now, that was a zoo. That's the only way I could describe it. I had to do a double-take because they all looked like sharks and piranhas just waiting to sink their teeth into Lincoln. Luckily for us the car windows were tinted. They had no clue that we had just driven right by them.

As we drove off, Lincoln looked back at the large contingent of media gathered in front of my office building and then turned to me with wide eyes. "So, that's how it's gonna be, huh?"

"I'm afraid so," I replied, administering a couple hard pats to Lincoln's back. "It's about to be a real circus. Get ready."

32

DA's
PRESS CONFERENCE

LINCOLN and I watched the press conference from his house.
I just knew it was going to be a circus outside his place when we
arrived, but to our good fortune, nothing. Not one blood-sucking
media member lurked outside. I guess therein lies the importance of
the gated community.

Dallas Smith stood on the steps of the courthouse in
downtown Atlanta answering various questions for about forty-five
minutes after making a fifteen-minute statement telling why they
chose to charge Lincoln with murder. As we sat, watching this sorry
excuse of a press conference, it became obvious to me that they
were, in fact, making an example of Lincoln. Since when is finding
a person's fingerprints, or semen, for that matter, a crime? Granted,
something like that usually warranted being thoroughly checked out.
But it just didn't seem like the evidence they had against Lincoln was
enough. It was obvious that Lincoln had had sexual relations with
Sullivan that night. Hell, I had the same relations with her just hours
before.

Andy's words about the DA, celebrity, and attention, seemed
on point. Through Dallas's constant smiles and addressing each
media member by their respective first names, I could have sworn

I saw him licking his chops on occasion while gloating over his newfound fame. After all, he was up for re-election, and this was his ticket.

Dallas and I knew each other, but not that well. Every now and then we would bump into one another at the barbershop. However, I can't ever recall addressing each other by our first names, even though our professional reputations preceded us. Our brief conversations always went something like this, "Hey, man, you doing alright?"

"Yeah, I'm doing well. You?"

"I'm straight."

"Good, good. Alright, man, hold it down."

"Definitely. You too."

And that was about the extent of it. One of us was usually coming as the other was going. We both went to Rodger, though, for our cuts.

If I had to guess, I would say Dallas was in his mid-thirties. I'll give him his props. He had a little style to him, especially considering his straight-laced profession. His mid-length afro blended nicely with his sideburns, and his soul patch, well, that really put him in there. He was what I'd call the new *hip* DA. His walk had a certain cool swagger to it. I don't think there was a person on the face of this earth who could tell him he wasn't the shit.

Yeah, Andy was on the money with Dallas's intentions. In fact, I bet he already sold the movie rights and handpicked the actor who would play him in the upcoming trial. Being on the other side of the demise of Lincoln Dix was big news in any environment, in every country, across every continent. He was that large. In certain circles, Lincoln's popularity dwarfed Michael Jordan's. Now, that's saying something.

"This a bitch!" yelled Lincoln, standing in front of his 70-inch customized flat-screen TV. He turned and looked in my direction. "Who's this clown?"

"Dallas Smith," I responded from the oversized blue leather couch I was sitting on. "From here on out, we're going to be seeing and hearing a lot of him. So, get ready. It's about to go down."

"He sounds like he has a gigantic hard-on for me, Matisse." Lincoln walked into the kitchen, grabbed a couple of beers out of the refrigerator and handed one to me before plopping down next to me on the couch. "They want to put me in the chair and watch me fry, huh?"

I took a swig of my beer. "Yeah, something like that, Lincoln."

"Damn!" Lincoln said, throwing his hands up in the air before sinking deep into the couch.

The press conference lasted only a couple minutes longer. Just before it ended, I turned to Lincoln.

"Do me a huge favor." Lincoln didn't respond. He just stared at the TV, but I knew he was listening to what I had to say. "Call all of the important people in your life right now."

"Right now? Why?" Lincoln asked, now looking down at the ground.

"Because I'm guessing all of your phones are about to start ringing off the hook, from family and friends to annoying media members."

"You think?"

"I can almost bet my last dollar on it. This is big news, Lincoln," I said, reaching into my pocket for my cell phone. "You know how large you are."

"Yeah, I guess."

"You guess? Oh, now all of the sudden you want to play the humble role. Usually you're the one constantly telling me how large you are."

"Whatever, Matisse. Who you calling?" Lincoln asked, finally giving me some eye contact.

"Andy," I replied in a matter-of-fact way, like who else would I be calling? "It's on, Lincoln."

Andy picked up on the first ring.

"What'd you think about the press conference, Andy?"

"I'm excited, Matisse; I have a boner as we speak. I'm going to hand that clown his lunch. Did you see what I was talking about with these overzealous DAs? Did you see how he was grandstanding?"

"Yeah, he seemed full of himself."

"Dallas Smith! He was in diapers when I started practicing, Matisse. And what's with the little patch of hair on his chin?"

"Fashion statement, I guess," I responded, thinking, *Man, this guy has an enormous ego, too. But it obviously works to his advantage.*

"How's Lincoln holding up?"

"All right, I guess." I stood and went into another room where Lincoln couldn't hear me. "He's a little shaken, but under the circumstances, who wouldn't be?"

"Yeah, I see it all the time. Tell him to hang in there. And, tell him to stay off Twitter too! We'll get this thing straightened out in no time."

"I hope so and good call on the Twitter."

"Listen, I was just about to call my staff. We're going to meet tomorrow morning at nine. Will that work for you guys?"

"Uh, yeah. Of course." I was a little puzzled when he spoke of calling his staff. I was under the impression that they were alongside him in my office conference room. "Did you all watch the press conference from the conference room?"

"No, we left shortly after Gail told us that you guys had taken off. We went back to the hotel."

"Oh, okay. Where are you guys staying?"

"We're staying at the Four Seasons on 14th Street."

"That's a good one."

"It'll work," Andy quickly responded. "Listen, Matisse, the more I think about all of us meeting tomorrow, the more I think we should probably meet at Lincoln's house. The media attention is about to multiply to astounding proportions. It's best we shield Lincoln from any contact with those vultures."

"Good idea. We're definitely on the same page there," I said, returning to the couch alongside Lincoln, where I witnessed him change channels every five seconds. All of the local and national newscasts began with Lincoln Dix as their respective lead stories. "Yeah, Andy, that sounds good. Let's meet here tomorrow morning at nine. I'll have Gail send a car over to your hotel to pick you all up."

"Great. We'll see you tomorrow then. Again, tell Lincoln to keep his chin up. Everything's going to be all right. His hard-earned money is not going to go to waste. I don't lose, Matisse."

"Will do."

As soon as I hung up the phone, Lincoln turned the television off and stood in front of me with his arms folded. "Well, what'd he say?"

"He said not to worry. He'll have you out of this mess in no time."

A slight smile appeared on Lincoln's face. "Really?"

"Yeah, really. That's what Andy said."

"He's the best, right?"

"Yeah, bruh! He's on top of his shit. Not only does he win, but he also has a stellar reputation, especially with high profile cases involving celebrities. He gets it done," I said, sensing it might calm Lincoln's nerves. It wasn't like I was lying because I wasn't. Andy was the real deal. He was the truth, in every way.

"Matisse, I didn't do it," Lincoln said, fighting back the tears. It was the first time I had ever seen Lincoln in such a state. It was also the first time that he seemed 100-percent sincere and serious.

"I know you didn't. Listen, man, it's all going to wash out. In the meantime, we have to stay focused and supply Andy and his team with as much pertinent information as possible. We're going to meet over here tomorrow at nine in the morning. Don't worry about the food. I'll have Gail call a catering service that's available to us all day long. You gonna be alright, man? I'm about to get up out of here."

"Yeah, I'm cool."

"Good. Remember, you have the security guards here twenty-four-seven."

As I showed myself out, Lincoln's phones, home and cell, began to blow up, just as I predicted. "Don't answer any of those calls," I cautioned. "However, think about what I said. Take a few minutes to call your loved ones so they aren't worrying about your well-being. Oh, and stay off Twitter."

"Alright, already, Matisse! Leave!"

Even though I was exhausted from the eventful, busy day, it didn't stop me from calling Miles on my way home to see if he wanted to meet for a nightcap at Al's. I definitely had the better end of that deal, seeing as how Al's was right next to my place.

Though I felt bad for Lincoln, my mood was somewhat upbeat. I had been formally cleared from the suspect list, plus I felt good about our chances now that Andy and his legal team were on our side.

It was weird. I thought Sullivan, may she rest in peace, may have been *the one*, but that turned out to be a total disaster. And now thoughts of Erica, and how badly I messed up with her, filled my head. But none of that negativity seemed to faze me or put a dent in my mood. In fact, I was grateful that the truth about Sullivan came out. Don't get me wrong; I wouldn't wish her horrible fate on anyone. Life's funny sometimes. You just wonder why things happen the way they happen. I'm an optimistic person by nature, so I'd like to believe things happen for a reason. There obviously was a reason why I didn't have a clue when it came to Erica. Why I didn't appreciate all of the great qualities she possessed is beyond me, but my being in the dark regarding her must have happened for a reason. It had to have. As a result, when it came to my future and romance, I had this overwhelming feeling of open-ended possibilities. And it felt good.

As usual, I arrived at Al's before Miles. It was busier than most nights, which was cool with me. I was kind of in the mood to do a little socializing. I had this burning desire to resume my life, and right all of the self-inflicted wounds that came with it. However, considering I was the agent of the biggest sports figure in the world, and also considering all of the day's news that surrounded him, I knew it was a pipedream.

I took a seat at the bar, and braced myself for all of Al's questions. Just as I saw Al making his way towards me, I looked up at the many televisions and found Dallas Smith and that pitiful press conference on every set.

"Matisse, I see they charged your boy, huh?" Al said, placing a napkin down on the bar in front of me, which was followed by a Stoli on the rocks.

"Yep," I replied. I figured if I kept my answers short, he wouldn't grill me too hard.

"How's he holding up?"

I took a sip of my drink. "He's doing alright, Al."

"How about you, Matisse? How you holding up?"

"I'm good, Al," I said in a muffled voice due to the piece of ice that swirled around inside my mouth. "Life's funny, man. It's full of curveballs."

"Ain't that the truth," Al responded before grabbing the towel that rested on his shoulder. He proceeded to wipe down the bar. "Y'all got your work cut out for you, Matisse. Murder is no joke, and murder raps are hard to beat."

"This is true, which is why we hired Andy Weinberg to represent Lincoln."

"What? *The* Andy Weinberg?"

"Yep, that one," I said, just as Miles and his sorry, always-late ass took the stool next to mine.

"What's up, Chief?" Miles said. We quickly exchanged pounds. "I don't know, Matisse, Dallas Smith looked like he had his game face on."

"That's what I was just telling him, Miles," Al stated. "In no way is this going to be a cakewalk, even if we are talking about Lincoln Dix. People haven't forgotten the O.J. fiasco. What are you having, Miles?"

"I'll do a Newcastle." Al turned and made his way over to the tap.

"You alright?" Miles asked. He placed his hand on my shoulder.

"I'm cool."

"Lincoln must be shitting bricks."

"Yeah, he hasn't been his usual cocky self, that's for sure." I put down my glass, which was about half full. "Hey, man, I know the whole Lincoln thing is today's hot topic, but do me a favor."

"What's that?"

"Tonight, let's take a break from it. I'm a little burned out on it all, and it's just begun. I'm going to be up to my ears in it in the following days and months. You know what I'm saying?"

"Yeah." Al placed Miles's brew in front of him.

"How are you and Shelby doing? You still going through with it?"

"Come on, man. Yeah!" Miles's body shifted a couple times in his stool. "Damn, Matisse! You ask me that every time I see you."

"Hey, I know how brothers get as that day approaches. I'm just trying to look out."

"Well, damn, man! How many times do I have to tell you? I'm ready to do this!"

"All right, bruh!" I raised my hands in the air. "My bad. That's good to hear. As soon as I finalize the women for the bachelor party, we should be all set."

Miles grinned from ear to ear. "You know what I like, right?"

"I know what you like, man. You like big titties and big asses, probably because Shelby has neither."

"That's cold. But, you're right," Miles said, giving me a pound.

"I mean, don't get me wrong. Shelby's tight. She's just not exaggerated like you like them."

"Yeah, you know how that goes, Matisse. I would never marry any of those big-tittied, big-assed girls. They're just for fun." Miles threw a couple of peanuts in the air, caught them in his mouth, and then took a big gulp of his beer in one fluid motion. "Shelby's the total package, looks, a well-proportioned body, and smart as hell."

"Here here," I said, raising my glass in the air until Miles did the same with his. Our glasses met, creating a ringing sound, and we each took large gulps, which practically emptied our glasses.

"Yeah, man, I can't wait until the bachelor party. I know when it's all said and done, you'll have all the honeys lined up. I know that, Matisse. You're my man." Miles popped a few more peanuts into his mouth before turning to me with a serious look on his face. "How about the cigars and liquor? Are we straight there, too?"

I took another sip of my Stoli and waited a few more minutes before answering his dumb-ass question. "Come on, Miles. I'm not even going to answer that stupid shit. You know how I do it, bruh!"

"True, true. My bad," Miles said, just as he began to go to work on another brew. "So, your boy Lincoln has you working overtime, huh?"

"That's got to be the understatement of the year. But, wait, didn't I just ask you not to mention anything about that?"

"Oh, my bad again," Miles responded. "So, what's going on with you personally? Any new women in your life?"

"Nope. I can't give a confirmation there," I said, swallowing my pride. "You know who's been on my mind an awful lot lately?

"No, who?"

"You'll probably laugh at me, but Erica."

"Laugh at you? Why? I always thought she was the one. Here I am talking about how Shelby is the total package. Shit, Shelby didn't have anything over Erica."

"You think?"

"Matisse, I know. Erica was tight. When you messed that one up, I mourned for you, dog."

"Yeah, yeah, yeah. That's so typical," I said, reaching for the bowl of peanuts in front of Miles.

"What is?"

"You! Us! Brothers!"

"Huh?"

"Brothers, man! Brothers always have to pour salt in the wounds. Constantly kicking the guy when he's down."

"Aw, whatever, Matisse. I was just being real. Hey, Erica was tight, no matter how you sliced it."

"Yeah, I know she was. I don't know what I was thinking. Seriously, I have no clue because she was amazing in every way. I was at a different place back then. You know what I'm saying?"

Miles thought about it for a moment before responding. "No," he said.

"A different place, meaning when it came to women, I really wasn't trying to do the right thing. I was so full of myself that I was the only person I thought about."

"Oh, okay."

"I'll never forget the day she walked out on me. I felt bad. I remember having this hollow feeling inside of my stomach. But, I got over it way too fast because at the time I wasn't overly concerned about anyone else's feelings."

"Damn, Matisse, you were cold," Miles said with a chuckle. "Pimps up and hoes down back then, huh?"

I laughed, but didn't respond verbally as images of Erica filled my head. It was a slow night at Al's. Not that it was always happening, but it was usually good for a few visuals—at least one or two honeys. However, on this particular night, Al's was a straight-leg convention. There were more dicks in there then a Richard Convention.

"So, you really think Lincoln is innocent, Matisse?" Miles asked hesitantly.

I set my drink down and turned to Miles. "Of course I do, Miles. This is a guy who had the world at his fingertips. Hell, he's Lincoln Dix, for crying out loud! What would he possibly have to gain from killing Sullivan?"

"I thought they said it looked like it may have been accidental."

"Well, yeah, that's the way it looks, but I believe everything Lincoln has said regarding Sullivan."

"I don't know, Matisse. The whole thing is kind of bizarre. Sullivan was a straight freak. I still can't get over the fact that you did her moments before Lincoln did her. She was out there, dog."

"Miles, why do you keep bringing this topic up? Haven't I told you, on two separate occasions, mind you, that I didn't want to talk about it tonight?"

"My bad, Matisse. I keep forgetting. It's hard not to talk about it, especially when it's all over the news, no matter the station."

"I realize that, man. I just thought I could meet my boy out for a few cocktails while we shot the shit. That's all."

"Alright, already. Fair enough, Matisse."

"Good. How's Shelby doing? Is she getting excited with the wedding almost here?"

"Oh, she's stoked. That's all we talk about. Well, that's all she talks about, anyway. I guess most women think about getting married from the time they were little kids. Shelby's always saying things like, 'I've always wanted this type of wedding and that type of wedding.' I mean, it's a big deal to her. But, like I said, I think it's a big deal to most women."

"This is true," I responded as I stood momentarily to stretch my legs. "I'm proud of you, Miles. You finally stepped up to the plate, and you haven't wavered one bit. Marriage is a good thing, at least from what I've been told."

"I was about to say, how would you know, Matisse?"

"Yeah, yeah, yeah. Hey, I even heard that married men live longer than single men."

"Really?"

"That's what they say."

33

A CALL FROM
AN AMATUER

AISLE from all of Miles's annoying questions about what was
going on with Lincoln's case, my visit with him was good and much-
needed. Though the cocktails numbed and relaxed me, I was still
emotionally and physically drained by the time I got home.

I treated myself to an extravagant gift last Christmas,
and hadn't yet gotten the use out of it I'd anticipated. However,
considering the state I was in, there was no better time than the
present to put it to good use. The Christmas purchase I splurged on
was a theater Jacuzzi tub. I had it installed in the bathroom of the
master bedroom. This thing was as tight as they come. A 50-inch
flat screen monitor was attached to the tub. It was literally a single
unit. I had never seen anything like it before, so in one of my rare
indulgences, I had to get it. I think what excited me even more was
the waterproof remote control. I thought that was the greatest. For
some reason, most men have love affairs with their remotes. And I
was certainly no different.

Relaxing in that tub with the water steaming-hot and the
jets flowing at full strength, I felt extremely relaxed as I watched
music videos on BET. I didn't want to watch anything that was going
to make me think. BET's *Afterhours Love* program was perfect. It

played great slow rhythm and blues coupled with out-of-this-world visuals. I don't know where they find all of those fine women, but somehow they do.

As much as I tried not to think, the thoughts that ran through my head were inevitable. I thought about Lincoln and how that ordeal was going to turn out. I thought about Miles and Shelby and their upcoming wedding. And I thought about Erica, and how I royally screwed that one up.

I felt pretty good about Lincoln, now that Andy and his legal team were on our side. There wasn't a whole lot I could do to help there. With Miles and Shelby's wedding quickly approaching, I knew that I needed to focus much of my attention organizing Miles's bachelor party. It was number one on my to-do list. I was never a person to force things when it came to women, but I had this feeling that just wouldn't go away, and that was that in spite of having blown it with Erica, she was now worth fighting for. So, it was right then and there—with the hot, bubbling water shooting up my ass and the soothing sounds and half-naked women on the screen in front of me—that I devised a plan of action regarding the very near future.

When it was all said and done, I had sat in that tub for nearly two hours, which brought me to about one in the morning. Just as I climbed into bed, my phone sounded.

"Hello," I said, wondering who in the hell was calling me at this hour.

A muffled male voice on the other end said, "Don't fall for the okie-dokie, bruh. Lincoln Dix is your man. He committed the crime."

"Who is this?" I asked. The next sound I heard was the dial tone. I immediately hit *69, but to no avail. The number was blocked.

What the person had said didn't faze me. I was more than convinced that Lincoln was innocent. He just had too much to lose, even if the ass was out of this world. I just didn't see him going temporarily insane over a great piece of ass, especially considering all of the choice ass he's had. Though I knew from first-hand experience that Sullivan was high-grade when it came to matters of the bedroom, it still wasn't enough to send my man, Lincoln, over the edge, just as it wasn't for me. I didn't commit that crime, and neither did Lincoln. I was sure of it.

The disturbing phone call prompted me to get out of bed. I made my way to the study, where I spent the next hour in front of my computer. The first thing I did was send an email to myself that I CC'd to Andy detailing what that clown on the phone had said.

I was startled to hear from Andy within seconds of my email.

"Do you have any idea who it was?" he asked via email.

"At this point, no," I wrote back.

"Interesting. Did you *69 him?" Andy inquired.

"Yep. Nothing."

"I'm getting a boner again, Matisse," Andy responded. "I love this shit! Whoever it is doesn't have much experience with this sort of thing."

"No? Why?"

"It's too simple. Okay, we'll at least give him credit for blocking his number—but the simplicity of his call, which said absolutely nothing other than implying Lincoln was the one who killed Sullivan, was elementary. Someone with more experience would have led us exactly where he wanted by using a series of hints. I'm telling you, this guy's an amateur. We'll track him down in no time."

"All right. This is your show, Andy. You know what's best. I'll see you tomorrow." I clicked "send," and once I saw that it went through, I immediately shut off my computer.

I made my way back into the bedroom, climbed into bed and turned my light off. This time it was for good.

34

BARBERSHOP ENCOUNTER WITH DALLAS

THE first thing I did when I awoke in the morning was call Andy. I knew there wasn't a whole lot I could do in terms of helping Lincoln. We were paying Andy and his team top dollar to represent Lincoln, and I figured the best thing I could do was to stay out of the way and just let them do their jobs. Don't get me wrong, I knew that my being there comforted Lincoln. I also knew that there were still questions I could answer to help the case. But on this particular morning I was being selfish. I needed a cut. I had a serious five o'clock shadow on top of my head. And that just wasn't cool. If you're going to do the bald-headed thing, not only should it always be smooth and soft as a baby's ass, but, most of all, it should have a certain shine to it.

After I explained to Andy that I wasn't going to meet them at Lincoln's until sometime after lunch, I threw on my workout gear and went for a light 45-minute run on my treadmill. I felt I needed personal time to get my body right. Over the past few days, I had neglected it big-time! In my experience, a healthy body lends to a healthy mind.

I watched the coverage of Lincoln's case on several of the local and national news outlets simultaneously as I slowly banged out four and a half miles on my treadmill. It was the story of the year. I was comforted to know that our press release had reached all of the respective media outlets because the word was definitely out about Andy and his legal team representing Lincoln.

I knew Lincoln was watching the same thing, so once I showered and dressed and was on my way to the barbershop, I called him from the car to see how he was holding up.

"You all right?" I braced myself for his response by turning down the volume on the speakerphone.

"Can you believe this shit, Matisse?" He yelled at the top of his lungs, just as I anticipated.

"Honestly, Lincoln? Yeah!" I pulled the car over to the side of the road. "I know this is a nightmare. And, I know you're thinking, '*Easy for you to say.*' And I really feel for you, man, but keep in mind, we have the best legal team on the face of this planet. Andy Weinberg is the absolute best money can buy. It's gonna be alright. I know it."

"Well, I'm glad to know somebody knows it, and not that it makes me feel any better. The only thing I'm feeling right now, especially after watching all these annoying reports on TV, is that I'm going to die in the gas chamber. And soon!"

"Lincoln, you didn't do it." I began driving again. "Justice will prevail. Besides, you're Lincoln Dix."

"I'm afraid that what's working against me this time."

"Unfortunately, you may have a good point there," I agreed hesitantly.

"So, I guess it is true about you abandoning me this morning, huh, Matisse?"

"No such thing. I just have to tie up a few loose ends and then I'll be there, man. Quit tripping."

"In case you forgot, Matisse, I have a lot of reasons to trip at the moment."

"True that. My bad. Listen, I'll see you later." I hung up the phone before giving Lincoln a chance to say bye.

When I got to the barbershop, Rodger already had a head in his chair, but I was up next. It didn't bother me at all. I had missed a couple of visits. While I waited, I used the time to get thoroughly reacquainted with the place. I thumbed through a couple of *FHM*s and *Maxim*s before moving onto the hard stuff. I soon found my fingers racing through the pages of *Playboy* and *Penthouse*. Aw, the beauty of the barbershop. Thankfully, Rodger had the stereo going instead of all of the televisions. I caught a major break there. Lincoln's case wasn't even a day old, and I'd already had my fill.

"You're up, Matisse." Rodger brushed off the chair as he awaited my arrival. Once I sat down, he draped an apron over me. "How goes it, Matisse?"

"I'm alright, Rodge. You?"

"I'm doing fine." He tied the strings to the apron tightly around my neck. "Not too tight is it?"

"Naw, I'm good."

"You sure about that? From what I've been reading in papers and watching on the TV, Matisse, it seems like you and that Dix boy may have your hands full. He sure has himself in a fine mess."

"Yeah, I guess it's all over the news, huh?" I shifted in my chair several times.

"You got that right. Well, did he do it?" Rodger applied the shaving cream to my head.

"No, he didn't do it. He'd have to be the dumbest man on earth. The world really is his playground." I looked up at Rodger. "I mean, think about it. Lincoln has fame, a boatload of money, and access to an enormous amount of the most beautiful women in the world. Why would he risk losing all of that?"

"I don't know, Matisse. As true as that may be, stranger things have happened." Rodger stepped from behind my chair to face me. "Look at that fool, O.J."

I didn't have a comeback for that. What could I have said? O.J., too, had a lot going for him at the time of that fatal night. And though he got away with it, in the aftermath it seems like he lost an awful lot. But I was sure Lincoln was way too self-absorbed to put himself in such a position.

"Now, let me get this right, Matisse." Using a straight razor, Rodger took his first two strokes. "She was your girl, but the hockey player was banging her?"

"Rodge, I really don't feel like going into it right now, but no, she wasn't my girl. And, yes, Lincoln was banging her."

"Were you banging her, too?"

"Yeah, I'd hit it a couple of times as well."

"She was a straight freak, huh?"

I let out a big sigh before pondering what Rodger had just said. "Yeah, Rodge, I guess there's no disputing or denying that now. It appears she was one of the biggest freaks this side of the Mississippi."

"And you had no clue that you and your boy, Lincoln, were tapping that ass at the same time?"

"None whatsoever." I sighed again. "Hell, Rodge, I'll take it a step further. Get this—I thought I was in love with her. And I just knew she was in love with me. What a fool I was, huh?"

"That's women for you, Matisse." Rodger stopped and stood in front of me again. "Women know when their man is cheating on them ninety percent of the time. You know how that goes. We think we're slick, and we aren't. But women, that's an entirely different story. They actually are slick when it comes to cheating and shuffling different men. I don't know what it is with them, but they pull it off an awful lot."

"You know, Rodge, I think you're right. Why is that?"

"I think a lot of it has to do with the man's ego. We have huge egos, and most of the time, it has nothing to do with how much money we make or occupation or anything like that. It seems if you have something dangling between your legs, then you automatically have an ego—and not a little one, either. And that's what gets in the way, Matisse. We think our women would be crazy to ever even think about cheating on us. The stuff we're bringing, both physically and mentally, in our minds, is so good, that it's inconceivable to think that our women would put us down for another brother."

I didn't respond to what Rodger had said, but as he went back to tending to my head, I thought about it. To his credit, it made a certain amount of sense to me. As men, I think a lot of us are cocky to a certain degree, and that cockiness stems from no other reason than being part of the male species. We're full of double standards, and clearly we aren't nearly as slick as women when it comes to doing things we have no business doing. It all boils down to this being a man's world and us believing it wholeheartedly.

"Here." Rodger handed me a mirror. "You straight?"

I studied my head, which was now once again completely bald. It had a fresh, shiny look to it, and, yeah, it was smooth as a baby's ass. And I knew this without even bothering to touch it. That's just how my man, Rodge, did it. I handed the mirror back to him. "Looks good, Rodge."

"Good. Let me line your goat up, so you can get out of here. With all of the shit you got going with Lincoln, I know your plate is full."

"Yeah, it's been pretty hectic, Rodge, but we hired one of the best legal teams around to represent him, which frees up some of my time. Don't get me wrong, I'm involved in Lincoln's case and I'm very concerned, but there isn't a whole lot I can do for him right now except just be supportive of him."

"It sounds like he's going to need all the support he can get, Matisse."

"I'm afraid you're right, Rodge." Standing in front of me, Rodger hit the lever—which made the chair I was sitting in recline to a 45-degree angle—before turning on the clippers and applying them to my face. It took Rodger about ten minutes to line and trim my goatee, but he still had to perform the finishing touches to make it perfect.

"Well, onto brighter topics. Did your boy ever get married?" He asked as he stood over me, holding the clippers in his hand, while rapidly chomping on a piece of gum. "The last time you were in here you were talking about how you were going to be the best man in one of your boys' upcoming weddings."

"You're talking about Miles."

"Yeah, I think that's the one."

"No, he and his fiancée, Shelby, postponed it due to Sullivan's death."

"Is that right?"

"Yeah."

"So, I take it they were pretty close with her, too?"

"They knew her through me, but I don't think they were that close. I think they postponed their wedding more for my benefit, you know, with me being the best man and all, coupled with my long-standing relationship with Sullivan."

"They did that all for you, huh? They sound like good people, Matisse."

"Yeah, they are. Miles and I go way back. He's been my man for a long time. And Shelby, well, I've gotten to know her over the years and she's great. She's the total package—you name it, she's got it. I envy the hell out of Miles. He came up big-time."

"Yeah, Matisse, every now and then we luck up. Not often, hell, you know the trouble I've had with women. But every now and then we get lucky."

"I'd say Miles definitely should thank his lucky stars to have Shelby. Not only is she nice and sweet, but she seems to have a lot of compassion."

"What makes you say that, Matisse?" He still hadn't begun to put the finishing touches on my goat as he stood in the exact same spot, holding those same clippers.

"Well," I started hesitantly, "the three of us went to Sullivan's funeral together and I was kind of taken aback by how hard she took the whole thing. I mean, I knew Sullivan the best out of the three of us, but it was Shelby who cried like a baby."

"Funerals are tough for a lot of people. Some people just can't handle funerals no matter how well they knew or didn't know the person."

"Yeah, I guess, Rodge. I just chalked it up as her being a really compassionate person."

"No doubt about it, Matisse, there are some good people out there, man."

"Shelby's definitely one of them. And Miles!" I shook my head as I thought about it. "That lucky bastard."

"Your day will come," Rodger offered before turning the clippers back on and putting the final touches on my goat. It took all of about three minutes. When he was finished, Rodger turned the clippers off and reached for the mirror in one full sweep. "Here you go."

"Thanks," I said, taking the mirror out of his hand and putting it up to my face. "That's why you have a customer for life, Rodge. On the money, like always."

He brought my chair back to its upright position and I stood, reaching into my pocket for my money clip. I pulled out a twenty-dollar bill. "Here you go, Rodge."

"Thanks, man," He said as he gave me a pound. "Stay up, Matisse."

"Oh, no doubt, Rodge," I replied as I made my way out. Just before I reached the door, in walked Dallas Smith like he was the king of the world. Hell, I started to ask him if he owned the place because it sure seemed that way from where I was standing.

"Y'all got your work cut out for you on this one, Matisse," Dallas said, stopping right in front of me with a shit-eating grin. Though he was inside, his sunglasses still adorned his face. The suit he wore looked expensive. It was a navy two-button slim fit, probably Armani or Boss if I had to guess. His shoes were black and freshly-shined. I'll give props where props are due: Dallas was a sharp dresser. And his little soul patch created a certain edge to his look.

"I wouldn't count the 'W' too fast, Dallas," I replied. "And I know that's what it's all about with you, the wins and losses."

Dallas chuckled. "On the contrary, my brother! On the contrary. You know I'm all about ensuring that justice prevails."

"Yeah, especially if you have a shot at furthering your career, right?"

"This is America. The land of opportunity," Dallas responded, still smirking.

"They haven't even thrown the opening jump ball in the air yet, or in Lincoln's case, dropped the first puck yet. There's still a lot of game left, my friend."

"That may be, Matisse, but the evidence we have right now is overwhelming."

"Come on, Dallas. You're obviously one hell of a poker player because you and I both know Lincoln didn't commit that crime, and you certainly don't have enough evidence to convict him. Hell, at this point you don't even have enough evidence to hold him in a jail cell. This case is just something to further your career, plain and simple."

"You're in for a rude awakening, Matt. May I call you Matt?" He lifted his sunglasses and perched them on top of his head.

"No, actually, Dallas, why don't you stick with Matisse?"

"Very well then, Matisse, I've already said too much, but rest assured your boy is gonna go down and for a long time. We're talking life. Believe that, player, because it's real."

I began walking toward the door again and replied without bothering to look back, "We'll see about that, Dallas. We'll see."

35

LINCOLN'S BREAKDOWN

I ran a few more errands, one of which entailed putting a deposit down on two large party buses for Miles's bachelor party, before finally making it over to Lincoln's place. I felt good about the progress I had made regarding Miles's party. All of the pieces were in place. I had secured a great location on Lake Lanier, which came with a boat, plus the transportation, food and drinks were now taken care of. The only thing I had left to do was make sure we had the dancers in place. I wasn't worried because that was surely forthcoming. The more I thought about it, though, the more inclined I was to go ahead and use the women from Jay's escort service. It was easy enough and it saved me a ton of time. And, I trusted Jay—well, sort of.

A mob of reporters gathered outside the gates of Lincoln's neighborhood as I made my way through. Two security guards stood in front of Lincoln's driveway, while another manned his front door.

"Can I help you?" asked one of the two who stood in front of Lincoln's long driveway.

"Yeah, I'm Matisse Spencer, Lincoln's agent." He reached for a clipboard that contained a list of names. After bumbling through it, looking it up and down to no avail, he looked up at me.

"Matisse Spencer, right?"

"Yeah."

He looked back down at the list. "Oh, here you are," he said while taking a pen and putting a mark next to my name. "I'll need to see some ID."

"Sure," I said, reaching into my back pocket for my wallet. "Here you go."

"Great. You're all set, Mr. Spencer." He turned and looked back at the guard who patrolled Lincoln's front door, and then pointed to me before yelling, "This gentleman's all right."

Once I got inside, I found Lincoln surrounded by Andy and his legal team, minus Tom and Big Jay, the two detectives. They were huddled in Lincoln's television room, which was just beyond the kitchen. Half-eaten food was everywhere. The standard buffet was in full effect, and of course it was catered.

"It's about time your ass showed up," Lincoln said, void of any grins or smiles.

"Look, I told you, I had to run a few errands; besides, Lincoln, how many times do I have to tell you you're in good hands with Andy and his team?"

Andy, who was sitting with his back to me, turned and looked up. "Thanks for the vote of confidence, Matisse." He then turned back around. "And you know, Lincoln, he's absolutely right. You're in very good hands with us. Believe me."

"That's what I keep hearing everyone say, but every time I look up at this damn television someone is talking about how I'm going to prison for a very long time." Lincoln stood and raised his voice: "So, which is it?"

Very calmly, Andy responded, "Lincoln, they obviously have a limited amount of evidence against you."

"Is that right?" Lincoln said, still standing. His voice grew even louder. The anger he was experiencing was evident. His body language and entire aura said it all: he was *pissed.* "Then why does every damn channel have me as the lead story? Why is there a boatload of media dickheads just outside of the gates of my neighborhood? And why does everyone think I'm guilty as hell?

Answer that, Andy. How about you Angela? And Stuart, I haven't heard a word from you since you guys showed up. And this is supposed to be the legal dream team? Well, you know what? I'm tired of hearing how you're the absolute shit! And yet, I'm a prisoner in my own house. I'm tired of this shit. I didn't lay a harmful finger on that stank-ass ho! And that's the truth, man! Damn it! Can't a brother get some ass every now and then without being accused of murder? Shit! How about that?"

Andy stood and made his way over to Lincoln. He placed his hand on Lincoln's shoulder. "As I was saying, if they really had sufficient evidence against you, Lincoln, you'd be sitting in a jail cell right now. I don't care how much money you have. And I certainly don't care about your celebrity. I know I'm not telling you anything you don't know. What, did they just give you those degrees? Come on, Lincoln, you have a J.D. and an M.B.A. You're obviously a bright guy. Hey, I know you're scared right now. You have a lot to lose. I'm not about to let that happen. I know you're innocent. Hell, I'd be surprised if this thing even makes it to court. We have two of the best private detectives around. In fact, do you see them anywhere in the room?"

Lincoln looked around. "No." You could barely hear his response. It was almost to a whisper.

"'No' is right. And do you know why?"

Lincoln looked at me and rolled his eyes as if to say, *What? Are we in kindergarten again?* "No, why?" He spoke up this time.

"Because as we speak one of them is tailing Hunter to find out what she's all about, while the other one is backtracking your every move, as well as Matisse's that night. Additionally, both are doing thorough checks on Sullivan and her whereabouts ever since she hit town. You see what I'm getting at, Lincoln? No stone will go unturned on my watch. None!"

Lincoln sat back down. "I just want this shit to be over. It's not right, man! It's not right."

"Things are rarely right, Lincoln," Andy said, as he loosened the lid from the bottle of water he was holding.

"Just earn your money on this one, Andy. Get me off. I can't do any prison time, and that's on the real real, dog."

Andy looked a bit puzzled. "The 'real real, dog'? Okay. Anyway, let's get back to work. Matisse, I'm glad you're here. I have a few more questions for you."

"Oh?"

"Yes, just a couple."

Joining them in the huddle, I sat down. "Fire away. Wait, before we get started, you're never going to guess who I just ran into at the barber shop."

"Who?" Lincoln asked.

"Dallas Smith."

"Really," Andy responded, smiling. "Did he look like he was ready to have his ass handed to him?"

"Just the opposite. He seems to be pretty full of himself. He mentioned some overwhelming evidence they have against Lincoln that's going to cinch the case for them."

Andy stood. His smile disappeared. "He's bluffing. They don't have jack! You hear me? Jack! You know what they have at this point? Lincoln's semen. That's it."

"Andy's right, Matisse," added Angela. "If they had something more concrete, Lincoln would be sitting in a jail cell right about now." She looked at Lincoln. "Don't worry, we're going to get you out of this mess."

"So I keep hearing," Lincoln said in a disbelieving tone. He crossed his arms tightly against his body like he was a stern coach who didn't take any crap, the kind that we all had at one point or another. The only thing missing was a whistle dangling about from his mouth and a red baseball cap with white lettering.

"Since you were the first one there, Matisse, did the scene look like it had been tampered with at all?"

"To tell you the truth, Andy, I wouldn't know the difference between a scene that had been tampered with from one that hadn't. Plus, I was freaked out. It's not everyday you find your lover lying dead in a pool of blood. Why do you ask?"

Andy took a large swig from his bottle of water, making a gulping sound as he swallowed. "Clearly someone is trying to frame Lincoln. That's not news. We already know that. But we often don't know our own enemies. Matisse, you've worked closely with Lincoln for many years."

"Right," I said, wondering what he was getting at.

"Who are his enemies? Who do you know that just can't stand Lincoln?"

"I've seen Lincoln piss off a lot of women throughout the years. But it's hard to say, Andy. That's kind of a loaded question because Lincoln's a public figure. Who knows who doesn't like him? Yes, it's true that he's immensely popular, but I'm sure there are people out there who don't like him."

Angela interrupted. "That's a good point, Matisse, but whoever is framing Lincoln knows him and has been in direct contact with him."

"How can you be so sure?" I asked.

"This isn't our first dance."

36

ERICA'S ICE CRACKED

WE worked from Lincoln's house for another two to three hours before knocking off. I was curious to see what Tom and Big Jay were going to come up with, if anything at all, regarding Hunter. And, even though she was completely out of my system, I wondered what other messed-up things Sullivan had done since reappearing back in the ATL.

On my drive home, many thoughts ran through my head. It was the holidays and I had a huge pile of shit on my plate. My personal life was a mess, thanks to Sullivan. And my professional life was in jeopardy, thanks to Sullivan as well. If Lincoln got convicted, my bottom line would be seriously affected. He was my cash cow. And in the midst of all of this, I had a bachelor party to throw, not to mention I hadn't done a lick of shopping.

However, for some reason I was feeling extremely bold. Thoughts of Erica permeated my head. I don't know what came over me, but at that moment, with the soothing sounds of Luther filling my car, I felt as though I had drunk man's confidence. I normally wasn't that aggressive, but I knew what was forthcoming.

I began dialing digits that used to be second-nature to me. Surprisingly, it was like riding a bike. I didn't have to refer to the stored numbers in my phone. Erica's number, it appeared, was in my head for life.

She picked up on the fourth ring. I was about to hang up, but grew a third testicle and manned up.

"Hello," she said, sounding like the Nubian princess I remembered her to be. Only this time I was picturing her with a halo around her head.

"Erica." At this point I felt like I was in a sauna. I could feel the beads of sweat on my forehead.

"Yes."

"It's Matisse." There was a long, uncomfortable pause. As I began to ask how she was doing, I heard a click and then complete silence before I could complete the sentence. By this time I was already home. I had pulled my car into the garage and was sitting in the dark. *I guess I deserved that*, I thought.

Now I really had a dilemma on my hands. *Should I call her back or just forget the scatterbrained idea entirely?* I wondered as I climbed out of my car and made my way into the house. Once inside, I headed straight to the bar, where I quickly poured a large Stoli on the rocks before plopping down on my couch. I didn't even bother turning on the television, which was rare for me. I was exhausted, both mentally and physically, and it probably showed in my appearance.

I reached for the phone and slowly entered Erica's digits again, cringing after pressing each number. At the very moment I hit "send," I felt like I was falling off of a cliff.

Erica picked up after the first ring, without bothering to say hello. "What do you want, Matisse?" She sounded irritated. *So much for the halo,* I thought.

Still sitting on the couch, I straightened. "You've been on my mind lately, Erica, and I just wanted to call and say hello and see how you're doing…."

Before I could say another word, Erica interrupted with, "I'll consider this your 'hello' and I'm doing fine, Matisse. Now goodbye."

"Wait!" I stood. "Erica, hold on!"

It was too late. She hung up on me again as I thought, *Damn, I should have sent her a text*. I certainly didn't anticipate such treatment from Erica, though I deserved every last bit of it. Had Erica changed? The Erica I knew was sweet as apple pie. In fact, I don't even recall a time when I ever saw her mad, except for the day she walked out on me. Whatever the case, I clearly wasn't on top of her favorite persons list. I desperately needed and, perhaps more importantly, wanted that to change. After all, I had had an epiphany. It was all crystal clear. Erica was the one. I let her get away, amidst a bogus set of circumstances where I thought the grass was greener. I undoubtedly was dead wrong. And now I was determined to get her back.

I took a big gulp of my drink, leaving only ice cubes in the glass before immediately dialing Erica's number a third time.

"What?"

"Look, Erica, will you just hear me out for a moment? Please?"

"Why should I, Matisse? I couldn't care less about anything you have to say. You have a lot of nerve."

"You're right, this is nervy of me. First off, I'm sorry…."

Erica interrupted with, "Tell me something I don't know."

"Okay, I deserve that. I regret how that whole thing went down. It was huge mistake on my part. I wish I could have that moment in time back because I surely would have handled it differently. I was the biggest fool to ever let you go and I can't say 'sorry' enough."

"Is this where I'm supposed to tell you, 'It's okay, we all make mistakes' or something like that? Well, it's not okay. You hurt me, Matisse. You hurt me badly. I don't trust men anymore because you all lie and play with our feelings and emotions."

"I messed up, Erica. What can I say? I messed up."

"You know what, Matisse, you did mess up." Her voice cracked. "I loved you and I was good to you."

"I know you were. And I loved you too."

"You loved me, but you just couldn't say the words, huh?"

"That was the biggest mistake of my life, Erica. Honestly."

"So, what do you want, Matisse? Is that all you want? For me to know how sorry you are and how you made a big mistake?

It doesn't work that way. I resent you calling out of the blue, saying I'm sorry about this and I'm sorry about that, and thinking everything is all right again. Well, it's not."

"Let me take you out to dinner, Erica." While I waited for her response, I braced myself. Something told me it wasn't going to be pretty.

"Dinner! Did you say dinner, Matisse?" My ear was ringing from how loud she screamed.

"Yeah, dinner."

"Matisse, let's get one thing straight. There won't be any dinners between us. There won't be any lunches shared and there certainly won't be any breakfast meetings, either. You made it abundantly clear that you wanted nothing to do with me that day I asked if you loved me. When you couldn't say 'yes,' that said it all."

Before I responded, I paused to let her words marinate for a moment. *Why couldn't she just get over it?* I thought. *I messed up, but now I'm back. And I want her back. Get over it!* But she was right. It doesn't work like that. It's not that simple. It was obvious that she suffered greatly because of my actions, or lack thereof. And I was quickly finding out that it was now my turn to suffer. If not on my own, Erica most certainly was going to make sure of it. However I was going to respond, I knew I had to be tactful.

"Erica," I slowly started. "I know I can say 'I'm sorry' until I'm blue in the face, and it probably wouldn't matter one bit to you. But, you have to crawl before you can walk. At this point, that's all I can say. I'm sorry. I messed up. Like I said, I wish I could have that moment in time back because I would have handled it differently, that's for sure."

"Well, let's just leave it at that, Matisse. You're sorry and you realize you messed up. Fine. Are you finished? Because, like I said, dinner or any other meeting between us will never happen. Okay?"

I started to try to convince her otherwise, but held off. Though her response to me was a chilly one and something I hadn't fully anticipated, I had broken the seal nevertheless. The ice was cracked. I was confident in my abilities to soften her over time.

Though I wasn't proud of it, my womanizing ways over the years rarely failed me when it came time to chase. Chasing was where most of the fun lay. She didn't know it yet, but I was about to woo her with all of my skills to the point where she was going to be right where she belonged: back with me.

37

A PLAN FOR LINCOLN'S ESCAPE

I woke up the next morning feeling rejuvenated and high on life, despite my horrendous phone conversation with Erica. For some reason, I looked at my glass as being half-full. At least we were in touch. Granted, she hated me, but we were in contact. And I was within striking distance.

I blew off my morning workout, showered quickly and made my way over to Lincoln's place to see how that was progressing.

The same zoo of reporters huddled outside the gates of Lincoln's compound. The same security guards manned his property, only this time, instead of stopping me and checking everything but my dental records, the guard at the foot of Lincoln's driveway said, "Hello, Mr. Spencer," and personally walked me into the house.

Once inside, the scene was déjà vu. I found Lincoln surrounded by Andy and his legal team. Big Jay and Tom were also in attendance. I sat down beside them and listened in. None of them acknowledged me, which I viewed as a good thing because I wasn't going to be around much in the following days. Hell, they didn't need me. Andy had everything under control.

"What have you guys come up with?" Andy asked, looking in Tom and Big Jay's direction.

Big Jay cleared his throat. "In tailing Hunter; she drives by Sullivan's house twice a day and slows down upon arrival. At this point, we don't know why, but there's definitely something there."

"Interesting," Andy responded. "Stay on top of that one. Something's bound to give soon regarding the lovely Hunter. Anything else?"

"Yeah, there's one other thing."

"Shoot," Andy said. He seemed to be in an upbeat mood.

"She met this guy for breakfast this morning," Tom stated. His face harbored an uncertain look.

"And, so? She's allowed to meet men for breakfast. Spit it out, Tom." Andy had a slight scowl.

"The guy looked familiar."

Andy stood. "Did he look familiar to you too, Big Jay?"

"Extremely. We've been wracking our brains ever since."

"How'd the pictures turn out?" Andy asked.

"They didn't," Tom responded hesitantly.

"Wait, what?" Andy glared at Tom and Big Jay, waiting for a response.

"We couldn't get a clear shot," Big Jay explained, "due to the angle and poor lighting."

"That's horseshit, guys," Andy said, raising his voice. "You mean to tell me he looked extremely familiar, yet you couldn't get a clear shot? We're going to have to do better than that. I don't think I need to tell you guys, figure it out. Our man here, Lincoln Dix's future is on the line." Andy sat back down and quickly jotted down some notes.

I looked over at Lincoln and our eyes met. His eyes rolled while his mouth smirked. I motioned with my eyes for him to meet me in the kitchen. Lincoln stood, made his way into the kitchen and I followed. "Excuse us."

Because the kitchen wasn't too far from where the group was meeting, we kept our voices low.

"You doing alright?" I asked.

"Man, for a guy who's as smart as you, Matisse, sometimes I wonder what in the hell is going through your mind."

"My bad. You're right. Let me rephrase that. How you holding up?"

"Thank you! That's better, man. At least have a little empathy for me. Damn!" Lincoln reached into the refrigerator, pulled out two beers and handed me one. "Here."

"Isn't it a little early to be drinking, Lincoln?"

Lincoln reached for a bottle opener, popped the top off and took a big swig of the ice-cold Corona Extra. "Awww! Nothing taste better than an ice-cold brew, bruh! Is it still morning?"

"Yeah, it's still morning," I said as I placed my unopened bottle of Corona on the counter.

"Since all of this nonsense began, Matisse, I've completely lost track of time as well as days of the month. It's the last thing on my mind. I'm going through serious stuff here, so if I want to crack open a brew in the morning, then so be it. And I need you to have one with me. All of this mumbo-jumbo that's going on in the next room is giving me the biggest headache. What I need right now is to get my mind off of the horrendous future I may be facing. You see what I'm saying, Matisse? I just want to share a brew or two with a friend. You know, take a break from the action and escape."

"Say no more, Lincoln." I cracked open my beer and took a seat on one of the barstools next to Lincoln. "Cheers."

"Thanks, man."

"How's the rehab coming along?"

"I haven't been able to concentrate on it at all. Luckily I had that ice rink built in the backyard. I'm gonna strap on the skates today and get a little work in. I should probably do it more often because even when I was a kid and had various personal problems, that was the only time those problems completely went away."

"That's funny, I hear that from a lot of athletes. I guess it's the time when you all are the happiest. It's your love and passion."

"Exactly." Lincoln upended the beer, sucking at the bottle until it was bone-dry. He stood and returned to the refrigerator. With the door cracked half open, he reached for two more beers and looked back at me. "You ready for another?"

I took a big gulp of mine, which was only half-full at the

time. "Yeah, bring it on."

"My man!" Lincoln responded. He shut the refrigerator
door and returned to his seat alongside of me. "So, how's your boy's
bachelor party coming along? Isn't that supposed to jump off in the
next day or two?"

"It's coming. Actually, I think we're ready to go."

"When's that gonna pop off?"

"Day after tomorrow. One of my football player clients owns
a great house on Lake Lanier. He also has a huge boat there. So,
we're going to make a weekend out of it. You know the drill—just
a bunch of guys hanging out, smoking cigars, knocking back some
cocktails while reaping the benefits of an occasional lap dance."

"Sounds like a great time."

"Yeah, it should be. Miles and I go back a long time. Hey,
now that I think about it, why don't you come? You're out on bail
and the only stipulation is that you don't flee the country."

Lincoln took another swig of his beer and pondered it for a
moment. "It sounds like a good-ass time, pimp, but I don't know."

"What do you have to lose? You said it yourself, you need
to get your mind off all this shit. It's only for the weekend. Andy and
his team can call us if they have any questions."

"I don't know, Matisse." Lincoln's apprehension was
apparent through his voice and facial expression. "Everything I do is
monitored. Hell, I might as well be in jail. I'm already a prisoner in
my own home. How do you plan on getting me out without anyone
knowing I've left the house?"

I let out a big laugh. "Is that what you're worried about?
Come on, Lincoln, how long have you known me?"

"A long time."

"Exactly! You should know by now how I do it. You have
this big-ass mansion, complete with a ten-car garage. Just off the
top of my head, here's how we'll do it. We'll bring in ten cars, all
heavily tented. You and I will be in one of those cars and when we
get outside the gates, each car will go in a different direction."

Lincoln considered it for a moment. "It could work."

I used that same moment to think about it further. But the

more I thought about it, the more skeptical of the plan I became. "How about this one, Lincoln. Instead of the ten cars pulling out of the garage at the same time, I think we're better off keeping it simple. The windows in my car are tinted to where no one can see inside. I've come and gone a few times and no one outside of security has stopped me. We'll lay you down flat in the back and I'll just drive out like I normally do. No one, especially those clueless media types, will catch on."

Lincoln polished off his second Corona, and then stood over me flashing a huge smile. "Now that sounds like a plan. Hell, yeah! Count me in. Shit, I haven't had any fun in a long time. Wait, but what about your boys?"

"What about them?"

"Are they gonna be sweating me? You know, asking all kinds of questions about the case and shit?"

"Man, please, none of those cats will even be thinking about your trifling, sorry ass. Did I fail to tell you that this is going to be a weekend of good food, good drink, good cigars and a lot of scantily-clad women doing their thing?"

"Right, right, my bad, Matisse. Shit, I feel better already. But why do I gotta be all of that?"

"What?"

"Trifling, sorry ass!"

"Because your ass is trifling and sorry."

"Whatever, bruh. But, really, Matisse, thanks, man."

"For what?"

"Aw, you know, including me."

"Please! It's no biggie. I'm glad you're on board. It's going to be a lot of fun."

"No, really, thanks. It means a lot."

38

PLAN "ERICA"
IN FULL EFFECT

WHEN I left Lincoln's place, I felt good about the fact that things were finally starting to come together regarding Miles's bachelor party, as well as Lincoln's case. Andy clearly had everything under control. With that said, my mind and attention immediately drifted back to Erica.

I wasn't by any means a glutton for punishment. But I knew that I had a few more at-bats left with Erica, and I damn sure was going to use all of my swings. What I didn't know was how to go about them. She seemed more than adamant about not having anything else to do with me ever again. Unfortunately for her, I'd been in that situation a time or two before, and prevailed each time. I know it sounded more and more like a game and to a certain extent it was. However, there was something inside of me that insisted she was the one. I'd made a terrible mistake the first time around with Erica and I was now determined to right that wrong. Sure, I could have taken what she said about leaving her alone at face value and walked away altogether, but I wasn't going to make it that easy for her. I also felt I owed it to myself and to Erica to try to get us back together. After all, in my mind we were soul-mates. Too bad it took so long for my dumb-ass to figure it out.

Still in my car on the way to my office, I picked up the phone and dialed Miles's number.

"What's up? Everything in place for tomorrow?" Miles asked. I could tell he was excited.

"Yeah, man, everything's in place. The question is, are you ready? It's the beginning of a lot of things, and the end to other things, if you know what I mean."

"Oh, I'm ready, Matisse. And, I know exactly what you mean. But like I said, and we've talked about it before, I'm ready."

"Well, good. It should be a lot of fun."

"I'm banking on it, Matisse. This is it for me, man. But no worries, I know you'll send me off properly."

"For sure! Hey, I hope you don't mind, but I invited Lincoln. Considering all that's going on right now with him I figured he could use a timeout to have a little fun."

"That's cool. By the way, what's going on with that?"

"He's out on bail right now. I told you I hired Andy Weinberg to represent him, right?"

"Yeah, but it seems strange for them to let him out on bail in a murder case. Doesn't it?"

I pulled into the parking garage below my office and sat there with the car running while I continued my conversation with Miles. It was too cold out to sit there without the car running. The warmth from the heater was doing me right.

"Well, all that says to me, and by no means am I an expert on the situation, is that they don't have much of a case."

"I hope for your sake and his, you're right."

"You know!" I responded with a slight chuckle.

"I thought that guy kind of got on your nerves, Matisse."

"Well, yeah, he does. I mean, he's arrogant, cocky and downright rude at times. But at the end of the day, he's still my number one client who puts a shit-load of money into my pockets. Plus, I wouldn't wish being wrongly accused of murder on anyone. I have to have a little compassion for the guy, Miles."

"Yeah, I guess. But what makes you so sure he didn't do it? Didn't they find his semen inside of her?"

"Well, damn, does that mean he killed her? What possible reason would Lincoln Dix have to kill Sullivan? I mean, come on! He's the top hockey player, let alone, professional athlete, in the world. He gets more ass than all of the toilet seats this city has to offer. I just don't see it, Miles." I turned my car off and slowly climbed out.

"Stranger things have happened, Matisse. You never know."

"True, but I'd bet my life on this one."

"Okay," Miles said. There was something uneasy about the way Miles said "okay." It was like he knew something I didn't. Like he had the inside track on certain information regarding the case, which proved Lincoln in fact did commit the crime. I wanted to press him about it, but that wasn't the reason why I'd called him in the first place. Plus I knew he was probably up to his old tricks of being nosey, instigating and playing devil's advocate.

"On another front, which is really why I called you, Miles, how do you suggest I go about getting back in Erica's good graces? She clearly doesn't want to have anything to do with me, but you know as well as I do that I've been in tighter situations regarding women and have come out on top. Hold that thought. I just got on the elevator and I'll probably lose you. I'll call you in a minute when I get to my office."

"Bet," Miles responded before hanging up the phone.

The moment I walked into my office and took one look at Gail, who was wearing a phone headset, I knew it was going to be a busy day. I looked down at the switchboard and witnessed nothing but red lights. I stood in front of Gail with my arms spread apart and whispered, "What's up?"

"Sir, I'm going to have to put you on hold," Gail said. She took off her headset. "This is insane, Matisse!"

"What in the hell is going on?"

"What else? Lincoln Dix!"

"Well, are you referring the calls to Andy's people?"

"Matisse, I'm not an idiot. Of course I am referring the calls over to them, but that still doesn't stop every Tom, Dick and Harry from calling."

"Who all's calling?"

"Let's see. There's every media outlet known to mankind. Then there's his enormous fan base, which, by the way, seems to consist primarily of women, both extremely young and old."

"Oh, so you know ages from listening to voices over the phone now, huh?"

"Yes, Matisse, and that's not the point right now. The point is it's crazy and I don't get paid enough for this abuse."

"Hire a couple of temps, Gail, to help with the phones. I'll be in my office if you need me. Oh, and don't patch any of those calls to me, either. I need a little breather from all of that mess."

"That's just great, Matisse. Glad to see you're overly concerned about your client."

I ignored Gail's last comment and made my way into my office. Once I settled into my chair, I immediately dialed Miles's number.

"What up?" Miles asked. I could tell he was in his car. The music was blaring.

"Why don't you try turning that shit down? What is that anyway?"

"You know how I like my old-school joint. "Rappers Delight"! Sugar Hill Gang, Matisse. Come on! You should know this. Last I checked we came up together."

"I wasn't sure because it was so loud. Anyway, getting back to Erica…."

"Oh yeah, Erica," Miles said, cutting me off.

"Yeah, Erica. How would you proceed?"

"Before I give out free advice, let me ask you this, Matisse."

"What, man." I reclined in my chair while resting my feet on my desk.

"Are you for real this time? Let's face it, you put her through the ringer last time. She was a great girl."

"Yeah, I'm for real, Miles. What kind of shit is that? You know me."

"That's the problem. I do know you and, quite frankly, that's been your M.O. with women, with the exception of Sullivan."

"What are you talking about, Miles?"

"I'm talking about your seemingly short attention span when it comes to women. You've always had to peek around the corner or see what's over the horizon. Since I've known you, you've had some real winners behind door one, but it's never stopped you from seeing what's behind door two."

I was silent for a moment, chewing on what Miles had just said. I removed my feet from the desk and positioned my chair in the upright position. "You're absolutely right, Miles. It's a conclusion I came to a few nights ago, but it kind of stings hearing it from someone else. You got me on that one. The answer to your question is, yes, I'm for real. My mind has never been clearer, and I've never felt such affirmation and reassurance."

"In that case, I'd probably start off with the traditional roses-to-the-job tactic. Here's the kicker, though. Does she still live in the same place?"

"As far as I know."

"Apartment or house?"

"Apartment."

"Good. That's good. Go over to her complex and see if they'll let you into her place."

"Come on, Miles, you know they aren't going to let me in there."

"Matisse, I know I don't have to tell you about the power of a few Benjamins. Line their pockets with a few C-notes. She's worth it, right?"

"Yeah, she is. But why am I going into her place?"

"There's one thing that rarely changes with women, and that is their love of receiving flowers. Have a flower truck follow you in and put rose petals all over the floor and have bouquets of flowers all over the place in every room. Place a large card on her refrigerator that reads, *Have dinner with me.* Now, you know it's going to be costly, right? But, like you said, she's worth it, right?"

I rose to my feet, smiling from ear to ear. "That sounds like a good starting point, Miles. And she is worth it."

"Try it out, Matisse," Miles said before answering what I

presumed to be a second cell phone. His tone automatically changed as he spoke to the person on the other end of the line. He sounded angry and irritated. "I can't talk right now. I'll call you back later."

"You rocking two cell phones these days?"

"Naw, I'm at home. That was my home phone."

"Funny, I thought I was one of the only people who still used home phones. Shelby lets you get away talking to her like that?"

Miles chuckled, "Please! That wasn't Shelby."

"No? Oh, I just automatically assumed. After all, who else would be calling your sorry ass these days?" I waited for him to elaborate, but not another word regarding that particular call emanated from Miles's mouth. Yeah, he was my boy and all, but I wasn't about to get into his business.

"Getting back to Erica, just try it out, Matisse. It's a guaranteed panty-dropper."

"It's already in motion, bruh. Wait a minute." My smile quickly disappeared. "I've seen that exact scene in a few movies lately."

"So!" Miles said, like I was crazy.

"So?"

"Yeah! So what."

"I'm trying to be original and creative, Miles. You know how it goes."

"Matisse, it goes like this. Just do it. That shit works. I don't care how many movies you've seen it in. Not only will she be going to dinner with you, she'll be footing the bill, giving you a smoker before the first drink has been ordered and calling you Daddy in her birthday suit by the end of the night. Trust me!"

"All right, Miles, but you heard it here first. It seems corny and played."

"Look, do you want Erica back or what?"

"Yeah, it goes without saying."

"Is she ringing your phone off the hook right now? Is she sending you little cute texts?"

Just as I started to respond to what Miles had asked, he cut me off before I could get the first word out.

"That's what I thought, player! Look, Matisse, you could be right. It may not be the most original approach at the moment. Like you, I've seen that shit a time or two as of late in the movies. At the very least it's a pleasant ice-breaker that should open up the lines of communication for you all. Right now, you're outside the door trying desperately to get in. Trust me, this is going to get you in."

"All right, I'm going to trust you. We'll do it your way."

"My man," Miles responded. "On the strength, glad you know who to trust."

"Whatever. Shit better work," I said before hanging up the phone.

39

BABY STEPS

AFTER talking to Miles on the phone, I was a bit antsy. I knew I wasn't going to get an ounce of work done for the rest of the day. I tried to calm my nerves by sprawling out behind my desk. I leaned back in my chair with my hands folded behind my head and my feet on the desk. It didn't help, nor did turning on the television.

How to proceed with Erica took up every bit of space in my head. I was swimming in a sea of Erica. I wasn't thinking about Lincoln. I wasn't thinking about Miles's bachelor party. And I surely wasn't thinking about Sullivan. It was all Erica. However, I was still indecisive about how I would make my next contact with her. How would I strike next? Or, based on my most recent encounter with her, strike-out next? She obviously was a tough cookie, and I'm a fairly bright guy. I knew the process wasn't going to be turn-key. And I certainly knew that there wasn't a whole lot I could do at this point to get her back. My brightest smile wouldn't work. My conversational skills would get the infamous Heisman. You know how women do it when they don't want to hear what brothers are saying. We get that all-too-familiar hand in the face. And most of the time we're left saying something like, "But, baby." Yeah, I was about to take another swing, but I knew a big whiff at the plate was probably waiting. I hurt that girl. Erica was a nice girl and I hurt her with my selfishness and self-indulgence.

Sure, I had told Miles that I would take his advice and do it his way, but I just wasn't altogether convinced that it was the best way to go about it. One thing was for certain: I didn't have the benefit of time on my side due to Miles's bachelor party, which was set to take place the day after next.

Finally it came to me. I likened it to a game plan, no matter the sport. Hitters usually struck out when they went to the plate swinging for a home run. Boxers usually got knocked out when they continuously went for the knockout punch. Basketball teams that lived by the three usually died by the three, and in football, the bomb rarely worked on the first play of the game.

It's all about taking it slow and steady, and, at times, setting up your opponent for the big play. Hitters normally fared better at the plate when they went up there looking to make good contact with the ball. Boxers set their opponents up with a series of jabs before they went for the knockout punch. Basketball teams that mixed in the high-percentage shots around the hoop with the low-percentage three-point shots were normally more successful than the teams that relied solely on the three. And most football teams usually spent a certain amount of time setting up the cornerbacks and safeties with a few down-and-out or down-and-in patterns before they threw for six with the down, out and up.

Well, that was my plan with Erica. I knew I had to come up big. I also knew that my work was cut out for me, and I didn't want to scare her away. I had already messed things up with her to the point where she didn't want to have anything else to do with me, so I thought it was best to take baby steps before I walked.

The lights on my phone kept blinking. It was Gail's extension, but I continued to ignore her. I kept brainstorming where Erica was concerned. My private life was in dire straits and needed immediate attention.

I remembered how Erica had a sweet tooth. She was particularly fond of gummy bears, chocolate and New York-style cheesecake with cherries on top.

I removed my feet from the desk and sat up straight before hitting the speakerphone.

"Oh, now you want to respond to my twenty calls. What's going on, Matisse?"

"I need you to come in here for a minute, Gail," I said, completely ignoring her question.

She let out a big sigh. "I'm on my way."

Gail walked in seconds later.

"Shut the door and have a seat."

"Is this where you fire me?" Her body language said it all. She wasn't worried one bit. In usual Gail-fashion, she was trying to be funny and sarcastic. I continued to ignore her.

"All right, here's what I need you to do." I stood. The desk still separated us. "I need you to find a place that sells gummy bears. I think there's a place in Lennox Mall."

"What?" Gail interrupted. "That's not in my job description, Matisse."

"Call up our courier service and have them do it."

"What's all of this about? Do you know how busy we are in here, on top of the mess Lincoln has gotten himself into?"

I pressed my index finger up against my puckered lips. I know no one likes to be shushed, but Gail had had it coming for a long time. Her eyes rolled as she mumbled something under her breath.

"I also need a box of Godiva chocolates and a slice of New York-style cheesecake with cherries on top. There's a Godiva place at Lennox as well. They can swing by the Cheesecake Factory for the cheesecake. Additionally, I need heart-shaped balloons and a greeting card. Once they get all of those things, have them come back here so I can sign the card, then I'll tell them where it can be delivered. Cool?"

"You're the boss, Matisse," Gail responded, sounding irritated. "I'm not even going to ask what this is all about, but I'm assuming you'll need some type of basket to place all of the items in. Am I right?"

I smiled. "Like always, Gail, yes, you are."

Gail flashed a crooked smile back at me before she stood and made her way out of my office. I felt good. It was like the smoke had finally cleared. *Baby steps*, I kept thinking.

I knew I had a good hour or so before the courier service would return with the goods. I grabbed the remote and turned on the television. Then I walked over to the couch and plopped down on it, fully stretched out with my feet dangling over the edge. Every station ran updates on Lincoln's case, mixed in with occasional sound bites from Dallas. No responses came out of our camp, which I viewed as a good thing. In my book, the cats who normally ran their mouths the most were usually the ones left holding the bag with dumb-ass looks on their faces and not knowing what to say next. It prompted me, however, to give Andy a call.

Andy answered in his usual upbeat fashion. "How goes it, Matisse?"

"Right back at you, Andy. How's everything going?"

"We're doing fine. Dallas Smith is something else, isn't he?"

"Yeah, I just saw him on television a second ago," I said, sitting upright on the couch.

"We've been seeing way too much of him today. He sure likes the camera. He really genuinely thinks he's going to win this case. I laugh every time I see him. With that said, Matisse, and keeping the holidays in mind, I sent him a fruit basket and a nice little greeting card."

"Yeah, what'd it say?"

Andy let out a big laugh. "It said, 'Good luck, but not in this lifetime. See you in court.'"

"That's funny." I tried to seem humored by producing a slight chuckle, but to no avail. Truth be told, though Andy was at the top of his profession, he was as bad as Dallas—full of himself! "So, everything is going as planned?"

"Of course it is, Matisse. Unless they can come up with better, more concrete evidence, this is going to be a complete cakewalk."

"How do you think Lincoln's holding up?"

"Honestly, Matisse, he seems to be doing alright. I've seen guys really crack under pressure like Lincoln is experiencing. He's obviously a tough-minded guy."

"Yeah, that Lincoln is a tough cat. I don't think I've said anything to you about this, but I'm hosting one of my buddies' bachelor party day after next. I hope you don't mind, but I invited Lincoln to come along with me to the party."

"Why would I mind? It sounds like a good idea. It could do Lincoln some good to get out a little bit more. It's always nice to be around your peers. You know you're going to have to come up with some type of escape route because we all know that the media is swarming."

I stood and made my way back over to my desk. "Good, then it's settled. And, yeah, we do have a seemingly good escape route that only I know about right now."

"I'm not even going to ask, just as long as one is in place."

"Yep, we're good to go in that area. And just so you know, the bachelor party is going to take place about an hour outside of Atlanta. Is that a problem?"

"Not at all," Andy responded. "The only stipulation at the moment regarding Lincoln is that he doesn't leave the country.

"On another front, Matisse, my guys are still following Hunter. She's definitely up to something and she keeps meeting that same guy at different places all around town for five and ten minutes at a time. My guys are close to coming up with some hard info that could help Lincoln's case. I don't expect anything to happen regarding the case over the next few days, so I'll just talk to you when you get back into town. By then, we should have some solid answers. In any event, have a good time. I'm in Lincoln's house as we speak, but he's been pretty scarce. So, if I don't see him between now and then, tell him I said to keep his head up. It's going to be all right."

"Will do, Andy," I said before hanging up the phone.

Gail walked into my office seconds later and, like always, didn't bother knocking. "Here you go boss."

She placed a basket on my desk with four oversized heart-shaped balloons attached to it. I stood over the basket, checking it for inventory. Sure enough, everything was there. The gummy bears, Godiva chocolates and New York Cheesecake with cherries on top

were strategically nestled in the basket amidst colored paper. I took
the greeting card from Gail and sat back down in my chair to sign
it. As the words crystallized in my mind, I could feel a set of eyes
burning a hole in my head.

"Gail," I said, looking up at her, "why don't you come back
in about five minutes?"

Gail let out one of her infamous sighs, complete with the
rolling of her eyes, "Oh, here we go, Matisse! Just hurry up and
profess your love for the girl so I can get it delivered to her before
the day's over. How 'bout that?"

I put my pen down and leaned back in my chair. "If you want
to continue working here, you'll leave my office now and come back
in about five minutes. How about that!"

"Works for me," Gail responded as she turned and quickly
made herself a memory.

I started to do exactly what Gail had said—profess my
love for her, but I was quickly reminded that baby steps were more
appropriate and more effective. I was on a mission to perfect the
"crawl before walking" theory. My pen hit the paper and when it was
all said and done, I had a message that read:

> *Erica,*
> *I hope this basket and card find you well.*
> *In life, we seldom get second chances. Those of us who are*
> *fortunate enough to get second shots are extremely lucky. I am no*
> *fool. If I ever had another shot with you, I'd hold on for dear life.*
> *Unfortunately, people tend to take people for granted. I*
> *did with you, and I'm now paying the price. Actions like that are*
> *unacceptable.*
> *I'm sorry for taking you for granted, and I'm sorry for*
> *hurting you.*
> *Best wishes,*
> *Matisse*

It was kind of soft and mushy, but heartfelt and real.
Gail re-entered my office.

"You ready, Romeo?"

"Here." I handed her a piece of paper with Erica's information on it. "This is her name and work address. Tell the courier service to put a rush on it. All right?"

"Yeah, Matisse, I got you. Put a rush on it. She'll have it in no time." Gail grabbed the basket, turned and walked toward the door. Just before she reached it, she turned back around and said, "For the record, Matisse, good job. I always liked Erica the most!"

I smiled and replied, "Thanks."

As soon as Gail shut the door behind her, I made my way into the bathroom. My body temperature had risen, I guess due to the anxiety I was experiencing. I can't lie, my being nervous probably had a lot to do with it as well. In any event, my palms were sweaty and the back of my shirt was damp. Fortunately, I had gotten into a habit of keeping several sets of extra clothes around, which enabled me to take showers when needed. This was definitely one of those times.

As the lukewarm water made its way down my body, I stood wondering if I did the right thing or not. Would the basket and card just infuriate Erica even further? Or would it soften her, creating a slight opening for me? I just didn't know. What I did know, though, was that all of the wondering and worrying I was doing was creating a huge knot inside my stomach. At this point, it was completely out of my hands. There was nothing I could do but wait. I just had to hope it would be well received.

40

NICE TRY

I never heard back from Erica, but I knew she received the basket of goodies because I had Gail check to see if she signed for the package. Sure enough, she did. Naturally, I was disappointed. I was certain she'd immediately call or, better yet, race over to my office or house, depending on the time of day, to take me back with open arms. No such luck. As a result, I didn't get much sleep that night. In fact, I probably set the record for the most tosses and turns in an eight-hour timeframe.

I woke up in a bad mood. Most of it had to do with Erica not responding to my gesture, but I'm sure the fact that I had gotten only about two hours of sleep heavily contributed as well. Regardless, I was off my game.

I lay in bed about an hour longer than usual. I ran through different scenarios as to why Erica chose not to respond, each time coming to the same conclusion. Hell, I wouldn't respond to my trifling ass, either. Not only did I hurt her, I dogged her too. At the very least I could have checked in from time to time so see how she was doing. Not me, though. After she walked out, life went on at the same clip and I rarely thought about her. It's amazing how we arrive at various moments of clarity. Unfortunately, for most of us those moments usually come after traumatic experiences. I was determined to capitalize on my clearer-than-usual view. Erica and I belonged together. It was that simple. I just had to convince her of it.

When I finally climbed out of bed, the first thing I did was check my phone messages, both work and cell, as well as emails. Nothing. No traces whatsoever of Erica. Disappointed was an understatement.

I knew I couldn't spend too much time obsessing about it because I had to get ready for Miles's bachelor party. I was comforted to know that Tanner Gibson was going to be there. He was one of Miles's former NBA teammates. I figured at some point I could get him to talk to Lincoln. At the height of Tanner's career, he was accused of raping a woman. The evidence that supported him was overwhelming. Though he was found innocent, it had to have been a troubling experience for him. I hoped he could conjure up some words of wisdom for Lincoln.

While thinking about Lincoln, images of Hunter kept popping up. Why would she be keeping tabs on Sullivan's place? And whom was she constantly meeting? I started to give her a call, but quickly thought otherwise. Andy seemed to be on top of things, and I certainly didn't want to get in his way. I was certain his detectives, Tom and Big Jay, would put us on the right path.

When I opened the door to retrieve the morning paper, my eyes locked in on a note that was taped to the door. I grabbed it and took a seat at the kitchen table. It was from Erica. She wanted to meet for lunch. I had an ear-to-ear smile. She'd made my day, or morning, anyway.

It's amazing how quickly our emotions can change. I went from one end of the spectrum to the other in a matter of seconds. I was pumped.

If I was going to be meeting Erica for lunch, I wanted to make sure I was at my best. This called for a good workout at the health club. I threw on my workout gear and took off. On my way there, I called to make an appointment with the masseuse. I also wanted to make sure I spent ample time in the steam room to clear out my pores. Yeah, I was stoked. But never once did I stop to think about how ambiguous Erica's note was. All it said was to meet her at the Buckhead Diner for lunch, with her name attached to it.

Just as I pulled into the parking lot of the health club, my forever-ringing phone sounded. It was Lincoln.

"Matisse, this bachelor party tomorrow is a weekend thing, right?"

"Yeah, so pack appropriately, bruh," I said, climbing out of my car.

"You said there's a boat too, right?"

"Yeah, man. Everything. We'll probably take the boat out, but keep in mind that it is December. Pack warm."

"Right, right."

"You doing alright, Lincoln?"

"I'm cool. There is one thing, though."

"What's that?"

"Andy's starting to scare me."

"Why's that?" I hung up my clothes in my locker and sat down on one of the couches in the locker room.

"He seems to be a little too confident."

I laughed.

"Why you laughing? I'm serious."

"I know you are, Lincoln."

"Does he know something we don't? I mean, we all know I didn't do it. But he's running around with a constant smile on his face and keeps talking about having a boner every time he sees that fool, Dallas Smith, on television. Talk about a dickhead, too. That guy Dallas really has it in for me, huh?"

"Don't take it personally, Lincoln. With Dallas, these are his 15 minutes of fame. You're a high-profile athlete and this is his shot to make a name for himself." I picked up the paper and began thumbing through it. "As far as Andy goes, bruh, all I have to say is that he is good and you're paying a pretty penny for his services. So, let's just trust him."

"Yeah, but...."

I cut Lincoln off before he could get the third word out of his mouth. It was something that I rarely did, but I really wasn't trying to hear his over-privileged, pampered ass complain about Andy. After all, he was one good ally to have. Plus, I had bigger fish to fry. Erica was waiting. "Hey, I gotta go, man."

There was no denying it. Andy was a cocky cat. But I liked it. I liked the fact that he was on top of his game and reveled in it. I loved the fact that he popped a boner at the mere thought of winning a case. And I especially liked that he was on our team.

I worked out hard that morning. The steam and massage were icing on the cake. They were definite treats. I showered quickly and raced over to the Buckhead Diner to meet Erica.

I was on time when I arrived, but Erica looked to have been there several minutes earlier. She had already been seated and had drained a cup of coffee.

As soon as I sat down, she started in.

"First off, I wanted to thank you for the basket of goodies." She looked dead into my eyes without breaking a smile. "You haven't forgotten what I like. That's impressive."

"It was the least I could do," I responded, admiring her physical beauty. She was gorgeous.

"But, here's the thing, Matisse."

Uh oh, I thought as I looked on, *here it comes*. Sure enough, she delivered a blow that would have staggered Muhammad Ali. It was lethal.

"We can't suddenly start seeing each other again. It's not that easy."

Ease into this, I thought. *Baby steps. Take it slow.* "You're right, Erica. I owe you so much more."

"Damn right you do, Matisse! But you know what?"

"What's that?"

"That's neither here nor there. It doesn't even matter anymore. I'm not even interested in going there with you, Matisse. I'd have to be a complete fool." While her voice grew louder, it also cracked. Erica's eyes welled with tears.

As I listened to her strong, venomous words, I studied her for a moment, thinking, *Damn, it looks like I'm gonna have my work cut out for me with this one.* However, Erica's resistance towards me was refreshing. Had she taken me back with open arms upon receiving a cheesy basket full of fattening foods, I, unfortunately and almost certainly, would have taken her for granted again, citing the words "too easy" as the reason. No, this was good. Her resistance and nasty attitude towards me garnered instant respect. We all like a challenge, and I was no different. I likened it to a game of chess, and I certainly had a game plan. I viewed her emotion as a good thing. It said to me that deep down inside she still cared, but was doing everything in her power to move on. Of course I wasn't going to let that happen.

"Erica, do you know what this is really all about?"

"What, Matisse?"

"If I ever had another chance with you, I would jump at the first opportunity. But, I know I hurt you, and as a result I know you despise me. And those are things that are bothersome to me and things that I'll have to live with for the rest of my life. However, I wanted you to know that I know I messed up. You are a gem and I'll probably never come across a woman like you again. I just wanted you to know that I've had my moment of clarity where you are concerned. And I'm sorry that it's a case of too-little, too-late."

A steady stream of tears rolled down Erica's face as she sat there not saying a word. *Gotcha!*, I thought. I figured I had delivered a blow for which there would be no recovery. I got greedy and went for the game-winner, and reached for her hand, which rested on table. Erica pulled away and quickly stood.

"Don't frickin' touch me, Matisse!" That was about as nasty as it got with Erica regarding expletives. Frickin' was her version of the F-word, which, in my mind, was another stellar quality she possessed. "This was a bad idea."

"What was?" I asked, looking up at her.

"This! Meeting you for lunch. Look, from now on, just leave me alone, asshole!"

Erica turned and ran out of the restaurant and, yes, everyone stared at me. I looked like the abusive dickhead who had just been unnecessarily mean to his girl. I looked down at the ground beneath me to see if there was a hole I could crawl into. I was out of luck. The stares and whispers continued. I sat there and took it like a man. It eventually died, and I ended up eating a decent lunch, feeling somewhat ambivalent about what had just happened.

Though Erica had called me names and blew me off in a loud, rock-star, Hollywood fashion, I got the sense that deep down inside she still cared. How I came to that conclusion is beyond me. I guess it stemmed from my optimistic outlook on life, intertwined with some good old-fashioned cockiness, undoubtedly fueled by testosterone, which obviously was my downfall.

Unfortunately, I was one of those cats who thought I could mack any woman, regardless of the situation. But I also knew that my track record of holding onto women was horrible. Erica had already gone that route with me once, and it was pretty apparent that she was determined not to ever go there again. I was holding onto something my mom had told me years ago when faced with adversity: "Where there's a will, there's a way," she said. Words I hadn't forgotten, and never will. In fact, it was a motto I adopted and now lived by.

41

SAFELY SPRUNG

WHEN I finally mustered up the energy to sneak out of the Buckhead Diner, no doubt with my head under my tail, I spent the rest of the day running errands in a last-ditch effort to get ready for Miles's bachelor party.

At last the time had come and everything was in place to send Miles off properly. Even I was excited. It was also time to put Erica and Lincoln on the back burner. I was tired of putting energy into things I couldn't control. This was Miles's time.

As much as I wanted that to happen, there was one more thing I had to do regarding Lincoln. I had to safely and quietly spring him from his house—or, as he referred to it these days, jail—without anyone, mainly the press, knowing.

Scrapping the original plan with me as the driver, the one I now had in place was fairly simple. I arranged with Andy to have his driver park in one of Lincoln's many garages when they arrived at the house in the morning. When they left at night, Lincoln was to be placed on the floor while Andy and the others sat in their usual seats. Lincoln undoubtedly would have to experience a level of discomfort, but I guess that's sometimes the price you pay for being in the wrong place at the wrong time. Not to mention that he had no business waxing Sullivan's ass just hours after I had gone there. Real talk: in his defense, that was on her. She shouldn't have been such a freak. Regardless, though, Sullivan didn't deserve to die, and I know Lincoln didn't do it. It was an unfortunate situation no matter how you looked at it.

When the car drove past the press, the only people to be seen would be the ones who had been going in and out regularly over the past several days. The tinted windows on the car also helped. After the car dropped the others off at the hotel, Andy and Lincoln would continue on to my place, where the driver was instructed to park in my garage. Since the bus for Miles's bachelor party was going to pick everyone up at my place in the morning, Lincoln was going to stay the night.

Knowing that Andy would probably want to come in and talk shop when they arrived, I made arrangements for Chinese food from P.F Chang's to be delivered. For a chain restaurant, that stuff is out of control if you ask me. I love that place.

When Andy and Lincoln finally showed up, it was apparent to me that Lincoln was in a good mood. And Andy always seemed to be having a good day.

"Well, how'd it go? Any problems?" I asked while escorting them into the kitchen where white cartons containing the food were lined up buffet-style and ready to go.

"It went off without a hitch, Matisse," Andy replied. His eyes were focused on the food. "Smells good. Looks good, too. P.F. Chang's. I know it well."

Lincoln went straight to the refrigerator, grabbed a beer and then stood over the food before helping himself to it. "Yeah, I like me some Chang's too. Right on, Matisse."

"So everything was cool then, huh?" I asked, still wanting to hear about the getaway that I had designed, as simple as it was.

"Worked like a charm, baby!" Lincoln said in between bites. He hadn't bothered to sit down. "Isn't that right, Andy?"

"We drove by them like we always do, Matisse."

"Good. Yeah, that's good shit," I said as I copped a squat alongside Andy at the bar in the kitchen. My plate was full, as was Andy's. Lincoln continued to eat standing up.

"We still looking good as far as the case goes, Andy?"

"Like I said, Matisse, I'm walking around with a permanent boner. Winning makes my dick hard. There's no way we lose this case. Do you mind?" Andy pointed at the beer Lincoln was holding.

"No, not at all." I began walking towards the refrigerator.

Andy rose to his feet. "I'll get it, Matisse."

It was too late. My head was already inside of the refrigerator. "Here you go."

"Thanks." Andy popped the top off of it before sitting back down. "They don't have anything concrete. If they did, Lincoln would be sitting in a jail cell right now. But that's not to say that they can't come up with anything over the next couple of days."

"Am I still alright to go to the bachelor party tomorrow, Andy?"

"That's exactly where I want you to be, Lincoln. Have a good time. But be smart."

"Be smart?" Lincoln had a confused look on his face.

"Yeah, wrap it up."

"Oh, it's not that type of party, Andy," I insisted. "These are respectable women, just shaking some tits and ass. That's all."

"Oh, that's too bad, Matisse. Give me a call the next time you throw a bachelor party. I've been using the same service for years and, quite frankly, it keeps getting better. The women are in awesome shape and, as long as you have the money, anything goes." Andy laughed, "The last thing I want is a bachelor party with respectable women."

"I'll definitely do that, Andy."

"Have you guys lost your damn minds?" Lincoln put his plate down. Andy and I both looked up at him. "My life is on the line, and you guys are sitting up here talking about bachelor parties and tits and asses."

"You're the one who started off the conversation by asking Andy if it was okay if you could go."

"Yeah, one question, Matisse. All it required was a yes or no response, not the super-duper deluxe conversation on bachelor party hoes."

"I'll say it again, Lincoln,"—Andy stood and applied a

couple of assuring pats to Lincoln's back—"everything is going to be all right. This one's ours. Besides, did you do it? Don't even answer it. I'll answer it for you. No. With that said, Lincoln, I'm a firm believer in the law. Justice will prevail."

"I sure hope you're right."

"I am right. Trust me. Dallas Smith bit off more than he can chew this time. Well, Matisse, thanks for dinner. It was great, but I'm going to have to get back to the hotel and get some sleep." Andy pointed in Lincoln's direction. Their eyes locked. "I meant what I said. Have some fun and try to forget about this mess. Okay?"

Lincoln stalled his response, then hesitantly replied, "All right, baby. Oh, and sorry I overreacted a second ago."

"It's understandable, Lincoln. You're under a lot of pressure right now," Andy responded.

"Yeah, it's tough, bruh," I added.

The fact that Lincoln was back to ending his sentences with "baby" was a sure sign that he was slowly regaining his old form. As annoying as it was for me, it was good to hear him saying it again.

I walked Andy to the door.

"Make sure that guy has some fun this weekend, Matisse," he said, whispering so Lincoln couldn't hear.

"I will."

"But keep an eye out for him, too. What we can't afford to do is allow him to have private lap dances."

At first I was puzzled. But then it dawned on me. "You're right. I never thought about that."

"Oh, absolutely. He's a target. Those strippers could definitely see him as their ticket to easy street. After all, you get him alone and it becomes his word versus hers. And, Matisse, I think it goes without saying, we don't want any part of that. I'm sure you're having them sign confidentiality agreements, right?"

"Yep, got that covered. Matisse or no Matisse, strippers and confidentiality agreements are a must!"

"Absolutely!"

After Andy left, Lincoln and I sat around and chopped it up for a bit. We mainly talked about what was going on in the NHL.

Being injured and not being able to play was already driving Lincoln crazy. And now he was being accused of a crime he didn't commit. You had to feel for the guy. And to top it all off, he was finally awarded a little freedom by way of this bachelor party, and now he wasn't even going to be afforded a private lap dance. Life's definitely full of ups and downs. And to take it a step further, sometimes it's just not fair.

42

GETTING THE PARTY STARTED

THE bus arrived at my place on time the following morning, as did all twenty of the bachelor party attendees. By looking at these cats, you would have thought there was a permanent supply of laughing gas in the air. They knew what was in store, which was why they all had smiles that spread from ear to ear.

I had the breakfast of champions waiting on the bus. We picked our poison by way of Krispy Kreme donuts, mimosas, Bloody Marys and brew.

Once we got going, the party started immediately. I had the DJ I hired for the bachelor party spin tunes for us on the way up to the lake. I also had two of the dancers accompany us to the party.

"Here," I said, yelling over the music.

"What is it?" Miles asked, studying the small glass and its contents.

"It's a shot of Patron!"

"You know I can't drink that shit, Matisse!"

"Just drink it and quit being a sissy before I do a Denzel on you and pull the bus over and threaten to send you back to the valley, Rookie!"

Miles laughed. "That was a tight movie, especially that

scene."

"Quit stalling and drink it, girl."

"I got your girl hanging to the left," Miles said before tilting his head back and slamming the drink. "Aw! Shouldn't I have some choice female parts in my face right about now?"

"Absolutely," I said, motioning for the girls, who, at this point, were already naked. "This is Miles. He's the groom."

"Say no more, Matisse," Linda responded. She had large, real boobs and excellent junk in the trunk – JLo-style. The other girl, Jada, had relatively small breasts, long legs and a surprisingly flat ass. I guess sometimes you have to take the good with the bad. Perfection just doesn't exist.

Rob Nice, the DJ, played one of Luke Skywalker's vintage cuts, and the two women simultaneously started doing their thing. As they took turns gyrating to the sounds of Luke and backing both asses up to Miles, the rest of the guys gathered around and watched. There was a lot of hooting and hollering going on while Miles sat there with a shit-eating grin on his face. And we hadn't even hit the outskirts of Atlanta at that point. Life was good.

In the midst of all of this, I looked over at Lincoln. He seemed to be having a good time. Hell, how could one not? Lincoln's situation was different, though. I could certainly see how he could be preoccupied. Either he was genuinely having a good time or he had his poker face on.

"You all right, bruh?"

Lincoln looked at me and nodded. "I'm cool," he said, giving me a pound. "I'm liking it already, baby!"

"Cool," I replied, digging into my pocket for my phone. I felt it vibrating, but I was too late getting to it. I checked my missed calls log, wondering who it could have been. Shelby's name appeared, which I thought was strange at first. *Why would she be calling me?* After further thinking about it, I just figured she wanted me to relay a message to Miles. Brides-to-be tend to get nervous and unreasonable on the day of the bachelor party. Shelby probably wanted me to deliver a message that went something like, "Act up, and I'll cut it off. You better behave, Mofo!"

I hit redial, but considering how loud it was with the music and all of the guys yelling and hollering, I hung up. It was pointless to call because I knew I wasn't going to be able to hear a thing. It wasn't like I could step outside for a moment. In any event, I knew that whatever she wanted, it couldn't have been too big a deal. Surely it could wait. For a moment, I thought about hitting her up with a text, but nixed the idea.

"Matisse, come join me, man!" Miles yelled. From where I was standing, I could barely see him. All I saw were the two dancers all over him. It looked like one of those late-night uncut videos on BET.

"I'm good right now, bruh!" I was bracing myself for a long weekend.

"Oh, you bullshittin'," Miles replied at the top of his lungs. "That's cool, though. I'll handle it alone."

"Considering this is it for you, Miles, you better enjoy. Remember, you're the one walking the plank. Not me. Your days are numbered."

"Right! Right!" Miles said as he playfully smacked Linda's ass before motor-boating her big-ass titties. "But you still bullshittin'!"

Surprisingly enough, everyone paced himself pretty well during our trip to Lake Lanier. When we arrived, even Miles was still in decent shape.

"I'll take that hour ride any time," Courtney said while helping me carry some things into the house.

"Yeah, it was a good one," I responded. "Miles seems to be having a blast, and that's all that counts."

"Not just Miles, Matisse. Everyone's having fun. The other girls should be here tonight, right?"

"Yep! It's going to be crazy," I said, popping the top off of a couple of beers. "Here."

"Thanks," Courtney said, taking the beer out of my hand. "That's a huge boat, Matisse. You know how to drive that thing?"

"Hell no. I hired a driver. I don't know if I would classify it as a boat. I think the more accurate term is yacht."

"I think you have a point, Matisse."

It didn't take DJ Nice very long to set up and the music was once again blaring. All the guys had formed a circle around Miles. The two dancers continued to put on a show, while Miles sat there in an oversized reclining chair, sipping on some type of adult beverage.

I'd forgotten how uncivilized bachelor parties could be. I could see these guys loosening up right before my eyes, and it wasn't even lunchtime yet. I knew I had to do something because if it continued at that pace, everyone would be fast asleep by dinnertime. I had a big night planned. That's when I came up with the idea of the male bonding ride on the yacht. I made sure the yacht was stocked with cigars, liquor and food. DJ Nice and the dancers had to stay behind. This was a guys-only cruise.

I knew I would be met with some resistance, but I didn't care. All of these cats would surely thank me later on. It was all about pacing ourselves.

I wiggled my way through the ring of guys that surrounded Miles and the dancers until I too was in the middle. I motioned to DJ Nice to cut the music. I began speaking when it quieted down.

"Guys, listen up."

"Matisse, what are you doing?" Miles slurred.

"Just cool out for a moment," I responded with the Heisman hand in his face. "All right, here's what we're going to do right now. The yacht down below is stocked with cigars, booze and grub. I know it's a little cold to be out on a boat, but trust me, this boat is like no other. For the most part, we'll be inside anyway. It's a good chance to do some male bonding before the festivities begin tonight. Plus, Linda and Jada need to get some rest because they have a long night ahead of them. Cool?"

Amidst loud dog-like barks like they were Omegas, and comments like, "Yeah, rest up girls!" and "You have a long night ahead of you!" I also heard a couple of jeers from cats who weren't too happy that this portion of the party had come to a halt. I wasn't worried about those yahoos because I was certain we were in for a night of big fun. For the most part, though, everyone seemed to be with it.

43

CHAOS AT THE CABIN

THE time on the yacht was well spent. No one got too wild. For the most part, we just caught up with one another amidst the cigars and cocktails. The food was good, too.

We had about an hour to spare before the night's festivities began. Most of the guys used the time to call their wives and significant others. I checked my cell phone for missed calls and saw that Andy had called shortly after Shelby had called. Knowing Andy, he was simply checking in to see how Lincoln was doing. I figured I'd wait until the morning to return his call. I wanted to make sure my boy's bachelor party went off without a hitch. I meant what I said about putting everyone else on the back burner.

"Miles, let's go for a walk," I said, tapping him on the shoulder.

"Huh, what's up, Matisse?" Miles had sobered up a bit from the morning. At least he wasn't slurring his words anymore. I knew that would change in a matter of minutes, which was why I wanted to get to him beforehand.

"Man, just come on."

We walked out onto one of the many decks attached to the house.

"What's up, Matisse?"

I brought a bottle of champagne out with us, popped the top

and poured each of us a glass. "Here."

"Okay, that's what I'm talking about." Miles took the glass.

I raised my glass in the air until Miles did the same. "Cheers."

"Right back at you. Cheers," Miles replied, lightly tapping his glass to mine.

"It all changes after this, Miles." We each took seats. Luckily, there was an outside heater on next to us.

"This is true, but like I've been saying all along, I can't wait, Matisse. Not to mention, my wild oats have been sewn."

"Is that right?"

"That's right, Matisse. I've had my fair share of women and I can now honestly say that Shelby is the only woman I desire. I can't wait to spend the rest of my life with her."

"That's great, man. I'm happy for both of you."

"I'm a lucky man, Matisse."

"That you are." Silence filled the air for a moment. "Well, I just wanted you to know that you're my boy, my dog, my ace! Simply put, you are my nigga for real! We've been friends for a long time, and it's meant a lot to me."

"Right back at you, Matisse."

We stood and gave each other a hug.

"I love you, bruh!" I said.

"I love you too, man."

"Well, enough of this soft shit. You ready to do this?"

"Am I? What! Please!" Miles put his glass down, grabbed the bottle of champagne and took a big swig before yelling, "Let's get this party started!"

"Oh, I almost forgot, Shelby called me earlier. I missed the call and haven't had a chance to call her back. I figured she was looking for you."

"Shelby called you? I wonder what she wanted. I better call her."

"Come on, bruh, you know she didn't want anything. You know how girls do the night of their fiancée's bachelor party. I'm sure it's nothing. Probably the worst thing you could do is talk to her right before burying your head between a bunch of big-ass titties. Come on, man, this is your bachelor party. We need to keep your mind right. Focus! Get it right, pimp!"

"You're right, Matisse. Let's do this."

I knew I had given Miles some old caveman advice and wasn't proud of it, but up to that point my experience with bachelor parties had been just that, archaic and barbaric. Besides, who was I to stop the format?

We made our way back inside. By this time, the rest of the dancers had shown up and DJ Nice was back to mixing his cuts. He appropriately started it off with Outkast's "So Fresh and So Clean."

Like earlier, we placed Miles right in the middle of the room. He sat in the oversized recliner, clutching the same bottle of champagne. The dancers came out one by one, each giving him a lap dance. Before long, it was a free-for-all. Miles was having the time of his life. He was also well on his way, as was everyone else. I kept a close eye on Lincoln. In fact, I bought him a couple of lap dances, as long as they were out in the open. No private lap dances for him. I managed to get in a lap dance or two my damn self. To DJ Nice's credit, he kept the beats coming.

As hard as I tried, I could no longer ignore Shelby's phone calls. She was blowing my phone up with calls and texts. My thigh was sore from the phone constantly vibrating and her texts were meaningless because they didn't say anything other than to call her. I made my way to one of the outside decks, where I found a few of the guys having private lap dances. When I found a deck that wasn't occupied, I answered the phone. I could barely make out what Shelby was saying because she was crying and trying to talk at the same time.

"Shelby, what is it? Calm down."

"I need to speak to Miles, Matisse."

"What's wrong?"

"I need to speak to Miles, Matisse," Shelby yelled at the top of her lungs while sobbing.

"Okay, okay. I'm going to get him. Hold on."

I went back inside where I found Miles, just as I suspected, with his head buried between a set of big-ass titties again! Only this time I was impressed by his motor-boating skills. The rate was rapid and somewhat artistic. I grabbed him by the shoulder. He looked up at me.

"What's up, bruh? You want in?" His words were slurred.

"Hey, Shelby's on the phone. It sounds like you need to talk to her."

Miles straightened up. His eyes were wide. "What does she want?"

"I don't know, but I think you should talk to her."

Miles stood and followed me out onto the deck. I probably should have given him some privacy, but my nosey ass had to find out what was going on. I stepped away, but just enough to where I couldn't be seen by him, but could hear everything he was saying.

"Shelby, baby, slow down, I can't make out what you're saying. Tape? What tape? What? Oh! Wait, baby, I can explain everything. Just calm down. Baby, please stop crying. I'll explain everything. I'm coming home right now."

For a guy who was shit-faced a few minutes ago, Miles had sobered up in miraculous fashion.

"What's up? Everything alright?" I asked.

"No, everything's wrong. I got a major problem at home, Matisse. I need to get back to Atlanta pronto!"

"What? It can't be that bad, Miles. You're talking about leaving your own bachelor party?"

"Believe me, Matisse, it's worse than bad."

At that very moment, out of nowhere, and at the height of the party, Atlanta's finest, along with Tom and Big Jay, appeared in the middle of everything. The members of the APD had their guns drawn, and pointed at Miles.

"Miles Keys, you're under arrest for the murder of Sullivan Williams," said Detective Miller.

"Wait, wait, wait!" I yelled, trying to intervene. "What's this all about?"

"It's about the murder of Sullivan Williams. And right now, Mr. Spencer, you're obstructing justice. Please step aside."

They placed the handcuffs on Miles, read him his rights and walked him out. Miles didn't say a word, and neither did anyone else. The place was pretty quiet.

"What's going on here guys?" I asked Tom and Big Jay.

"We don't have time to explain everything to you right now, Matisse, but Lincoln is off the hook."

I looked over at Lincoln. He looked like he was going to faint. It was probably one of the first times I had seen a black man turn ghostly white.

44

SOMETHING JUST ISN'T RIGHT

WHEN I showed up at the police precinct in Atlanta, I didn't know what to expect. Nothing made sense. On the way down, however, I listened to the messages that Shelby and Andy had left that morning. I couldn't make out what Shelby was saying because she was crying uncontrollably. The only thing Andy said was that Lincoln was off the hook and that he'd explain it to me later.

How is Miles involved in all of this? I wondered as I sat, waiting to see him.

"Follow me, Mr. Spencer."

I stood and followed Detective Miller to Miles's cell. Each of our steps echoed against the cement floor. The hallway that led to the cell was dark and drafty. There Miles stood behind bars, sobbing like a baby. He looked like he had just been through a war. His eyes were bloodshot red and his shirt was un-tucked and wrinkled. The constant clanging of the heavy doors that led in and out of the various cells reinforced the fact that this wasn't a dream. It was very real. I was visiting my boy in an Atlanta police department precinct, and he was locked up in a jail cell.

"What in the hell is going on here, Miles?"

Miles wiped his eyes and took a deep breath. "You tell me,

Matisse. I don't know what any of this is all about."

I stared at him for a moment without saying anything.

"Honestly, Matisse, I don't know what's going on."

"Well, I take it you know they have you locked up in this damn jail cell for the murder of Sullivan. You do know that much, right?"

Miles put his hands on his head and began pacing while mumbling something under his breath.

"What?" I asked, trying to make out what he was saying. He continued pacing and mumbling to himself for a few more minutes before finally erupting.

"Shit!" Miles yelled while kicking one of the walls of his cell. "I didn't do it, damn it! You have to believe me, Matisse. I swear."

Though I had an abundance of questions for Miles and the police, I tried to say as little as possible. I was just as confused as Miles.

"How could you even be linked to Sullivan? I mean, yeah, you knew her, but that was through me."

Miles wiped his eyes again. He looked exhausted, almost as if he had aged in a matter of minutes. "I was at her place the morning she died," Miles said in a whisper with his head down.

"What?"

He looked up at me. "Yeah. I stopped by her place that morning."

I scratched my head and took a step back. "Wait a minute, what?"

"I went by there looking for you. I had trouble sleeping that night. I guess you could say I came down with a case of cold feet regarding the wedding, and needed someone to talk to."

"How'd you know where Sullivan lived?"

"You mentioned it to me a time before."

At this point, I didn't know what to think. I didn't say anything else. And I certainly didn't remember telling Miles where Sullivan lived. But, in his defense, maybe I had given that information to him. Miles and I had shared many cocktails together before and after Sullivan's death.

"Just because I stopped by there looking for you, Matisse, doesn't mean that I killed her. You have to help me out here."

"Well, in order for them to be able to hold you in here, they have to have something substantial on you. I'll see what I can come up with in the meantime."

"Thanks. Your help and support mean a lot."

"I'll be in touch," I said before walking out. I had an uneasy feeling.

45

THE VISIT

I opted not to answer my phone on my way home. I needed some time to think. I didn't know what to make of any of it. On one hand I was glad to know that Lincoln was off the hook, and was even happier when I thought about how much money he and I would continue making. But there was still this very real problem. My man, Miles, was sitting in a jail cell for Sullivan's death. The police were being tight-lipped, so I was at a loss on that front. All I really had to go on was Miles's word, which I wanted desperately to believe, but it damn sure didn't seem to add up.

I knew Andy probably had some additional information on the matter, what with him blowing my phone up every ten minutes and sending me annoying texts saying to call him ASAP. I simply wasn't in the mood to hear from anyone. When I finally got home, I went to my room and lay down flat on my back. I did absolutely nothing but stare up at the ceiling, running various situations through my head.

Unfortunately, about an hour into it I was interrupted by the ringing of my doorbell. Ordinarily, I would have taken the time to put some clothes on before answering the door, but I just wasn't feeling it. In fact, I was put off that someone would just show up at my door without having the decency to call first.

I opened the door wearing nothing but a pair of boxers and a t-shirt. There stood Shelby bundled up in a thick overcoat involving some type of fur. As always, she looked flawless. Her makeup was perfect. She played her look down by pulling her hair back into a ponytail. I can't say that I was totally surprised to receive a visit from her, but, all things considered, I would have expected her to be sobbing much like Miles was in his cell, but her eyes were dry.

"Hey," I said, pulling her inside. I gave her a light peck on the cheek and shut the door behind her.

"What a fine mess this is, huh?"

"I don't know what to make of it, Shelby." I took her coat from her and hung it up in the hall closet before leading her into the kitchen, where I put on a pot of coffee. "You seem to be holding up pretty well."

"Please! I'm so mad right now, Matisse, I could scream." Shelby settled on one of the barstools. "What are we going to do?"

"That's a good question. First Lincoln is accused, and now Miles. What in the hell is going on, Shelby?"

Shelby didn't respond. She sat there with her head down staring at the granite countertop.

"Shelby!" Still no response. I walked over to her and gave her a slight nudge. She looked up at me, appearing startled. "I lost you for a moment."

"Can I use your bathroom, Matisse?"

"Of course. It's right there," I said, pointing.

Shelby stood. "Thanks. I'll be right back."

"I'm going to have a little Irish coffee. You want one?"

"Definitely," she responded on her way to the bathroom.

I sat on the stool next to Shelby's after pouring a couple large cups of coffee. I made sure each cup had plenty of liquor in it. I think we both needed it. For some reason I watched Shelby as she made her back down the hallway to the kitchen. It was a short distance, but it seemed like a slow-motion movie. She had this look on her face and didn't take her eyes off of me.

"Here you go," I said, pointing at her cup of coffee when she got back into the kitchen. Shelby didn't respond, nor did she resume her position on the barstool. I felt a pair of warm hands on my shoulders, which soon ran up and down my chest. Shelby stood behind me, where she leaned over and straddled me. Her perky breasts were pressed up against my back as she began tasting my neck with her tongue.

"Shelby, what's going on here?" Startled, I didn't know was going on.

"Shhhhh. Just enjoy it, baby."

"Baby?" I said, spinning my barstool around and looking up at her like she was crazy as hell. I wasn't about to bone my boy's girl. I grabbed her hands, which were in overdrive massaging my chest. "Stop!"

Shelby let out a loud sigh. "Just enjoy it, Matisse."

I stood and quickly distanced myself from her. "Enjoy what, Shelby? You're engaged to my best friend, who, at the moment, happens to be sitting in a jail cell. What is there to enjoy?"

Shelby began to cry buckets of tears. I walked back over to her and hugged her while she continued to sob in my arms. After a few minutes, when the crying ceased, Shelby reached into her purse and pulled out a DVD. "Here," she said, slamming it onto the countertop.

"What's this?"

"Miles is a dirty slimeball, Matisse!"

Instead of trying to carry on a conversation with this woman, who was crying like a baby in my kitchen, I turned on the television and popped in the DVD.

I couldn't believe what I saw. Not only was I at a total loss for words, it sickened me beyond measure. My body temperature rose to the point where I felt light-headed. I stood there for a few more minutes, trying to regain my composure. Finally, after cooling off a bit, I pressed stop, quickly threw on some clothes and headed for the door.

"Where you going, Matisse?"

"Where do you think? Miles has a lot of explaining to do."

46

SMOKING MIRRORS COME TO LIGHT

I couldn't get to that jail cell fast enough. When I arrived, I found Miles in the exact same state. He looked like shit. But that was the least of my concerns.

"Do you want to explain this?" I yelled, clutching the DVD.

"What's that?"

"What's that, my ass!" I grabbed hold of the bars of Miles's cell and rattled the door. "Miles, don't play dumb. You know damn well what this is. So, think long and hard before responding."

"Hunter?"

"Yeah, Hunter!"

I saw tears forming in Miles's eyes. "It was an accident, Matisse." Miles wiped his eyes. "I didn't mean to do it."

"So, you did it?"

Miles hesitantly shook his head. "I'm telling you, Mat, it was an accident."

"Wait, I don't understand this at all. What in the hell were you doing at Sullivan's house that morning in the first place? And none of this bullshit about you looking for me."

Miles began crying. "All right, here it is. I'm tired of sneaking around and lying." He took a deep breath and got the crying

under control. "When I was living in New York, I had a brief affair
with Sullivan. At the time, she was living there, too."

"What?"

"Yeah. I didn't think much of it. You know, I was just sowing
my oats. I knew I was about to get married, and I loved Shelby to
death. Don't ask me why."

"Damn, Miles, what in the hell is wrong with you?"

"It gets worse."

"Great!"

"Anyways, when she found out I was moving down here, she
ended up transferring here as well. I had no idea the girl was going to
get so sprung. She knew what the deal was between me and Shelby.
At that point, I didn't know what to do about it."

"So, you killed her?"

"No, Matisse! I'm telling you, it was an accident. Right
before she moved down here, she went through my things one night
unbeknownst to me. Well, you know how I started getting into
videotaping my sex sessions awhile back?"

"Yeah, and?" I said, not believing what I was hearing.

"Well, here's where it gets worse. Shortly after you and
Hunter broke up, I ran into her one night in New York. She was still
in love with you, but she was hurt. We spent all night talking about
you over cocktails. The next thing I know, we're at my place, butt-
ass naked making home movies. In Hunter's defense, she had no idea
the cameras were rolling."

"Sure could have fooled me. Remember, I just saw the damn
thing. Shit, Pam Anderson, Paris Hilton and Kim Kardashian have
nothing on you guys. Hunter definitely seemed to have a camera
presence."

"Mat, I'm sorry."

"From what I've heard so far, your ass is sorry, and you're a
piece of shit. So, what happened next?"

"Sullivan stole the DVD I made of Hunter and began
blackmailing me. She said that if I didn't call the wedding off, she'd
make sure Shelby saw it. When I told Hunter about the whole thing,
she freaked out. She didn't want anyone to know about the DVD.

That's when Hunter befriended Sullivan. She thought that she could get her hands on the DVD that way. No such luck. Sullivan was too smart for that."

"So, that's how she and Sullivan became friends, huh?" I said, remembering my brunch when they showed up together.

"Yep. We were desperate, Matisse."

"You guys are imbeciles, is what you are."

"I messed up! I know!"

"Right about now, I'd say that's an understatement."

"I thought for sure that you and Sullivan would fall back in love with one another. So while you guys were hanging out, I thought she'd forget about me and give up the DVD. I seriously thought I was off the hook. That's why I went over to her place that morning. I thought she'd willingly hand it over, but she wasn't falling for that shit. We argued and I accidentally pushed her and she fell and hit her head. I didn't know what to do so I ran out."

"I guess it's safe to say you were the one making those ridiculous calls to me, insinuating that Lincoln was the one responsible for Sullivan's death."

Miles nodded his head slowly up and down.

"Wow," I replied, shaking my head in disbelief. "So, you were willing to let an innocent person go to jail on your behalf? Mind you, I was a suspect, too."

Miles began sobbing again. "I'm sorry, Matisse. I don't know what else to say. The hole just kept getting deeper and deeper."

"I don't want to hear that shit, Miles! The whole thing is pitiful. I guess it's also probably safe to assume that you were the one Tom and Big Jay kept seeing with Hunter."

"We didn't know what to do, Matisse, especially after Sullivan died. All we knew was that the DVD still existed."

"Did Hunter know you were the one who killed Sullivan?"

"No. She had no idea. All she was concerned about was retrieving the DVD."

At that point, I didn't know what to say to Miles. I just turned and began to walk out, right as a storm named Shelby blew in like a hurricane, but this time the tears were gone.

"You sorry piece of shit! How could you, Miles? How could you?"

"Baby, it's not what you think. I'll explain it to you later."

"It's not what I think." Shelby turned and looked at me. "Did this fool just say 'it's not what you think,' Matisse?"

I didn't say a word. I just looked at her, wondering if she smuggled a gun or knife in to smoke this fool. That's how mad she was. I was mad too.

"'It's not what you think.' That's your thing, huh, Miles? I remember you saying the same exact thing that morning I followed you over to Sullivan's house."

"That's enough, Shelby," Miles said, sternly. His voice grew louder.

"That's enough? Please! Honey, I'm just getting started. Here I was in love with my husband-to-be, and you were giving Hunter the high hard one—in full color, I might add. Would you like to see the DVD?"

"Shelby, be quiet. Don't say another word."

"I have to give it to him, this guy is slick," Shelby said, looking in my direction. "He said he wasn't doing Sullivan and, like a fool, I believed him, even after finding him in her house that morning."

"Shelby, what are you doing? Don't do this, baby. Please. Please don't do what I think you're about to do."

"You see, Matisse, I'm not stupid. I knew Miles was up to something between the secretive phone calls and him constantly saying he had to go meet you. Obviously, I now know the calls were between him and that skank Hunter, who he kept meeting while using you as a front."

"Dammit, Shelby, that's enough!"

Shelby's lips smacked and her eyes rolled. "Really, Miles? I think it's time for you to shut up and listen. I'll give you your props, you're good because I was completely in the dark about Hunter. Hell, even when I followed you over to Sullivan's house, I had no idea whose place I was tailing you to. I just had a strong hunch that you were involved in something that wasn't right, and I had a stronger hunch that it involved some skanky bitch! I guess the joke was on me. I loved you so much that I forced myself to believe your lies when I knew deep down inside that you and Sullivan were involved in some way, and seeing your hands wrapped around her neck when I got there pretty much confirmed it."

"Baby, please stop talking. I'm begging you."

"My conscience can't take it anymore," Shelby began to sob as her voice cracked. "You know, Miles, I would do just about anything to be with you, even if I knew it was wrong. And that's sad because it says a lot about me and how little I value my self-worth. But, I now know, you aren't worth it. Nobody is. It's over, Miles. I'm turning myself in."

"No!" Miles yelled. "Shelby, baby, listen to me, we can get through this. I promise."

"It's too late, Miles. I wouldn't be able to live with it. We both know I was the one who pushed Sullivan that morning. I don't know what came over me. The simple fact that my fiancé was in another woman's house arguing like they were man and wife fueled a rage me. Even with her in your grasp, my first instinct was to protect the man I loved. I panicked and reacted. Clearly, I didn't mean for her to fall and hit her head, but I can't say it was an accident. I was so damn mad and enraged. I'm ashamed of myself, Miles. And, had that DVD not arrived on my doorstep this morning, I would have gone along with your plan and we would have been married in a few days. It sickens me to think about it. Was I that weak, that you could tell me anything and I would believe you, even if it was the most illogical thing I'd ever heard? Believe me, Miles, I'm disgusted with myself for letting it get to this point. I had to see a video of you having sex with another woman to open my eyes. No, this isn't for me. I'm clearing my conscience on this one."

Shelby turned and walked away without saying another word. I looked at Miles as the tears steadily rolled down his face.

"Matisse, I know I messed up. Just hear me out. Please!"

At that point, I had heard just about all I could hear. In fact, I couldn't believe what I was hearing. Who were these people? Surely, this wasn't my boy, Miles, whom I had known and loved forever.

And sweet Shelby, whom I had always thought was nothing but perfection. No, I couldn't hear anything else he had to say. I followed Shelby's cue and, without saying another word to Miles, turned and left. The hurt and disappointment I experienced cut like a knife. It was painful.

47

SLOW DOWN AND
TAKE A LOOK AROUND

As sad as the situation was, I have to give Sullivan credit for being a smart cookie. She had instructed a friend of hers to send a package containing the DVD, along with a note, to the police, to Shelby, and to Hunter's boyfriend, Jeff, if anything ever happened to her.

Miles had a monstrous temper, but only a select few people (me being one and, obviously, Sullivan another) knew that side of him, which was why she had made such arrangements. It still didn't stop her from loving him. Although Sullivan's actions regarding Lincoln and me were pitiful and shameful, they acted as distractions from the pain Miles caused her.

In the end, Shelby did exactly what she said she was going to do. She turned herself in to the authorities. Regardless of what she said about it not being an accident, my gut told me otherwise and the jury concurred. Though it wasn't premeditated and was committed in a moment of rage, it was manslaughter no matter how you sliced it. Shelby got five years in prison, as did Miles. He received three years for his role as an accomplice, a year for obstruction of justice and a year for slander for his part in implicating Lincoln. There was nothing I could do for either of them, nor would have if I'd had the opportunity. Though it was an accident, they still had to do the time.

Miles and Shelby both deserved what they got. If you ask me, I think they should have been punished even further. Life these days doesn't seem to mean much to a lot of people—just look at the nightly news.

I look at Miles and Shelby and can't help but to wonder, *What happened* and, worse yet, *Where was I when this transformation took place*? Maybe it wasn't a transformation. Maybe the two of them have been crazy ever since I've known them. The point is that here were two people I've known for a long time, Miles in particular. Never in my wildest dreams would I suspect him of boning my girl, or even an ex-girl for that matter, let alone plotting some crooked-ass scheme that affected innocent people. It certainly wasn't the Miles I knew. However, had I listened more intently to what he was saying during our many conversations or paid closer attention to his actions, maybe I would have seen the signs. Maybe. I always sensed this but never really knew, though I'm now convinced that more often than not, things aren't the way we perceive them to be, and neither are the people with whom we surround ourselves and think we know. Unfortunately in life, we tend to take people and situations for granted instead of taking a close, hard look around to see what's really going on. I get the feeling that taking the necessary time to deeply understand people and their situations is a big part of what life is really about.

It's funny; I had a conversation with a friend of mine the other day. Her version of what life is really all about entailed jumping out of planes and climbing mountains, while she scoffed at the notion of assessing situations and proceeding with caution. To her, taking the time to look around meant that you weren't living life to the fullest. While I see the importance of taking risks in life and doing things you've always dreamed about doing—like jumping out of planes and climbing mountains—it means very little if you don't have strong and meaningful connections with others that are built over time and are not impulsive or self-serving. Taking the necessary time to look around and assess and understand situations, more often than not, could save you from a lot of heartache by the time it's all said and done.

In the aftermath of Sullivan, Miles and even Lincoln, I've

experienced a certain amount of clarity regarding my actions where women are concerned. I now know that my commitment issues were a direct result of my failed relationship with Sullivan. Unfortunately, Hunter, Erica and many others had to bear the brunt of it.

I don't know if I'll ever fully come to trust people unconditionally, considering what I've recently gone through, and having been betrayed by people I thought I knew. All I can do is try in the future. I certainly want to sustain a meaningful relationship and to do this I know that trust is a very important element.

As far as Erica and I are concerned, who knows? I know she's softening. And I also know that I still have a lot of growing to do where relationships are concerned. I'm a strong advocate of always looking at the glass as being half-full rather than half-empty. So, I'm optimistic that things will work out for the best between us.

Through it all, I've learned a valuable lesson, and that is that sometimes we don't really know the people who we feel are the closest to us. I thought I knew Miles inside and out and had to learn the hard way that I didn't.

And, perhaps more importantly, I learned that sometimes we need to slow down and take a good look around, specifically at the people we surround ourselves with on a daily basis, and realize that the grass isn't always greener. Had I done that a year ago, I wouldn't be in the predicament I'm in now with Erica.

It's hard sometimes to appreciate just how fortunate you are. If you have deep feelings for a person who reciprocates those feelings and treats you well in every way, shape and form, then cultivate them, nurture them, and revel in them. While we're going a hundred miles an hour trying to find that perfect mate, the one we're supposed to be with could be staring us in the face. Yeah, I've learned that the hard way but, fortunately, I've learned.

Look around.